THE WOMAN WHO FOUND HERSELF

Chris Cutler

For Ariane.

Death does not close the book,
it only turns the page.

1

Dordogne, 1943

The moon rises over distant pine trees, causing the shadow of the church steeple to point an accusatory finger. Watery light spills through the French window to find carvings on a massive chestnut wardrobe. Faded sepia paper peels from the walls — Arcadian scenes hand-painted in hope before the Great War. A hope that never came.

Esther stares at her reflection in the wardrobe. She sees a young woman with cropped hair wearing clothes borrowed from her brother. Her soft hands tremble as she buttons the jacket.

On the far wall, a tall, elegant figure detaches herself from the hand-painted wallpaper and watches. Esther's simple brown jacket contrasts with the *belle époque* dress. Yellow satin with short bouffant sleeves, the skirt flows from tiny waist to ankles, long hair pinned up to expose neck and shoulders, pale as alabaster.

Why have you cut your hair?

Esther's gaze shifts to the image behind her, but the vermillion lips have stopped moving. Every muscle tightens as she listens to the silence. The painted figure listens too. Esther slips a flashlight into one of her coat's many pockets and leaves.

Passing through the door, the ghost drops a note into Esther's pocket. *Ne meurs pas, c'est un piège.* (Don't die, it's a trap.)

The resistance is active in this part of France. Esther is meeting Jean to guide down a Lysander with nothing but moonlight and flashlights. The moon hangs low in the rain-soaked night, dancing off the sharp needles of the pines to warn anyone foolish enough to reach for it. Pale light flits behind the tattered shrouds. Esther times her exit from the shadows, taking the path beside the old Templar house. A lone guard sleeps whilst, beneath the trees, darkness oozes its resistance to the moonlight. A man is smoking, the single red eye dilating at the end of the tab.

Esther takes the cigarette from Jean's mouth before the smell of tobacco betrays them. Crushing it into the soft earth, they kiss, then he leads her to the rendezvous. Hearts pounding, he pulls her towards him. Warmed by his embrace, her hands search for naked flesh. Finding it, she gasps as he pulls at her clothes. There's no thought now of the Lysander.

'Now,' she whispers.

Jean is too gentle a lover to hurt Esther, but cannot hide his urgency. When he enters her, she cries out, making him clasp his hand over her mouth. A twig snaps in the distance, but Jean has passed beyond thought. Deep inside her, he sighs. In the darkness, there is another. The girl in the *belle époque* dress returns to the wallpaper. The Lysander pilot sees the gathering clouds and aborts the landing. With no plane, the lovers drift towards sleep, only to be woken by a boot.

Esther whispers its owner's name. 'It's us, we were...'

'I know what you were doing. Regular little love birds, aren't we?'

The accent is unmistakable.

2

John, November 2002

'Are you happy?'

It's the only question she asks these days. I have never lied to my mother.

'In our own way.'

She reaches out a thin hand. 'You can't be happy in your own way, only unhappy. I want to know about you.'

'I am happy.'

It's the first time I have ever lied to her. She smiles her disbelieving smile.

'I'll go now, but I will be back.'

She has stolen my line, and in doing so, I know. Clasping the thin hand, I stroke the liver marks, the raised veins, the arthritic knuckles.

'I love you, Mum.'

'I love you, too. Be happy.'

She closes her eyes.

A month later, Cathy is leaving for work. Most days she wears a jacket over a T-shirt and skirt. This time, makeup, and a business suit. As she bends to kiss Peter, the fabric of her skirt pulls, showing the zip.

'Don't forget I've got my work do tonight.'

'The Christmas party? I thought that included partners.'

Cathy avoids eye contact. 'Sorry. Yes, it does. That's next week. This is a leaving do.'

I say nothing. Even Peter can tell his mother is lying.

'She's got going-out clothes in her bag,' he whispers, before adding 'Boys' night in.'

Bangers and mash with Dad in front of the television is a seven-year-old's remedy for everything.

The TV meal cannot lift our mood. He looks at me with his child's questioning frown as he takes both plates to the kitchen. I put him to bed, but I can hear he is still awake when Cathy comes home.

'How was your evening?'

She drops her coat on the sofa, spreading a telltale smell of aftershave.

The three of us studied at the same university. Richard went to work abroad, then he came back, and Cathy started seeing him again. At university, I waited for it to burn out, but this is different.

At first, she is indignant, but something in her expression tells me she is glad I have put my foot down. Now that my mother is gone, I persuade Cathy to let Richard go, and in exchange, we will fulfil our lifelong dream of living in France.

She kisses me whilst I hold my breath against Richard's aftershave.

'I'll go take a shower.'

This is code. I am not sure I want sex, but to refuse would be to lose the ground just gained. Afterwards, lying awake listening to her night noises, I am far from certain she will stick to our plan, but there's only one way to find out.

Cathy, January 2003

John wants us to move to France. I think I am cool with it. It's a way out of the mess I've made of my life. I suppose I better sort through all our junk. The first box I open is my box of treasures.

HOLDEN, Ben, and Laura. Congratulations on the birth of Catherine Demelza, born April 30th 1969, at York Royal Infirmary. Weight 8lbs 7oz.

I smooth out the folds of the faded newspaper cutting, hidden beneath a soft cloth with a rabbit's head. That comforter was my constant companion until I was eight. Mopsy's familiar, comforting smell has not changed. I am a child again. Dad opens my bedroom door and comes to sit on my bed. Why does it have to be our little secret? Eyes stinging, I push the rabbit and memory back into the box.

A loyalty card from Cooplands, full of coffee bean stamps. I'm shopping with Ma. Me periods have started, so that makes it what? 1981? We are in Browns, getting my first bra. I have to tell her.

'Can we get a brew?'

I tell her what Dad does. Ma puts down her mug.

'I'll never forgive you.'

Never forgive *me*? She must mean never forgive *him.*

Mum sold up, and we moved to Holgate. I don't know where Dad went. Me and Jan went back to sharing a bedroom.

Three cinema stubs for the Odeon, Clifton. *Who Framed Roger Rabbit?* 1988. A sliver of moonlight shone through the uneven towers of the new Catholic cathedral, spilling into the small bedsit. Flicking on the light, the room fills with a harsh glare. It illuminates the cracked and crumbling walls, hidden beneath peeling woodchip paper. I try to dress in front of the mirror that John rescued from a skip. Propped against the wall, all I can see is the bare light bulb.

The woman in the mirror has put on weight since she was a schoolgirl. I struggle with the jeans' zip, give up and reach for a skirt. It rides up, but Richard likes a bit of leg. He smacks my bum, takes the piss out of my accent and says summat about too many chip butties. John puts his arms around me and tells me he loves me just as I am. That's why I moved in with John.

The photo of me in that skirt gives me one of those looks. *"Summer of Love" my arse. You were doing it to spite yer da.*

John would have liked me all to himself, but he never asked. Don't ask, don't get, that's what I say.

Bloody hell, *The Joy of Sex*! All those cute drawings of bearded men showing their willies seem so dated now.

John wanted me to marry him when we graduated. I told Richard, but he wasn't that bothered, saying Inuits share their wives so John could share his. We were having drinks after the film, my arm looped around each of them like Jessica Rabbit. When they both plonked a G&T in front of me, I laughed, put on a Southern drawl and said, 'I'm not bad; I'm just drawn that way!' It became our in-joke.

John's diploma! 1991 — I was in year two then. Richard got a job in life insurance. I suppose if you can con your best mate into sharing his girl with you, you can sell people insurance they don't need. Here's a picture of John and me at the Poll Tax march. Richard made an excuse and stayed behind.

John's first business card: John Cartwright, Programmer, Efficient Chips, 12A High Street, Cirencester. Bless him, he was so proud! Getting married seemed more like me saying sorry for putting up with me and Richard.

If I felt guilty, I would've dumped Richard, but I couldn't. He destroyed my self-esteem, then gave it back to me in exchange for what he wanted.

A pregnancy-test kit. Expiry date September 1994. We'd been married three years, but I always pushed the conversation about starting a family away with some new excuse.

That night, John brought it up again. He poured me something brown and frothy that had been in a plastic bucket under our stairs. My bottle of Liebfraumilch was because I needed something more than his attempt at homebrew.

'I'd like us to try for a baby.'

My finger traces the blue glass, stroking the sad-looking girl on the label.

'I know. So do I, just not...'

'Just not what?'

The girl's expression changes from sad to guilty. 'Richard's gone but, you know...'

He doesn't answer.

'OK. I'm not Saint Mother Fucking Theresa! That's why I never told you. We are not students anymore. I didn't think you would be as cool with it as at uni.'

Frost forms on his glass. I'm tempted to tell him everything, but cannot do that to the man I love.

'I'm sorry.'

He lets the silence ferment like that god awful bucket under the stairs.

Looking him in the eye, I say it. 'I'll come off the pill.'

A Valentine's card, 1995. I've been off the pill for five months, plotting my fertility cycle. After we finished, John said he had a good feeling about it.

At the weekend, I was with my boss meeting backers for the contract for the Cheung Kong Centre in Hong Kong.

'Nice dress. Are you bad, or are you just drawn that way?'

My innards turn to water. 'Richard! What the fuck are you doing here?'

He shrugged. 'Lending money to your boss.'

'Liar!'

'Well, you always knew me better than anyone else. They are sending me to Hong Kong until the handover. I'm flying out on Monday. Fancy a fuck for old time's sake? The rest room cubicles are very comfortable.'

I throw my drink in his face. He is right about the restrooms.

Loads of postcards between 1995 and 2000. Richard did the rounds: Hong Kong, Manilla, Singapore, Abu Dhabi. Of course, I went to see him when he came back.

'It's like the Wild West out there.'

'I don't understand.'

'Nothing for you to worry your pretty little head about.'

'What's that supposed to mean?'

That was the nearest I ever got to standing up to him.

'Easy tiger!' Somehow, he made it sound like a threat. 'Remember the Cheung Kong deal?'

How could I forget the Dorchester restroom? He rambled on,

trying to blind me with financial jargon. If he ever had money, he hadn't now.

'I'm a mum.'

'Yeah, you told me.'

'You should meet him. And John.'

He took a shine to Peter, offered to babysit, stuff like that. Most of the time, he was polite. He seldom referred to our misspent youth and never to the Dorchester restrooms.

A pair of open-crotch panties. I must have put them here to hide them. Yes, I've gone back to my old ways. John and I were getting ready to go out. He caught me in front of the mirror, lifting my breasts to where they were ten years ago.

'I love you just as you are.'

Your husband's opinion doesn't count. Even Richard seemed more interested in our son than me.

'Richard will be here soon; you ready, pet?'

The doorbell rings. Showtime!

Richard's jaw drops. 'Wow, you look fantastic! What's the special occasion?'

I smile. 'I've got a date with me husband.'

That's not it. I want Richard to see me like this. I want him to want me like he did at uni - like he did at the Dorchester.

'John's a lucky fella!'

I close the box. John knows. At first, we both pretended nothing was happening. I kidded myself that Richard had settled down and regretted treating me as his fuck buddy at university. John isn't stupid, just not confident enough to face Richard. I am far from certain I can go through with John's plan, but there's only one way to find out.

3

John, February 2003

I'm taking Peter to France for some father-son bonding, and to look at houses. Cathy needs time to adjust to our new life, but I wish she had shown a bit more enthusiasm. She is back in England, getting Richard out of her system. At least she is on board with the project.

The ship smells of diesel, chips, and beer. Its deck is uneven where they have painted over the rust. I bend to get through the cabin door, knees cracking from an old rugby injury.

Peter gives me a brave smile. He looks worse than when he got food poisoning.

'It's still damp, but I've got the sick out.'

I hand him back his favourite Mario Brothers T-shirt. It's a pity for my trousers, as I only bought one pair.

'You're lucky Mummy's not here.'

'Why is that soldier?'

'She would have a go at you for being scruffy.'

He's right.

'Why did you call me soldier?'

I shrug. 'Because you are being brave about the seasickness.'

'I didn't enjoy being a soldier.'

He is asleep before I can ask what he means.

Dordogne

I'm glad Peter got some sleep on the ferry, but he still looks rough. I opened the window a crack to let the fresh air in, and to carry away the smell of vomit. The rain runs like tears down the glass, dripping onto my leg.

'I still feel sick.'

He has been staring at the hedges ever since we left the main road.

'Concentrate on the horizon.'

He goes back to sleep. Woods, fields of cows. Is brown their proper colour or is it just mud? More woods, piles of timber, immense trunks all the same length, piled higher than the car. Peter wakes.

'It can't be much further,' he says.

I ruffle his hair.

'You've been saying that for hours.'

There's a deviation sign, but I am going by the sat-nav. A large tree blocks the road giving me a *told you* stare in the headlights, forcing me to do one of those weaving reverses where the engine over-revs. I'm past caring. We follow the deviation sign but still get lost.

'Where's the atlas?'

Peter pulls it out from under him. It's damp and smells of sick. 'Why did you put it there?'

'Sitting on brown paper is supposed to stop car sickness, but we didn't have any.'

At least the rain has stopped.

'Look up Mareuil in the atlas.' I spell it for him whilst trying to keep the car on the road in this mist.

'Look, Daddy, there's another sign. What does Strasse Gesperrt mean?'

'I can't see anything.'

'It is in front of us, next to a man in a hat. The man is pointing, telling us to stop.'

I'm too tired to deal with Peter's imaginary friends.

'You just ran him over!' he exclaims. 'Well, I think you did, but it was like we went straight through him.'

'If I had run someone over, I think I would have noticed!'

All the same, I check the rear-view mirror. That is when we hit something.

'SHIT!'

A boar swerves, so he only half hits us before clattering up the road whilst the car slides to a halt in a ditch.

'I told you!'

'No. You said there was a man. Now I've hit a boar, and we are stuck.'

'Why didn't you see him?'

There's a sound of distant barking, then dogs, followed by their owners in an old van. A man gets out.

'Mon cousaing va vous aider.' He twangs the word cousin in a typical *sud ouest* accent.

The hunter jerks a thumb over his shoulder before following the dogs.

'Even if the boar nearly killed us, I'm sorry for him,' Peter says. 'But I'm not sorry for the man who helped because he tried to kill the boar.'

It's hard to disagree with him. I love that boy so much. We are back on the road, and the hunter has gone in search of his companions.

'Are you going to give him something because he helped us?' he asks.

By the time I find my wallet, the young man has disappeared, so I hurry along the road and dive into the bushes.

Stopping to listen to see if I can hear the hunters, the forest listens right back. There's a distant hum of a light aircraft, then a shot so near that I fall over. I am not hit, but can feel something across my chest. There's a man standing over me, holding a revolver.

Regular little love birds, aren't we?

He moves the pistol towards the imaginary weight. I cannot explain why that's the side of my body that feels warm. Another shot, then nothing. He just melts away like a scene change in an old movie.

I can't move. The world around me spins as if I am about to faint. Then the hunter who rescued us runs up, shouting things I don't understand.

Peter leaps out of the car to hug me when I get back. OK, I should not have left him, but why is he so upset?

'I saw you in a beret with a cigarette. You were with a girl dressed as a boy. Was she a ghost?'

'There is no such thing as ghosts,' I reply.

We are going to a strange house, and I don't want him to have nightmares.

'At first, I didn't see the couple walking up the road behind me,' said Peter. 'One was wearing a raincoat, smoking and wearing a beret like in the old films.'

That doesn't sound like me. He grabs my hand for reassurance. 'With him was a teenage girl in boys' clothes. I could tell it was a girl from the way she waved her arms about as she ran. I thought they were going to steal the car, but they didn't even notice.'

Peter has a vivid imagination, but I can't help peering into the darkness. Maybe there are more hunters.

'As they walked past, something fell out of her pocket. I went to get it because if someone drops money, you should always give it back, but it wasn't money. It was a piece of paper with writing on it.'

Breathless, he thrusts the scrap into my hand. *Ne meurs pas, c'est un piège.*

'Even if it is not money, it might be important, like a shopping list. They didn't hear when I called, so I put it in my pocket. That is not stealing, is it?'

'No, it's not,' I reassure him.

'You told me to wait in the car. I wished I'd gone with you, but thought I might get lost. If that happens, I have to stay where I am until someone finds me.'

His voice is monotone, reciting by rote what we taught him.

Hushed now that the rain has stopped, the leaves whisper in the wind that chased the clouds away. Moonlight shines through the trees, almost as if searching for something. I remember the gunshot. He must have been terrified.

'I called with the trees, "come back!" but you couldn't hear.' I squeeze him tight. 'Someone came back, but it wasn't you. He was older and fatter but wearing the same style raincoat. He walked straight towards the car carrying a revolver like the ones you see in cowboy movies. I hid. He was walking away when I looked again.'

We have a cuddle. Eventually, he is calm enough to sit straight and put his seat belt on, so we drive to the gîte.

After what happened, I put Peter in my room to stop him from having nightmares. I ought to phone Cathy, but leave it until he is in bed.

'Hello.'

'Oh, hiya. Y'alright?' The voice sounds thin and distant.

'Did I wake you?'

Richard is there, I can tell.

'No.' She pauses before adding, 'How was the trip?'

I can't do this.

'OK. Look, I'm exhausted; I'll call you in the morning.'

Peter sits up and makes his teddy bear wave at me. 'Bedtime story?'

'Yes, of course.'

'Winnie the Pooh?'

'Of course.'

Peter spotted the house at the agent, abandoned like the fat boy nobody wants in their team.

'Please, Daddy! It has a balcony, so I could stand on it like a pirate looking for enemy ships.'

When we get there, he jumps out of the car.

'Look, there's the girl in the boy's jacket, standing on the balcony.'

Something caught my eye too, but I do not want to fuel his imagination. 'That's the wind catching the curtain.'

'No, it's the girl. She doesn't scare me because she looks sad.'

The agent has seen nothing. 'I thought you said the house was empty,' I say.

'It is, but I have the keys.'

If there was a girl, she has gone when I look back at the balcony.

Peter heads towards the front door. 'Can we look inside?'

'That is the Italian's door. The entrance to the main house is round the back.'

'What Italian, Daddy?'

Esther

What a strange sound in the square beneath my window! I often sleep now that I am dead. Jean died like me, but I am sure he was reborn. Is that what woke me? I would run to the balcony if I were alive. Now I glide, but I am still tingling, desperate for my first sight of his new body. He looks up but does not recognise me. Have I faded so much? Come inside! I have picked wildflowers for the bedroom. I'm sure Jean remembers because he's leading the boy away from the collaborator's door. You can't get in that way.

There's a weight of history in these walls. It's a pity I didn't keep it tidier, but at least the bedroom is light and fragrant. I fade into the mirror as the door opens. How stupid to be so shy! He turns to go. I'm scared he will not recognise me from his new body. A boy enters. This time, I step out of the mirror.

Hello!

He stops, looking surprised but not scared.

'Hello, I'm Peter. Do you live here?'

He heard me! *Yes, I live here.*

What is your name?

I remember my manners. *My name is Esther, and I am a French resistance fighter. They killed my boyfriend.*

'I'm sorry.'

He looks confused, so I continue. *When they shot him, I wanted them to shoot me too so we would meet on the other side.*

'Did you?'

No, don't die, it's a trap! There's nothing there. I came back to find his reincarnation.

I feel the lady in the wallpaper watching as he pulls a scrap of paper from his pocket.

'What's reincarnation?'

When someone dies, their soul has nowhere to go, so they go into a baby, and that baby becomes their living self.

He screws his eyes and frowns, as if solving a complex problem. 'Did you do that?'

Yes.

'I don't understand. If you are born again, and you are here talking to me, that makes two of you.'

There's only one. The real me is my living self, so what you are seeing is an echo from the past.

'But I can see you.'

You can see a rainbow, or moving images at a picture palace, but that doesn't mean you can touch them.

'Can I touch you?'

Try.

He reaches out his hand as if he might get an electric shock. I step forward and the outstretched hand passes through me.

'That's really cool! So, how come you can talk to me in English?'

I can't.

'Yes, you can, because I can hear you.'

Are my lips moving?

He studies me. 'No. How do you do that? Are you a ventriloquist?'

I am thinking, and you are picking up my thoughts. Because you are English, you hear me in English. Few breathers have that gift.

He scratches his head. 'Was your boyfriend reborn too?'

I believe so. That is why I am looking for him.

'Why?'

Because if I find him and introduce him to my living self, they will be happy.

He nods. 'I saw you the other day. You were with a man.'

I shimmer with excitement. Peter's father opens the door. I'm sure it's Jean. He walks straight through my outstretched arms and ruffles the boy's hair.

'The man is waiting for us.'

I cannot bear to be invisible to him. His voice is unmistakable — the English accent suits him.

Peter looks up. 'She's lovely.'

He means me. How sweet!

'Who's lovely, Peter?'

15

'The girl in the boy's jacket.'

'Have you seen her?'

'I told her she was pretty, then asked her why she looked unhappy. When a sad face smiles, it is still lovely.'

I love this boy! He is how I imagine Jean before the war.

Peter pushes his hair back from his face and smiles. 'They killed her and her boyfriend in the war, and she is waiting for him. Are we going to buy this house?'

Jean cannot see me, but I am sure he senses my presence.

'I would like to.'

'Good, then I can talk to her again. She's the one I saw when the car broke down.'

In my endless sleep, I dreamed of bearing Jean's child. He has returned, I'm sure. I must find my living self and tell her.

The next day, Peter is by the fountain in Touriac.

Hello! How are you?

He jumps. 'Oh, hello! I'm fine, thank you. Daddy is talking to the estate agent.'

I come out of the fountain. *Is your father going to buy the house?*

'Yes! Imagine living in a house with a real live ghost! OK, make that a real dead one.'

I think he is making a joke. My Jean arrives.

'Daddy! Can I have an ice cream?'

Jean takes Peter to an ice cream shop for a hot chocolate. The shop belongs to Ariane who is a friend of my living self. He is called John now, so I should use his living name.

'We are thinking of buying an old house in Saint Etienne. I'm sure it has a lot of stories to tell,' John says.

Ariane replies. 'Talk to Francine in the library if you want stories; she is an expert in local history.'

I have to learn more about Peter's mother. The chair opposite seems to move unaided.

Does your father likes the house?

'Yes, he does; we just hope Mummy will too.'

Is your mother with you?

Peter looks down, dredging chocolate from the bottom of the cup. 'She was busy. Daddy wants Mummy to try again. She said she couldn't if Richard is still around.'

I don't understand. Who is Richard?

'Mummy's boyfriend.'

I am shocked to learn that John is married to Cathy, and she has a lover, but what can I do?

I am visiting the spot where Jean and I died in 1943. Between the hunter's tyre tracks are prints of boar and deer, overlaid with those of the dogs that chase them. Tall pines edge the path, their topmost needles coated in white candy floss.

I can show you where Jean and I hid. I know who did it, but not why. 'Regular little lovebirds, aren't we?' He sounded so cruel. Today, a blackbird sings, summoning the dawn chorus. Later, Jean will visit the library where my living self works.

Peter is with Ariane, finishing a second pancake. Francine is in the library, swimming in the quietness. Our lover comes in, tall as when he was the brave resistance fighter, helping refugees find their way into Free France. He was slimmer in the forties; his living self is older. Deep-blue eyes have faded to slate. I hope she recognises him.

'Are you Francine?'

My living self nods, frowning as if trying to place an uncatalogued book. John asks about the house he is buying.

'Yes, I know it.'

'What should I look out for?'

'I cannot say. It depends for what you are looking.'

'Will it fall down?' he asks.

'I cannot say, but all the same, it has been standing since the revolution, so it will outlive us both if you fix the roof.'

'How did you know about the roof?'

She shrugs. 'In rural France, everyone knows everything.'

John looks down, unable to hold Francine's gaze, then takes a breath. 'Would you like to see it with us?'

'I am working' she answers.

What is she doing? Just say "yes"! I can't kick her, so I spill the library cards. She stands after a brief, one-sided conversation behind the counter.

'If you're still there, I'll come during my lunch break,' she continues with a smile.

An enormous pickup drives into the square.

Our lover strides forward with his hand out. *'Bonjour, Francine!'*

'Enchanté. Je m'appelle Peter,' the boy adds.

Francine turns to him. *'Oo la la, tu parles Français!'*

He is showing off, but I like him.

Francine points. 'They added a new façade a century ago.'

She shows them an old photo. 'This is the church with the old steeple that fell in 1911.'

Peter studies the picture. 'Why is this steeple bigger?'

'It had to be bigger than the *église* in the next village.'

John takes the photo. 'Why?'

She gives him a mischievous smile. 'The priest was a man. Every man longs to be bigger than the next. If you are a priest, you want a bigger steeple.'

Peter does not understand, but still joins in. 'It's not just bigger, it's on the other end.'

The librarian smiles at him. He looks so like his father. 'The mayor has demanded it.'

She has lost John too. 'How can he do that?'

'The taller steeple may fall on the house.'

Peter frowns. 'Why is that important?'

'It was the house of the mayor!' she exclaims.

Everybody laughs.

John wants to show Francine inside, but her lunch break is over, so she excuses herself and leaves.

Peter looks sideways at his father. 'She seems nice.'

All these years, I have waited for our lover to be reborn, to reunite him with my living self. Now I discover that someone got to him first. If Peter's mother is who I think she is, I am going to have to rethink my strategy.

4

John

I'm sorry Francine had to go. Why? She's young and pretty. Isn't that a good enough reason? No. Not if you are married, and especially if you are on a mission to save that relationship. I couldn't believe it when she went on about priests' penises. OK, she didn't say the word, but that was what she meant. Thank goodness Peter didn't get it.

I wonder if Francine fancies me? I've been off the market so long I can't read the signals any more. Not that I ever could. My first encounter with Cathy was at the University Buddhist Society. I was talking to her about reincarnation when she put her finger on my lips and whispered, 'Fancy a fuck?'

I'm buying this house to stop Cathy from seeing Richard, so there's no way she'd let me have a girlfriend.

Peter and I have another look around the main house. The hand-painted wallpaper is beautiful, and the ceilings are super high with amazing black beams, like someone has chopped them with an axe. The wardrobe in the bedroom looks like it might lead to Narnia. Reflected in the mirror is the *belle époque* debutante from the Arcadian wallpaper.

Peter is in the loft surrounded by rubbish, old magazines, and school exercise books. He hands one to me.

'This one is in English.'

The copperplate writing is as crisp as ever. *Crossing The Line* by Jenny Wren.

'Is that her real name?' he asks.

'I doubt it. It was a nickname for girls in the Navy.'

A bookmarker falls out.

Vitium est temporis...

Peter picks it up. 'It's like what I found on the road, but it is not in French or English.'

'No, it's Latin: The fault is in the age.'

'What does that mean?'

'*Vitium est temporis potus quam hominis.* The fault is owing to the age rather than the person.'

'I didn't know you could speak Latin.'

Neither did I, but then I didn't know someone once rented the apartment at the front to an Italian.

'It's a way of saying you are not to blame, that circumstances forced you to do something.'

'What, like when Craig says "Khalid made me do it"?'

'No, more like when there is a war on, and people do terrible things, then it is the war that is to blame, not them.'

'What things?' he asks.

'Peter, I don't know. Someone probably wrote it during the war.'

'I'll ask Esther. She will know.'

'Who's Esther?'

'The ghost, silly. Resistance Girl. She gave me this book to give to Mummy.'

'OK, but don't say that a ghost gave it to you.'

We are back at the holiday home.

'Can I call Mummy and tell her about the house?' asked Peter.

'I'll do it,' I answer.

I don't. It has all gone much faster than I intended. I should not have put in an offer without Cathy at least seeing the house. Peter pushes the phone into my hand. He has already dialled.

'Hi, Cathy.'

'Christ, John. I thought you had died!' she responded.

'No such luck.'

'That's a horrible thing to say. I'm missing you.'

'Are you?' I asked.

'Please don't start that again; I'm looking forward to moving to France.'

'Are you?'

'For fuck's sake, John. I said, don't start. You know I've always wanted to live in France; you know what I am giving up.'

'I'm sorry, Cat,' I said. Then, 'I love you.'

'I know you do.'

She is supposed to say "I love you too", not "I know you do". I pretend not to notice, talking instead about the house.

'See you on Sunday. Love you,' I say, ending the conversation.

'Love you too. Bye.'

I stare at the phone after she hangs up. She said it; maybe things will be alright after all.

That was two days ago and now we are driving back to England. Peter's jobs are holding the atlas, telling me where we are, and holding my phone to my ear when it rings.

'Who was that?'

'The seller. He's accepted our offer, but we have to sign tomorrow.'

'But we are on the way home!' he objects.

'I'll come back with Mummy next week.'

'Can't you sign on your own?'

'I want Mummy on board. She hasn't even seen the house,' I explain.

'Can I ring her and tell her?'

'No, I'll tell her when we get home.'

Things could still go either way with Cathy. I need to be careful.

Cathy

They're home. John didn't phone until they got to Newbury, which only gave me a quarter of an hour to get rid of Richard. I'm still wearing the work suit and stockings I wore for our cosplay. The skirt is a bit too short and a lot too tight, but men like that, don't they?

Peter rushes out of the car, yelling, 'Mummy, Daddy bought a house!'

I knew it!

Peter hugs me. 'Your hair smells of shampoo.'

'I washed it for Daddy,' I tell him.

'Those glasses make you look clever.'

'Thanks very much! Aren't I always clever?'

'Not always, no. Did you buy biscuits?'

'In the cupboard.'

Peter switches on the games console and pretends not to listen. Out of guilt, I make mugs of tea, which is the limit of my skills in the kitchen. John is trying to read me. I was on board with the France project, but needed to spend time with Richard to check I was doing the right thing. He was all smiles when we told him.

'I'm so pleased for you guys. You'll love it, Cathy. You must invite me over when you have settled in.'

It was all total fucking bullshit, but John smiled and said, 'Of course.' In his shoes, I would drown Richard in the pool. I wonder if there's a pool? I should listen to what John is saying, but God, he's wittering away, going on about the countryside, village, and house. Friggin' eck, give it a rest! Do I want to do this? When I'm with Richard, I'm not sure. Richard makes me feel alive. John makes me feel loved. I want to make it work, but do I love him?

Peter is pretending to be lost in his game. I can't bear to think of living without him. He and John are a package, so I must try to make the best of it. There you go; we are that clichéd couple staying together for the children's sake.

John is still babbling on about the house. His jumper has crisp crumbs on it. I think of Richard in his double-breasted suit. John sees me looking and tries to brush them off with the mug still in his hand, spilling tea everywhere. I fetch a cloth. He's like my favourite record — old, scratched, but I love him.

The needle scrapes across the vinyl as his words pull me out of my daydream.

'Hang on, next Monday?'

'I'm afraid so. It's a condition of acceptance.'

'But I'm at work,' I complain.

'Don't you have any holidays you could take?'

'Aye, but that's not the point.'

'What is the point?' he asks.

'I feel rushed. The place has been empty for years; why the urgency?'

He takes a swig of tea. 'Maybe he thinks now he has a bite, he has to reel it in quickly.'

I shake my head. 'You offered too much.'

'Have you seen the price? It wouldn't buy a garage here.'

'Summat has made him desperate to sell now. We need to find out what it is.'

He shrugs. 'We may never know.'

'We will know, or we don't sign.'

I need a drink. The bottle of wine opens with a satisfying pop as John goes to the kitchen to find some glasses. I couldn't do this when Richard was around. All my life, I wanted John to show some balls, to put up a fight for me and demand exclusive rights. Instead, he acted hurt — constantly trying to make me happy. He is hot chocolate with too much sugar. He never made a fucking decision, yet now he comes up with a plan to tempt me away from Richard. France is a new start for him, a way of dragging himself out of his rut, but he is doing it because he loves me.

I pour the wine. 'When's the appointment with the solicitor?'

He gives a slight frown. 'A week tomorrow. Ten o'clock, I think.'

'Change it to afternoon; I want to speak to the mayor. He'll know what's going on.'

John puts his glass down. 'Let that breathe. I've got some bubbly I bought on the ferry. We can celebrate over supper.'

Cooking is not my thing. "My turn" means picking up a takeaway on the way home.

'What are you making?' I ask.

'What have you got in the cupboard?'

'Not much.'

He picks up the wine cork. 'Peter will be at school and we'll need someone to look after him.'

'I could ask Richard.'

The words drip like paint on to a Persian rug as I rush to get the white spirit.

'He said if we need to spend time together, he would look after Peter. Richard could sleep here, get Peter to school, and still get to work. He works flexitime so he could pick him up as well.'

I'm overdoing it, I'm sure. The white spirit of Richard helping us spend time together sinks into the carpet.

'It's a solution.'

'I'll call him,' I say.

'I'll see what food we have in the cupboard.'

He is hovering in the kitchen while I make the call, and back the instant I hang up, so I know he was listening.

'I'll pop to the supermarket,' he says.

'Richard says aye to the babysitting.'

Peter pauses his game. 'Hey! I'm not a baby. I want to come with you.'

We have a quick tennis match. I serve. 'You have school.'

Bop. 'Don't want to go.'

Bop. 'It's football Mondays.'

Bop. 'Have you washed my kit?'

Bop. 'It's on the bed.'

He misses. 'Thanks, Mummy.'

Advantage Mrs Cartwright.

I serve again. 'Time for bed.'

Bop. 'I'm hungry.'

Bop. 'Go get ready, and I'll do you a butty.'

Bop. 'Chocolate spread.'

Bop. 'Cheese.'

Bop. 'Triangles.'

Bop. 'We don't have any; I'll do Cheddar.'

Bop. 'Don't like Cheddar.'

Bop. 'I'll toast it.'

He misses again. 'Thanks, Mummy.'

Game set and match Mrs Cartwright.

John is putting his coat on. 'See, you can cook.'

'Aye, I even managed spaghetti once.'

He grins. 'From a tin!'

I go over and kiss him. 'Cheeky bugger.'

Peter pushes between us. 'Eugh! Get a room!'

John picks Peter up and plonks him onto the stairs. 'You, bath. I want you in your pyjamas by the time I get back.'

He wriggles away. 'It's not bath night.'

Peter is in bed. We've finished the meal and drunk most of the wine. John has left a book on the coffee table.

'What's this?' I ask.

'Peter found it at the house. It's a World War Two story. He thought you might like it.'

There's no cover design, like it's a proof copy or something.

'How sweet. Why did he think that?'

'Well, it's set in the part of France we are moving to. It's a chance to find out some local history.'

Local history is the last thing on my mind. I take the glass out of John's hand and he gives me one of his looks.

'I missed you,' he says.

'And I missed you. No, John, don't look like that; I honestly did.'

'I'm glad. Well, you know what I mean.'

I knock back the last of the wine. 'Aye, I know exactly what you mean. I'll wash.'

I need to check Richard didn't leave any of his stuff in the bathroom. There's a bar of Yardley's lavender soap I've not seen before.

Are you honestly going to leave him?

I jump. The reflection studies me.

'I love John.'

I am not sure whether I am convincing myself, or my reflection. Am I doing the right thing?

European Cup Final, Twickenham

'John, me ole mucker! How was France?' Richard swings his mobile to the other ear so he can pick up the tickets. 'I've got them.'

'Got what?' The voice is staccato. Richard thinks, not for the first time, that John needs to get himself a new mobile.

'Three tickets for Twickers.' He doesn't say Twickenham because he knows the diminutive term annoys John.

'Oh, fuck. I'd completely forgotten. We've got to go back to France. We've bought a house.'

The pause is almost imperceptible. Richard regroups and laughs. 'Yeah, Cathy told me.' She didn't, but Richard wants John to wonder when Richard and Cathy had spoken.

'Look, I know rugby's not really Cathy's thing, so I thought you could give the other ticket to Donkey,' says Richard.

'It's not Donkey, it's Horse, and he's already got one. I'll ask Tree. He might take mine too.'

'Fucking hell, John, where do your mates get their names from?'

'Tree is six foot six, and if you'd been in the shower with Horse, you wouldn't need to ask.'

There's a roar of laughter from Richard's end, turned on like the canned laughter on a sixties comedy show. 'I'll remember not to drop the soap.'

Richard's fake laddish humour draws John in against his will. 'We fly out on Monday. I'll check that Cathy is alright for me to be out Saturday.'

'Bloody hell, John! Tell her you are going out with the lads, and she'll have to look after the sprog.'

'Our marriage doesn't work like that,' says John. 'She may have something already planned.'

'OK, mate. Check with the trouble and strife if you must, but I'll see you and Tree in the Cabbage Patch before the match.'

John puts the phone down and thinks how stupid cockney slang sounds in a Surrey accent. The nearest Richard ever got to the East

End was his prep school. There older boys bullied him from when he was seven until he was big enough to do the bullying himself.

By the time he went to Carlsborough, an irrational sense of entitlement replaced any empathy he might have been born with. He should have gone to Oxbridge. That he made it to Bristol owes more to the old-boy network than native intelligence.

Supporters packed the Cabbage Patch. John and Tree missed the early train and would have gone straight to the stadium if Richard hadn't got their tickets. They found him at the back, surrounded by Hooray Henrys talking out of their arses. Richard refused to take any money for the tickets, so John bought a round of drinks then checked his watch.

'We need to get going or we'll miss the start.'

Tree downed his Guinness, leaving the Quins' supporters to their Pimm's. Richard never made it to the match, and they met him afterwards.

'How were the seats?' He made circular movements with a bottle of Champagne.

'OK, if you like being behind the posts.'

'Sorry I couldn't make it. Bumped into a few Quins' fans who blagged a box off Will Carling. Free booze. Fucking brilliant.'

John's lips narrow. 'So it seems. What did you think of Rob Howley's grubber kick?'

Richard is having trouble understanding the question. 'Fucking brilliant. When was that?'

'At the end.'

'Yeah, yeah, fucking brilliant. What happened?'

'He beat the fullback to the ball and scored the winning try,' explained John.

'Yeah, yeah, of course he did. Fucking brilliant. So Wasps won then?'

'Yep.'

'That explains why all them Frenchies look like they've got garlic stuck up their arses.'

'Possibly.'

'What was the French team again?'

'Toulouse.'

'Yeah, yeah, fucking brilliant. Still, the French never do well when they play away.'

This is the most insightful sentence Richard has managed.

'Yep. Look, Richard,' says John, 'are we heading back to yours? You said we could crash there tonight.'

'Sorry, guys. Didn't I tell you? These guys are holding a post-match party at Hampton Court. I'd love to get you in, but it's all a bit hush-hush. You don't mind getting the train back to Reading, do you? Give Cathy a snog from me.'

John minded. If he was sober enough to give Cathy a snog, it would not be from Richard.

Tree leans in to John as they make their way to the station. 'What's a hush-hush party?'

'Dunno, but I imagine it involves white powder and strippers.'

When John gets home, Cathy is reading the book that Esther asked Peter to give to her.

5

England 1941

To be RAF flying crew is single status only, so Flight Lieutenant Jennings cannot marry his sweetheart. They pledge their troth in the village church at Cobham, witnessed only by the image of Mary Magdalene, standing impassive in the window above the altar. The smell of leatherette Bible covers, polished wood, and cold stone struggle to whisper: "All things shall pass." Jennings experiences a crisis of faith, questioning if it's the Englishness of the life the church clings to, not the evil of this world, that will soon pass away. His girl drops onto a kneeler depicting a small Kent cottage, the kind she hopes he will buy for them when this terrible war is over. His kneeler has poppies stitched with love by a war widow. Jennings prays fate will spare his mother a similar task.

Outside, the couple consummate their union, rough granite pressing into pink flesh. Turning her head away, she reaches down and parts her lips. It's not how she imagined it, but war changes things. Her parents raised her well; she had not pictured lifting her skirt without a ring on her finger.

Rain beats against the grey Nissan hut, corrugated iron rusting against the relentless waves of British weather. The commanding officer stands erect, his handlebar moustache bristling, voice loud enough to drown out the wails of the doubting wind. Born to exude the confidence he does not own, he taps a map pinned to the hardboard wall. It shows where he is about to send another group of England's elite to their death.

Air Commodore Maxwell slaps Jennings' shoulder as he leaves. 'Third time pays for all.'

The pilot is living proof that some return. After one final sortie, Maxwell will put him in charge of training. Then he can marry the slip of a thing that he is sure he has hidden somewhere.

France

Whatever the outcome, this will be Jennings' last flight into hostile territory. The cockpit smells of aviation fuel and Duraglit. Instruments are polished to within an inch of their lives to show the Allies' superior air power. He pushes the joystick forward to lose height. The wooden wonder shudders as Jennings pulls back, levelling out beneath the cloud base. He enjoys flying Mosquitoes. The Rolls-Royce engines give off the reassuring purr of a lioness guarding her cubs.

This is not just the usual drop. 'You OK, Jenny?' The navigator's tone is gentle even though he has to shout. Jennings takes his eyes off the instruments for a second.

The navigator is talking to me, wedged between the cargo boxes. Little Jenny Wren they call me. I had a name before the war. Jennings does not ask. It's harder when they die if you know someone's real name. Jennings knows neither the contents of the boxes nor my mission.

I tremble inside my flying suit. This is my first time. My French grandfather evacuated Mamy from Dijon to Surrey during the Great War. I mutter under my breath, rehearsing my lines. The only qualification I have for the mission is my perfect French. At Abingdon, sadists pushed a row of petrified girls from the top of the training tower. I was the only one to survive without injury.

I'm delivering radio valves to a safe house near the demarcation line. It has a balcony facing the square. I am to approach it by the back door and say, '*Les grues sont en retard cette année.*' The person there should answer, '*Ils viendront quand le soleil reviendra.*' If they do not... I feel for my service revolver.

Jennings peers though broken cloud. 'Unstrap the cargo; we must be almost there.'

A silver snake glints in the moonlight. 'Bates! Is that the River Isle?'

The navigator studies the map pouch on his knee. Before he can answer, a trail of tracer bullets flies towards them. Jennings pulls on the joystick; Mossie responds with a steep banking climb.

'Get her out!' he screams.

He levels out as soon as we reach the cloud base. 'NOW!'

The manoeuvre catapults me and the boxes to the back of the plane as Bates opens the bomb doors. Jennings thrusts the joystick forward again, sending the cargo out of the underbelly.

I hang in the night air. The boxes will land where they will. I don't suppose the resistance will find them before the Germans do. Jennings' job now is to get home alive. The dive has dropped them below the cloud base. Anti-aircraft fire resumes. This time they are hit.

The tracer bullets, engines, aircrew, and cargo all erupt in a chaotic symphony. Here, suspended between earth and sky, the conductor's baton brings an abrupt silence. Boggy ground breaks my fall. I hide the chute as best I can. Dressed in peasant clothes under my jumpsuit, I realise many things can still betray me. I check for the British service revolver and the wireless valves hidden inside a baguette. The small bar of Yardley's lavender soap was my idea. The locals will spot my Dijon accent, but not the Germans, I hope. If they do, I have an additional item. Wrapped in a twist of paper like a scotch mint is a cyanide pill.

With a flick of my wrist, the revolver spins into the river. I enlisted to meet men, not kill them. RAF pilots are way better than the conchies mincing around the land army girls. Now I will meet French men. I know what will happen to me if captured, but Germans are not on my dating list. That is what the pill is for.

The lion wakes. The growl of the Rolls-Royce engines screams its death throes, pulling me out of my teenage dreams. I look up to see a de Havilland DH.98 bury itself in the adjacent field. If either Jennings or Bates has survived, their welfare comes before my mission.

A fireball billows upwards as almost two hundred gallons of aviation fuel ignite. Dark red against the sky, flames billow, their edges black with unburned petrol — a shroud to mourn yet more wasted lives. Something draws me forward. It's not a heroic desire to remain there until I see that the two airmen are beyond rescue. Nor yet a macabre wish to look at the mangled remains from which fate ejected me. It's an unreasoned reaction to an unfamiliar situation. Already, behind me, is the sound of a motorbike.

I wrench the rough linen shift free from the brambles, but before I can spring forward, a broad hand wraps around my ankle. Dragged backwards, skirt pulled up over my torso, my pale legs streaked with mud kick against my attacker.

When he has enough of me in his grasp, Jennings clamps his other hand over my mouth. 'Bates is dead. In that fire, they will be lucky to find a body. If they do, the fire will have left nothing to identify him.'

There's a forced intimacy: my skirt lifted like a wanton plough-girl, the airman's face close to mine. My body confuses adrenalin with endorphins, making me shake my head to dislodge the feelings.

'I can't leave you. Are you injured?' I say.

Jennings releases me. 'You can, and yes, I am. They did not mean for us to meet again. You must complete your mission. Do you have your revolver?'

'Yes,' I lie.

'Good.'

He empties his own gun, leaving a single bullet.

'Take these. I have all I will need.'

The handful of brass cylinders feel heavy in my hand.

'But how will you...?' I stop and try another question. 'Where are you hurt?'

Inappropriate thoughts return. There are worse ways for him to die.

'Where?' I ask again, pulling us both out of the shining tunnel.

He shifts. 'My ankle; broken or a severe strain. It makes no difference; I can't walk.'

I place the bullets on the ground between us to show the negotiations are far from over. 'Not on your own. Stay here. I will go, but I'll come back.'

He grabs my wrist. 'You will not. That is an order.'

I don't answer, twisting my hand to escape as if he were an

overeager schoolboy playing kiss chase. 'Let go of me.'

I rub my wrist that still shows signs of his grip. 'Forgive me. I lied. I do not have my revolver. Give me yours.'

Whatever the difference in rank, I am fit, and he injured. I will not let him take his own life. I hold out my hand. He hesitates, then complies.

'My chances of survival are zero. Yours are slim. A weapon might shorten your odds. What does it matter if, when they find me, it's a German or British bullet?'

I turn to go. I have no answer to his logic, only a determination to prove him wrong. The safe house can't be that far. I need to find a road, but the sound of the motorbike engine is growing louder. Running away from both crash site and bike, I hear the engine cut close to where the airman lies hidden. Then I spot a gate.

Praying that the crash will draw the soldier away from Jennings, I set off. All that HQ has told me is that the village of Saint Etienne contains the safe house and a garrison of German soldiers. "Hiding a tree in a forest" was the expression they used.

Saint Etienne

The Templar house is neither a farmhouse nor a chateau. It now plays grudging host to the German garrison. Without authority in Free France, Pétain has invited them to police the demarcation line. Herr Schneider would know that Mosquitoes only have two crew members, and neither is likely to have survived. With luck, he will only send one dispatch rider to check. I set off towards the village. It's the only location they have given me for a safe house. Let's hope it's the opposite direction to the one the Germans expect. Rounding the corner, I see the abandoned motorbike and pick it up. My brother taught me to ride, so I know the kick start is the hardest and could attract its owner's attention. I tuck the hem of my skirt into my knickers and turn the machine to face down the slope. Selecting second gear, I hold in the clutch and push, letting it out when almost running. Euphoria floods me as the engine springs to life. By the time the German reaches the road, I am out of pistol range. However, my relief is short-lived. Riding towards an armed German garrison on a German Army motorbike, I turn the corner and run straight into a checkpoint.

Cathy, 2003

I brought the book, but I can't read in a car that smells of plastic and air freshener. John and I are both trying so hard that it forces the intimacy. Mechanical coupling at the hotel airport, minds elsewhere. What does Peter understand? He was weird when Richard came to babysit.

John shrugs. 'Was he? Probably sulking because he wanted to come with us?'

'Maybe. He used to love staying with his gran.'

John's lips pressed into a thin line. He misses his mum. The inheritance is her act from beyond the grave to bring us together, so I owe it to her to give this my best shot.

The Mairie is old. Modern furnishings strip the room of charm, but Madame le Maire's welcome washes away the municipal sterility. She does not seem to mind that we are late. I am wearing my business suit; John, his usual jumper. It infuriates me when he tells her the offer price. Maybe it's just the jumper. Anyway, I get all the information I need. They are OK with us being English, and John is not offering too much.

Outside, he is like a toddler showing a picture, desperate for my approval.

'There it is.'

I stop short. 'What, that? All of it?'

'Yep, from the barn to the letterbox.'

Is he kidding me? Our entire house in England would fit in the barn. Naturally, John has not thought about getting the keys, so we can't go inside, and he hasn't even booked a hotel. I let it go. I am trying to let this be his project because, strange as this may sound, I love him, and yes, if he wants this house, I'll support him.

'Did you hear that?' he asks.

There's a mournful honking noise. High above, hundreds of birds circle to no apparent purpose. The calls grow as one breaks away, followed by another. Gradually, they form into a perfect V formation. The cries grow as they move off, each bird finding its place.

Les grues sont en retard cette année.

I turn, expecting to see the mayor behind us.

'What did you say?' John asks again.

So he heard it as well.

'Nothing,' I reply. 'Do you think they are geese?'

'Maybe. They made quite a racket. Why did you say they were late?'

'I didn't, but we are. Let's see if we can find a Chambre d'hôtes before we go to the solicitor.'

She makes us wait, which puts me in a mood.

Finally, she opens her door, scattering apologies like spiders that scuttle away to weave their webs in unseen corners.

John would have signed the *copromis de vente* without reading it, so I take the papers while he looks for his pen.

'That's not the price we agreed.'

The solicitor explains it's some kind of tax dodge where we pay the difference in cash while she looks the other way. This loses John, so I nod to him to show I am happy and ask where I sign.

She offers her heavy Mont Blanc pen to John. 'It is Monsieur Cartwright who must sign.'

I am livid. We were supposed to be joint owners.

'We both sign,' I say through gritted teeth.

'That is not possible because it is Monsieur Cartwright who pays the money from his mother's estate. It is to prevent money laundering. We have to be very careful when money comes from outside France.'

John signs a separate document to give me the legal right to live with him. I'm still cross.

'Who made these laws?' I ask.

'Napoleon. He was an excellent general and made good laws, but I think he was *un peu misogyne*.'

'No shit! More like a right twonk.'

'Excuse me?'

'You heard,' I say. 'Just give John the fucking pen and show him where to sign.'

Outside, John is finally cross with me for swearing.

I kick a pebble that skitters under an oncoming car.

'She deserved it; she treated me like a little girl.'

'Maybe that is how it is in France — only men can sign.'

'Why, do they sign with their nobs?'

He bursts out laughing, which stops us from arguing. He's mistaken about only men signing. It's something to do with the money not having cleared probate, and me not being a beneficiary. I didn't explain because it was more fun being angry with the solicitor.

We go back to the Chambre d'hôtes, where I sulk into my book. I like that Jenny Wren. Is she going to escape the Germans?

6

1941

Unconcerned, a guard turns towards the sound of a motor. He is expecting the dispatch rider's return and pulls the barrier aside. I will have to test my cover sometime, but not riding a German bike. I rev the engine. The guard sees his mistake too late to draw his gun, and I slip through the gap. Pure terror drowns the adrenalin as I feel a bullet clip the faring. I throw the grey NSU into a right-hand bend up a narrow lane, but the track soon becomes too thin and rutted. Abandoning the bike, I make for the cover of the woods.

Soldiers are flooding out of the house, so I dive into a ditch, thanking my brother for teaching me to ride his motorbike. And for playing endless games of hide-and-seek with me. The Germans do not see me as they hurry past, but there's no guarantee of a better hiding spot if I break cover. Stiff with cold, water finds its way into every orifice. I lift my head, letting the cool air fill my lungs. Far away, someone barks an order. Footsteps return. The water in my mouth, brown as wood bark and rough as gravel, reminds me of how thirsty I am. I swallow. Voices. Clipped Germanic syllables, harsh and efficient as a Beretta, force my head back down into the water. Controlling my heart rate, bubbles trickle from my nostrils. When my lungs are empty, and I can bear it no longer, I raise my head, gasping. The woods listen, cold and silent as a corpse.

I have not become that corpse. Waiting until I am sure they have gone, I climb back onto the track, heading for the safety of the woods. Finally, I loop back until I come to another road that leads to the village. My shoulders finally relax when I see a house with a balcony and an alley beside the barn.

Stone steps lead up to the back door, a faint light behind a curtain. The door opens a crack to reveal half a face, red as a gammon.

I blurt out, '*Les grues sont en retard cette année.*'

The face replies with a grunt. '*Ils viendront quand le soleil reviendra. Entrez! Vite!*' adding, 'were you followed? I heard shots.'

Shivering muddy water onto the dark ochre tiles, I search for my French. 'No, I hid in the woods until they gave up.'

Tall chestnut doors of unguessable antiquity cover huge cupboards built into the thick stone walls. An enamel-fronted range reminds me how cold I am.

Louis pushes me towards the fire. 'Undress!'

His wife comes out of hiding, holding a towel and spare clothes. 'That is no way to talk to a mademoiselle. Here, put these on. Turn your back, Louis!'

I open my bag. The bread has disintegrated, but the two radio valves survive. I set the wet packet of soap to dry.

'There is an injured airman near the crash site.'

Louis looks doubtful. 'Is he badly injured?'

'A sprained ankle, possibly broken.'

Louis lifts his eyes towards the ceiling. 'Can he get up there? There are no stairs.'

He takes me outside where there's a tiny opening under the eaves. Louis produces a rope tied to a mangled piece of metal. Tossing it through the opening, it catches. After testing the rope, he hands it to me.

The loft is large, with just enough light to show there's no other way in or out. Straw covers rough floorboards, and a wireless transmitter sits on an upturned crate, cover removed. Last of all, I notice the man sitting on the stool.

He holds out a hand. '*Bonjour. Je m'appelle Jean.*'

I hold out my own, wondering if it's normal in France for strange girls to climb through one's window. 'Jenny.'

Jean picks up a blackened object, rotating it between finger and thumb. 'Have you brought the valves?'

I cross my arms, upset that the young man seems indifferent to my arrival. 'They are downstairs.'

'Good. Your friend, do you think he will be capable of passing by this window?'

I glance back. 'He broke his ankle. Perhaps with a ladder and some help.'

Jean stands. 'Then we must find him. You must remain here.'

Positioning my body between him and the window, I cross my arms. 'How will you find him? I'm coming with you.'

The farmhouse kitchen welcomed all in happier times, but the cavernous hall of the Templar house is forbidding. Germans have stripped the panelled walls of anything of value, replacing them with maps fixed with thumbtacks. Lines in red pencil mark the demarcation line, often redrawn to wrong-foot the resistance. The commanding officer sits at a heavy oak table whilst the dispatch rider cowers before him.

'I know there was a survivor; you let them steal your motorbike.'

The *oberleutnant's* withering stare turns to contempt when he learns it was a girl.

It's past midnight when we get back to the safe house. Finally, the airman collapses on a horsehair mattress in the loft.

Without stopping to think, I kiss the pilot. 'I'll see if we can have some food,' I say.

He nods, neither accepting nor rejecting the kiss.

I return with bread, Louis' home-made saucisson, cheese, and wine. We would be lucky to get potato soup and vegetable pie in England. Jean and I eat with the airman, which gives me the chance to check out the young Frenchman.

Jean, however, turns his attention to Jennings' injury.

'I cannot tell if it broke, or is just badly sprained. You must stay here until the swelling subsides. In the meantime, I will bind it.'

He fetches a towel, a bucket of water and some comfrey. He applies the bandage, then turns to me.

'I have brought you your robe.'

I fix him with the stare of a magician's assistant, daring him not to look away. This time Jean obliges. There's little entertainment during the war, and where's the harm in giving him a free show?

'The pilot is hogging the mattress. I would not mind sharing, but he seems too unwell. Is there anywhere else I can sleep?'

My eyes make it quite clear where I have in mind.

Jean looks uncomfortable. 'I have a bed at the next house, but it is tiny.'

My smile switches to full beam. 'Good. The night is chilly. You can keep me warm.'

I am not a virgin, but have never slept with anyone before. My best friend at boarding school was a girl, so it does not count. Now I am lying beside someone I find attractive, but whose interest in me seems only superficial. He tries to make conversation.

'What pulled you to this work?'

I struggle with one of his shirt buttons whilst he readjusts the blanket in my favour before trying another approach.

'Your family?'

Jean seems to want to get to know me first. There has to be a first time, but at this rate, it will not be tonight.

'My mother was French. Grandfather produced mustard in Dijon. When the Great War broke out, he sent his daughter to Richmond, where she met my father. He was at medical school. They married, and we moved to Plymouth. He was a naval doctor by then, so after I left school, I joined the Royal Navy.'

Satisfied with the introduction, Jean finally becomes interested in my naked back. When his fingertips touch me, it sends a soft, tickling sensation through my body. I take his hand and push it between my thighs. It stops the tickling and may speed things up a bit.

'What about you?'

I clench my thigh muscles so I can concentrate on his answer.

'I was eighteen when Franco massacred the Republicans in Madrid. Those who survived walked to France. Hand carts creaking, donkeys shitting their owners' fear. With soft footfalls, columns of people with exhausted expressions shuffled into the village.'

I had not realised Jean was poetic as well as handsome. I release my thigh muscles.

'Next came trains from Alsace, disgorging their cargo onto dusty platforms at Périgueux. Les Périgourdins welcomed all, even Parisians.'

'Why do you say even Parisians?'

Jean takes his damp hand from between my thighs and places it on my waist.

'In rural South-West France, Paris is as mysterious as Frankfurt or Madrid and its occupants are no less foreign. Whole families slid south in their black Citroëns, like snails with their possessions tied to their backs and suitcases on their tails. The shells rust in the fields with no petrol, their owners vulnerable as slugs. War spread like hoarfrost, freezing souls and sucking life from the soil, dividing France.'

There was a hardness in his voice that betrayed a fierce love of French soil and a bitter hatred of those who defile it.

'The demarcation line bisects my parents' farm. We hide all: Jews, deserters, airmen.'

I move my mouth close to his. 'And English spies.'

Louis makes no comment the following day. Mrs Gagneaux comes in with bread and an undrinkable brown liquid that is supposed to be coffee. Her husband throws it into the sink before filling the cup with water. I drink mine without comment. Louis notices my cheeks are flushed, and the young man will not meet his gaze. He smiles.

I break into the unspoken conversation. 'I was told not to go to the front door. Why is that?'

Louis looks up. 'Not our door. There is another apartment.'

He jabs his thumb backwards. 'Behind this wall. Two up, two down. Steer clear of it.'

'Why?'

Louis snaps shut the clasp knife he has been using to cut his charcuterie. 'Fucking I-tai lives there. Watch him. They're fucking fascists, those I-tais. We are surveying him. One day we will get proof.'

'I don't understand. Proof of what?'

Jean answers for the older man. 'We think he may be an informer. One day, he will talk.'

I hide a half-smile. 'I could get to know him. You could introduce me as a new farm worker.'

'What good would that do?' Louis asks.

I lower my eyelids and look up through my lashes. 'I could pretend to fancy him, then he might open up, like Jean did.'

Flushing, I realise my mistake. 'Jean said nothing. He was asking me questions. You know, checking that I was genuine.'

It does not convince Louis. War does that; you mistrust your friends. I hurry on, saying too much.

'Italians are different. In bed, I mean. They might say something when a Frenchman would not.'

My voice trails off. Both men know bullshit when they smell it.

Louis sniffs. 'If that is your *metier*, we better get you a job at *Le P'tit Chou.*'

I look at Jean for help. 'It is a restaurant just outside the village. That's where the Germans congregate when they are off duty.'

Louis splutters. 'Restaurant? That is one word.'

It's easy to guess another. I take some bread to the airman to allow Jean and Louis to talk behind my back. You can hear everything in that loft.

Jennings is sleeping. Rearranging the blanket, I kiss his cheek as close to his lips as his sleeping position will allow. He starts, tries to get up, finds he can't, and then recognises me.

'Don't you Navy girls knock when you enter an officer's quarters?'

I hide a smile. 'I do, and I salute, but not today.'

'Why not today?'

'I salute the badge, not the man. Neither of us are wearing our uniforms. We are equals.'

I sit beside him, holding out the baguette. 'Am I forgiven?'

'What for?'

'For kissing you.'

There's a twinkle in his eye that in happier times might accompany the chink of glasses or a dinner table anecdote.

'Did you? I was asleep, so how would I know?'

'If you don't know, then I will leave you to wonder,' I say, hiding a smile.

Downstairs, Jean convinces Louis that he has passed no information to the English girl.

'It was the other way round. She's an SOE. It's her first mission, so they have not trusted her with intelligence.'

'Special Operations Executive. Isn't that the Secret Intelligence Service? Is she a spy?'

'That's what I thought. Apparently, the SIS hates the SOE, but Churchill loves them, so that's what we are getting.'

'What we are getting? Is she staying?'

'She has an open brief to remain in France if she can be helpful to the resistance.'

Louis roars with laughter. 'So, you are taking advantage of her open brief! Make the most of it. She's already talking about chatting up that Italian, Ricardo, to find out what he's passing on to Fritz.'

7

Cathy, 2003

It's morning. The shower down the corridor has two settings: C (cold) and F (freezing). I cannot make the old lady understand we need to leave early to catch our flight. Breakfast is not ready, so I do a jam butty for the car, then try to pay the old biddy while John fetches the suitcase. She doesn't take cards, so John has to get cash from Touriac. We miss our flight.

To give John his due, he takes over, hires another car, drives to Calais, and we make the last crossing as foot passengers. I call Richard and beg him to pick up Peter and stay an extra night. He says it'll cost me, but for once, a shag is the last thing I fancy.

We finally get home and find Peter acting strangely. He should be in school. Richard is eager to get to work. I understand Peter is cross with us because we promised to pick him up yesterday and let him down, but why is he taking his anger out on Richard?

I was thinking more about the book, if I am honest. Jenny is my kind of girl; I like her. Is it a memoir? I hope so, because that would mean she survived the war, at least long enough to write it. Strange that she did not want to put her name to it. It makes sense that it's in English if she is an SOE, but she was taking an enormous risk. What if the Germans had found it?

1941

Louis got me that job at *Le P'tit Chou*. I said I was a refugee from Dunkirk. The Germans bombarded the port during the evacuation, so it will be almost impossible to authenticate my papers.

I soon gain a reputation as a flirt, but turn down requests to go upstairs. Even at the bar, I get valuable intelligence for a kiss. Does Jean know? Probably, but he says nothing. He can't when the information serves the war effort.

The airman is another matter. His ankle requires surgery. That's a daunting enough prospect in peacetime; in the present circumstances, it's impossible. He's still in the loft, which bothers Louis. The Germans don't know the location of the cache, but guess it exists. The longer we hide him, the greater the risk.

While he's stuck up there, I have a bit of fun. I give him a look I learnt at the café.

'Is there anything I can do for you?'

At the bar, I am guaranteed to get an inappropriate response, but the airman does not take the bait.

'Not unless you can haul a steaming hot bath through that window.'

I accept the challenge. The next day I am up there with hot water, a towel, flannel, and my bar of lavender soap. I undress him, brushing away his objections by saying I am a FANY.

'No, you're not! Bloody stupid acronym, sounds rude. First Aid Nursing Yeomanry, my arse.'

I give the said body part a firm smack. He must be in pain because he is usually polite. Lathering the flannel, I slap it on the area most in need of attention.

'Ow! The last time anyone handled my bollocks like that was my first day at Cranmore.'

I giggle. 'Tell me.'

'The initiation ceremony for new recruits was to smear their crotch liberally with black boot polish. It took me a week to remove mine.'

They have accepted me into the resistance cell, but my real initiation would happen after the visit from Herr Schneider.

The *oberleutnant* leaves his guards outside and raps the tortoiseshell tip of his swagger cane against the glass. The formal politeness with which he announces his arrival covers smouldering anger. Louis opens the door, knowing better than to speak first. The German looks around him, taking in every detail. Madame Gagneaux has hidden the sausage. He spots telltale traces of grease but says nothing. The longer Louis remains silent, the more prominent the vein on the German's neck becomes.

'We shot an enemy aeroplane down for violating our airspace.'

Still no response.

'The pilot survived and is being hidden. I am pleased to say one of you has been patriotic enough to share with us his location, so I am here to invite him to surrender to our hospitality.'

He draws a metaphorical arrow from his quiver. Fitting it into his bow, he pulls back his right arm, feeling the tension mount in the bowstring. His left holds the bow motionless as he sights the Frenchman along the shaft. Still, Louis does not speak. Above his head, Jennings can hear every word. He's glad that Jenny and Jean are not there, but even more pleased that Jenny has returned his revolver. He stretches out towards it while holding his breath. Below him, ferns of frost unfold between officer and butcher, searching for the tiniest sound. When it comes, it floats down like the first snowflake. The German's eyes move from the Frenchman to the ceiling.

Finally, Louis speaks. 'We have rats.'

Like the arrow loosed from the metaphorical bow, Schneider draws his pistol and discharges six shots into the ceiling. Unable to bear the weight, a branch dips, sliding a wedge of snow to the ground. Silence. The German raises an enquiring eye towards the ceiling, inspecting the pattern of holes. One darkens, the rim turning brown like a boxer's eye and a drop of blood falls to the floor between the two men. Schneider studies it and replaces his gun in its holster.

Looking Louis straight in the eye, he smiles. 'I appear to have killed a rat.'

Turning in a single parade ground movement, he marches from the house.

Jean's bedroom overlooks Louis' garden. We were in bed when the *oberleutnant* arrived, so I only found out later what happened in the kitchen. I let out a cry when the gun went off.

Jean holds me. 'You do not know.'

I push him away. 'What? That Louis was shot? What other explanation is there? I'm going to see.'

Jean already knows better than to stop me.

Herr Schneider has left, taking all but one guard with him. I recognise him as the one that shot at me as I drove through the barricade. In other circumstances, we could be friends, maybe even lovers. Now society expects us to hate each other, to kill each other if required. He doesn't look capable of killing anyone. No more am I.

When I realise he is there to stop escape, a tiny ray of hope forms like dew on the grass, trickling down the blade, searching for my soul. Taking a deep breath, I enter the courtyard, my heart pounding in my chest as I try to think of what to say if challenged. I nod to show that I have seen him and then walk up the steps. The guard will report back, but he has not stopped me.

Louis is watching and opens the door as I reach the top step. The kitchen clock grumbles in the silence towards a conclusion nobody can imagine. Madame Gagneaux is wiping the drops of blood from the floor. Every time she squeezes the cloth into the bucket, another drip falls from the ceiling. There's no sound from above. Louis is silent. I cannot be glad he is safe. Before the war, I might have been friends with the German outside and an enemy of Louis.

Finally, with his voice lowered, he tells me what happened. 'He does not know the hiding place; it must rest like that.'

I have other priorities. 'What about the airman?'

Louis shrugs. 'I think he's dead. If not, he soon will be.'

'I'm going to see.'

Louis grabs my arm so hard I feel the bruise. 'If you do that, you will reveal our hiding place to the Germans.'

'And if I don't, Jennings may die.'

'We wait until the guard leaves.'

I wrench my arm free. 'By which time Jennings will have bled to death.'

Another drop of viscous claret strikes the floor in silent admonition.

'Then we have to get rid of the guard.'

Rubbing my bruised arm, I ask him how.

Louis makes an exasperated gesture to accompany the Gallic shrug. 'We are in a war; how do you usually get rid of someone?'

He doesn't scare me anymore, so I look him in the eye. 'I have never killed.'

'Then you must learn.'

He goes to a row of sausages curing over the fire, curved like scimitars, and hands me the only straight one. I am surprised by the weight.

'You want me to kill him with a sausage?'

A smile flickers across his face as he goes to his knife drawer.

'If you must kill someone, this is the knife.'

Holding a long, narrow, filleting blade, he moves close to me as if to put an arm across my shoulder. With a forefinger, he traces my bottom rib. 'You plunge it in here.'

His finger pushes just above my solar plexus. 'It must go just to here.'

Running his hand upwards, he cups my entire breast. He now has his other arm across my shoulder.

'Twist the knife to sever the major artery as if you were cutting the heart from a pork.'

I have never butchered a pig, so do not know what he means.

'The difference is that the pork is dead. Your victim will jerk away, so you must pull him down onto the knife.'

He pushes down on my shoulder as he twists the handful of breast.

I pull away from him, murder in my eyes. 'Ow! That hurts!'

He smiles. 'Good! You must be in anger, or you will fail.'

He places the filleting knife next to the sausage. 'You were asking how you kill a man with a sausage. You hide a knife in it.'

I pick it up, but Louis turns it around. 'Hold the handle, not the blade. Just use it as a knife; the meat will fall away when you drive it home.'

I pick up the sausage and turn to go before the anger in my breast subsides. 'I hope you're right.'

'Are you hungry?' The guard avoids my gaze as I stride up to him.

His eyes say 'yes'; his lips 'no.'

'I do not eat on duty.'

He speaks in broken French, stumbling over his words.

I smile, as if he has just asked me to dance. 'Then you must save it for later. Where shall I hide it?'

The French sausage slides into his trousers as I search for the German one. My eyes switch to full beam, leaving him in no doubt about my intentions. He staggers backwards, so I put my arm across the back of his neck, pulling his head down so I can kiss him. As I plant my lips on his, I feel him grow. Kneading him with my right hand, I pull his face into mine, forcing my tongue into his mouth.

The lad is inexperienced or has not had sex for a long time. He groans, then spasms. Unprepared for it to happen so fast, I release the German sausage and grab the French one, pushing it upwards as Louis showed me. The guard's eyes widen. My mouth still clamped over his, I pull him towards me with all my strength, remembering to twist the knife. We stand locked in this macabre embrace until his blood is in my mouth. When he goes limp, I release my grip. He drops to the ground, the knife still embedded deep in his torso. Falling to my knees, I vomit.

Louis and Jean are by my side in an instant. The older man is full of praise for how I killed the German, whilst the younger wanted to know if I was OK.

'I need to wash. I'm covered in blood — and other things.'

Louis suppresses a smile. 'He died with a smile on his face, at least.'

I turn to the older man, wishing I'd killed him instead. 'C'est un chose vraiment vulgaire à dire.'

The butcher shrugs and turns away, muttering. 'I was only trying to lighten the mood.'

Jean is unhappy about my "special operations", but Louis is more practical. They need an intelligence gatherer. Now that I've proved I can kill, I am a fully paid-up group member.

There's a more pressing problem now: we must move the corpse before the change of guard. Jean looks at the well and then at Louis. Madame Gagneaux will be furious that they plan to poison her source of drinking water.

Meanwhile, I am trying to get the grappling rope through the window. Fumbling in the gloom, I happen by chance on a broken ankle, relieved to find it's still warm. The airman's breathing rasps as he tries to speak.

'I never even knew your name, Jenny.'

I kiss him. 'Nor I, Jennings.'

'It's the war. It's over for me. There is a photo of my girl in my uniform. Find her. Tell her I thought of her at the end.'

I turn until my lips are close to his ear, smelling the sweet smell of death on his breath. 'What is her name?'

He forces the words. 'Susan. What is yours?'

I wish I was Susan so I could ease the airman's passage to the next life.

'Cathy. And yours?'

His breathing catches into a death rattle.

'Peter.'

8

John, Summer 2003

I'm crashed out in my favourite armchair. The journey back washed me out and the last thing I remember is Cathy curled into the corner of the sofa with that book. There's a scream. It wakes me just in time to feel the book hit my chest.

'Whatever is the matter?' I ask.

'It's that book; it's minging! So many dead!'

I rub my eyes. 'It's about the war. People die in wars.'

'I know. I don't want to read anymore.'

'Then don't.'

I retrieve the book. Cathy doesn't know Peter claimed the ghost gave it to him, and that she wanted Cathy to have it. Maybe I should have checked out the book first, but Cathy was saying, 'Oh, how sweet that he brought me a present.' When she started reading, she was saying how it sounded just like our house, and what a coincidence that it mentioned the village. If the ghost gave the book to Peter, I need to know why. I don't believe she means us any harm. Peter seems quite taken with her. A lot of children have imaginary friends at his age, but hats off to Peter for choosing a ghost. It makes a change from Pooh and Piglet. I don't get the feeling she means me harm, either. Peter said I was her old boyfriend or something. To be honest, I didn't listen. The whole idea of a ghost falling in love with me is laughable.

But somebody had been on the balcony the first time we visited. We both saw them. And I knew things like the front door not connecting to the rest of the house. It's difficult to explain, but I feel the house wants us back. I need to read that book; it may help me understand what is going on.

Jenny, 1941

The rain falls in torrents, washing away the blood of the murdered sentry. Louis says a silent prayer of thanks to Saint Medard, grateful for this small mercy amongst his mounting problems.

The replacement guard arrives, finds the post deserted, and returns to report. Herr Schneider storms into the courtyard, smacking his swagger cane against his boots. Louis stands, arms crossed, legs apart. As mayor of a commune in Free France, he has some influence. The Germans are only here at the invitation of the Vichy government.

'I cannot be responsible for the behaviour of your soldiers,' he says.

The *oberleutnant* bristles. Louis smiles through clenched teeth.

'It is my duty as mayor to cooperate with you. I do so despite the discourtesy you paid me last night. There is a new peasant girl; I saw her speaking to your soldier before they left together for the woods.'

'And what would they be doing there?'

Louis shrugs. 'What do young people usually do in the woods?'

Schneider mutters under his breath. '*Ist das die Pilotin?* Is this the female pilot my soldier was supposed to guard? It's beneath the stupidity of my most junior soldier.'

His eyes narrow as he studies Louis. 'Maybe I only injured the pilot when I fired into the ceiling and she escaped when the guard abandoned his post.'

The *oberleutnant* barks an order; the replacement salutes and takes up his position.

Rocking, overcome with grief, I crouch beside the corpse for twenty-four hours, only shifting to check on the guard. Finally, he leaves. Getting a corpse down from the loft will be difficult.

Jean arrives. 'How is Jenny?'

Louis is in no mood to indulge him. 'As you see.'

'And the airman?' Jean asks as an afterthought.

'Dead.'

Jean looks around as if expecting to see him laid out for burial. 'Where?'

Eyes thrown up to the ceiling, Louis growls. 'Where do you bloody well think?'

Lady Macbeth is on her knees again, scrubbing the kitchen floor. Louis pushes her away in irritation. 'Take Jenny to meet the others. She has earned her place on our team.'

I am being sent away. The butcher has also found an errand for his wife. I can guess why. He needs to deal with the airman. Rolling his knives in an oilskin, he slings the bundle around his neck and climbs to the loft.

When Jean passes the news of his death back to London, I make sure that the commanding officer respects the dying man's wishes. Air Commodore Maxwell meets Susan, at her request, in the church at Cobham, noticing the instinctive motion of the girl's hand to her stomach. Something of Jennings still lives in the green fields of Surrey.

Cathy, Summer term 2003

I've put that book out of my mind. I wanted to burn it, but John said no. Something about an important primary source. It's in his study and it's staying there. He's gone back to France to sign some papers, so I've got to do Peter's parents' evening on my own. He's being difficult.

'But you like these evenings, all them teachers saying how clever you are.'

He doesn't even look up from the games console. 'I don't want to go, alright?'

'Fair do. I'll get Richard to babysit.'

He slams down the controller. 'OK, I'll go.'

Richard turns up anyway.

'I don't want to be any trouble, so I'll make myself at home whilst you two go.'

Peter is scowling. I think he could be a bit more grateful.

These evenings are usually sitting listening to teachers saying nice things about him. This time is different.

Mrs Georges squirms. 'There is no doubting his ability, but he seems not to be trying his best. The art teacher's comment sums it up: Basically lazy.'

I shrug. 'He's clever, so he doesn't need to work so hard. Maybe you should give him stuff that stretches him.'

Mrs Georges ignores the dig. 'The art teacher would like to have a word.'

I give her the Cartwright stare. 'The one who thinks my son is basically lazy?'

Peter smiles his approval as Mrs Georges goes red and shuffles the papers on her desk. 'The school counsellor would like to see you as well.'

Peter says something under his breath. It's not a word we taught him.

By the time we leave, I'm seething. Peter drew a picture which the art teacher showed to the counsellor. He had to paint a picture of *Les Misérables*. It's on the desk, so I pick it up. Very good, although it owes more to Münch than Monet.

The counsellor arranges her papers. 'Mr Toni showed me that picture because he was concerned Peter was trying to express some inner frustration or anger. Forgive me, but is everything alright at home?'

I snap. 'Fine. Perfect. Peter's clever. A teacher asked him to paint a picture showing how bad it was for the working class in France, and that's what he did. If it looks like a horse and sounds like a horse, that doesn't make it a fucking zebra.'

I storm out. Peter follows, trying not to smile.

Back home, Richard's still here, waiting for a shag to pay for not babysitting.

Peter scowls. 'Why is he still here?'

I throw the car keys into the bowl on the hall table. 'He's going now, so you can get ready for bed.'

Peter sulks off and Richard moves in to kiss me. 'Am I?'

I turn my head away. 'Are you what?'

'Going now? It's just that I didn't know when you would be back, so I ordered a takeaway.'

For once, sex is the last thing on my mind, but I give in and phone the Raj to add to the order.

'We eat, and then you go, OK? I'm not in the mood tonight.'

While I go to the car to get the bottle that I picked up on the way home, Richard puts on our song. Olivia Newton-John is singing "there you are with yours, here I am with mine."

I throw the bottle on the settee, putting my hand to my face. 'I said I'm not in the mood.'

He stops the record and comes to hug me. 'What do you want?'

'To live in France with John and Peter, you to be happy for me and to be happy yourself.'

He picks up the wine and pulls out his sommelier's knife. That's fucking typical — to have a bottle opener but no condom. Well, he will not need one tonight.

'I'm supposed to be happy that you are leaving? That's a big ask.'

'I know.'

We talk about the counsellor while we eat. 'Like her social work degree counts more than my love for Peter.'

He puts his fork down. 'I love him.'

Did I hear right? 'Perhaps you do, but he has a dad; you can't take that away from him.'

Richard's stare freezes my fork mid-way to my mouth. 'I could be his father.'

No, I'm not going there.

'Peter wouldn't accept you. See how he goes on these days? He didn't use to be like that.'

He's still staring at me. 'Has he said anything?'

'You heard. Peter doesn't like you babysitting.'

'Has he said why?'

'Nah. I think he is being unreasonable. I mean, you're only trying to help.'

The tension leaves the room as he nods his agreement. 'More wine?'

I drink whilst he leans back. 'I don't like the idea of a counsellor.'

'It's not your place to say.'

His look returns. 'Is it not?'

I swallow the wine and hold out the empty glass. I just want someone to talk to. It's obvious where this is going. I'll get drunk, and before long, it will be "I love you. I'm sorry about knocking you back; you can stay the night." I will have stopped thinking about the man with a penknife and no condom.

I might as well get it over with. 'Sorry, Richard. You can stay.'

He puts on his coat. 'That's very kind, but I'll take the answer you gave me when you were sober.'

He kisses me on the forehead. 'Goodnight, Cathy. See you soon.'

I stare after him, wondering what had just happened.

Watch him. He's not what he seems. He wasn't during the war. He isn't now.

I spin round. There's nobody there.

John, the following summer

The restoration is taking ages. We should have moved by now, but finding tradespeople has been a nightmare. Francine has been a godsend, but I have to be careful. Cathy is watching me open my emails, so I tilt the screen to show I have nothing to hide.

'The electrician can't start before September.'

The temperature drops.

'Why don't you ask Francine to help?'

Cathy has a new phone that does text. When it pings, she goes outside to read it. Peter comes in.

'Ask Francine what?'

'To find an electrician.'

'Esther says Francine is her reincarnation, and you are her boyfriend.'

'Peter, I am not Francine's boyfriend.'

His lip quivers. 'You are the reincarnation of Esther's boyfriend, and Francine is the reincarnation of Esther.'

'Even if that was true, Francine and I can't be boyfriend and girlfriend because I am married to Mummy.'

Peter is fighting a losing battle with tears, so I give him a hug.

'We are moving to France so Mummy and I can make a fresh start. You want that, don't you?'

Enthusiastic nodding.

'Then please stop talking about Francine being my girlfriend.'

Cathy comes in, slipping the phone into her pocket.

'I've run out of holiday. You go to France with Peter and I'll come down later.'

I don't answer. An elephant appears in the room. Cathy does a little hip shimmy to pull her skirt lower.

'I need to keep some leave for Christmas,' she adds.

The elephant's chewing invades the silence.

'You could take it unpaid.'

'We can't both do that, not with you spending money like water.'

A large grey head turns, pushing me off balance.

'I thought you were going to stop seeing him when we bought the new house,' I say pointedly.

'I will, when we move down proper.'

Cathy finally arrives in France, and we pick up where we left off.

'The lawn mower needs repairing. The library should have a list of repair shops.' I try to sound casual.

Cathy, who has been sunbathing, turns over and tips her sunglasses. 'Watch her; she fancies you.'

'I'm old enough to be her father.'

'Not quite, but she is a lot younger than you. And me.'

I let it go. Like a pan of milk, our words are simmering just below the rim. Removed from the heat, the milk subsides without boiling over.

She slaps on more sunblock. 'As you're going anyway, I forgot to pack any holiday reading. Can you get something in English?'

'I'll check the local history section.'

'Nah, get a novel. I'm on holiday.'

Holiday reading delivered, Peter and I go back to work. The front door only leads to Peter's bedroom and the new bathroom. It was a separate dwelling once, like the apartment in the story. We will need a proper mason to knock a hole in the original façade to connect it with the main house. While we wait, we decide to knock down the little wall in the loft. Peter loves using a sledgehammer.

I come back from the garden where I was stacking the bricks to find he has made a hole in the wall next to the living room chimney.

'Have you got a torch?' he asks.

I put down the bucket. 'We can bring the inspection light over. What have you found?'

He points. 'It must be the kitchen loft. You go first.'

It's empty apart from a mattress. Time has left nothing but strips of material and bunches of straw.

Peter pokes through the rotten hay beside a wooden box.

'Look, an old light bulb.'

'It is not a light bulb; it is a radio valve.'

'Does it still work?'

'I very much doubt it.'

'There's something else, a tin or maybe a soap dish.' He rubs it, trying to make out the writing. 'Yardley's lavender soap. Can I give it to Mummy?'

'I don't think Mummy likes lavender.'

'I'll give it to Esther. Do ghosts wash?'

'Maybe you should ask her.'

He turns back to the radio. 'How did it work without electricity?'

'I don't know. Batteries, I suppose.'

He looks at the radio valve again. 'But they would need to be recharged. I'll ask the ghost how they did it.'

The next day, Peter watches me clearing away the brambles round the well.

'What are you doing?' He has the radio valve in his hand.

'Putting a lid on the well so you don't fall in.'

'I'm not a kid. OK, I'm a kid, but I don't do stupid things like that.'

He pokes around. 'I can't see anything. The ghost said there was a windmill. They made it look like it was for pumping water, but it was for recharging the radio battery.'

9

I am hiding inside the coffee machine at the ice cream parlour. It's lucky that ghosts don't have bodies.

Francine is with her best friend, Eimear. Ariane is making pancakes. She finishes serving, then turns to my living self. 'Francine, I was just thinking about you! A man was here with his wife.'

She puts a little biscuit in the saucer and hands the cup to her friend.

'He is Jewish; his family were fleeing the Nazis during the war. They stayed at the house the English couple are buying.'

'*Et alors?*'

Eimear smiles to herself, exchanges a knowing look with Ariane, makes her excuses, and leaves.

Ariane turns to Francine. 'The old man doesn't speak English. When he asked about the current owner of the house, the mayor gave him John's phone number, but when the old man called, he couldn't make him understand.'

'I don't know what that has to do with me.'

Ariane checks no customers are waiting to be served, then sits down. 'I phoned for the old man. John is happy for him to visit if you act as a translator.'

The coffee machine gives a brief hiss of excitement.

'And you said yes.'

'I said I thought you would be interested. You are, aren't you?'

'I suppose so.' Francine blushes.

'He's very nice.'

'He's very married.'

Drifting over the Perigord countryside, I think of Ariane's words. Chateau de Mareuil rises beyond the woods, its stones close-laid to withstand the trebuchets of forgotten wars. Centuries later, the Germans commandeered it. How could I forget the part it played in my story? I wrote it all down, then gave it to my little brother for safekeeping. The chateau looks the same, but everything else has changed.

Peter rides up to the castle and then turns towards the woods. He is near the place where that man murdered me. Spring sunshine makes shafts as sharp as pine needles through the crowding woods. Propping his bike against a tree, he stretches out on the bank. Branches rustle in the breeze whilst he looks up the road as if waiting for someone. Well, I must not disappoint him. Gliding forward with the sun behind me, he sees nothing. My shimmering grows as I get closer. Peter shields his eyes, now sure there's somebody there. Finally, I am standing in front of him.

'Hello!'

Hello. Did your mother like her book?

'No, she didn't like the airman being called Peter.'

That's her fault for trying to seduce him when he had a sweetheart back in England. I don't say that, of course. Instead, I change the subject.

Your bike looks fantastic.

He beams. 'Thank you. It is my birthday present.'

Happy birthday.

A puzzled expression eclipses his sunny smile. 'Thank you. Why do you always wear boy's clothes?'

I rustle inside the brown tweed jacket my father made for my brother.

Because dresses are not very practical in the woods. Also, I wear my brother's clothes when I am avoiding the Germans. If they are looking for a young woman, they leave me alone.

'Doesn't your brother need them? Anyway, the Germans would never mistake you for a boy; you are way too pretty.'

Peter is too young to flirt with me! I'm glad ghosts cannot blush.

He changes the subject. 'I saw you here the day Daddy crashed the car. You were with a man. Was it your dad?'

Fading with sadness, I grow again. *No, that was Jean; he was my boyfriend. My father is in Lyon, I think. That is where his last letter came from. Mum went there with my little brother, Benjamin.*

Peter is studying me. 'Why didn't you go?'

I flicker beneath his stare. *I stayed to be with Jean.*

'Why did you say, "was my boyfriend?" Did you argue?'

Nothing like that. They killed us in the war.

'That must have happened a lot.' He gives me that look again. 'Can we be friends?'

My image puffs up with happiness. *I would like that.*

He gets up and goes to his bike. 'I have to get back; we are expecting visitors. I wasn't paying much attention, but I think it was someone who thought they had stayed in our house during the war. Daddy wants to invite Francine from the library so she can translate.'

I smile. Jean may be with his wife, but he is already thinking of my living self.

Peter gets on his bike, then turns back. 'The airman Peter — was that me?'

No.

He nods. 'I didn't think so. Mummy thinks it was. Can you tell her?'

I don't think she can hear me.

I watch Peter cycle away and think again about the visitors. Hundreds of refugees hid in that safe house. And yet... I go to the house.

My living self pulls into the square and almost runs into Peter.

'Hi, Francine. The others haven't arrived yet. Come and see the stuff the last owners left in the loft.'

John waves. 'Hi, Francine!'

He doesn't come over, acting differently when Cathy is there.

Upstairs, Peter lets out a sigh of frustration. 'It's all gone! They must have come back and taken it whilst we were in England.'

Francine looks around the loft, trying to orient herself compared to the house below.

Peter taps his foot. 'This is over the living room; where you are is the main bedroom.'

He takes Francine's hand, dragging her to the wall at the far end. 'There is another loft behind, so we are knocking the wall down to make it bigger.'

'It looks large enough already. What's that hole?'

'We did that in the summer. It goes to the loft above the kitchen. Remember the book that Esther gave me to give to Mummy? They had a loft just like this. I think it is the same house, and this is where the airman hid.'

So he, too, has read the book.

Noises downstairs tell me the others are arriving.

I watch from above while John helps the couple up the steep wooden staircase. My little brother is so old, I don't recognise him at first. That is the difference between us and breathers. We stay forever at the age we were when we died. It must be hard to grow old.

Benjamin gives Francine a strange look when she introduces herself.

'Sorry to stare; you remind me of someone. I must be mistaken. The last time I was in Dordogne was before you were born.'

Francine smiles. 'Maybe it was another life.'

He returns the smile. 'That must be it. Leah, did you bring the folder?' They speak in German.

'Of course.'

She hands him a sheaf of typed papers, which he sets aside whilst he studies several sheets which are folded and re-folded. I recognise these, for my tiny handwriting covers every inch. He offers them to my living self, smiling.

'The diary starts in Alsace, before I was born. My brother and sister were born there.'

Francine nods her understanding.

'We had little paper,' Benjamin continues. 'My sister wrote this.

63

It's a mixture of German and French.'

Francine takes it from him. 'I recognise some French words,' she says, 'but many are German. Most of the nouns are Verlan.'

Peter moves to look over Francine's shoulder. 'What's Verlan?'

She explains that it's slang, a word with two syllables transposed to make a new secret word.

His eyes light up. 'Like cockney.'

He explains East London slang. It sounds more complicated than Verlan.

Benjamin nods. 'One reason Esther wrote like that was in case the Germans got hold of it. The crisscrossing was because we had no paper.'

Francine hands it back. 'That makes perfect sense, but I'm afraid I can't read it.'

'That is why I have typed it all out in French. I thought our English friends would like to hear the story. It is not as Esther wrote it. She had a child's eyes. They see more and understand less. Perhaps it is the other way round — who knows? Over the years, I have woven into it the wisdom of hindsight and the foolishness of old age.'

10

The diary of Esther Fröhlich. Alsace, 1935.

I am ten years old, and have lived over my father's shop all my life. My earliest memory is of his workshop and Mother's cooking. Imagine the scene: the arched door beneath a giant bobbin and needle to advertise my father's profession.

One day, he was plastering the brickwork between the timbers. 'Esther, come and help me,' he called.

Each upper floor overhung the lower so that, but for the steep-pitched roof, you would think they had built the house upside down.

He put down the bucket in the manner of a Rabbi about to explain some nuance of the Tora. 'A proper Alsace house customers will want to visit. If they see you take pride in your premises, they know you will take pride in the work they commission.'

I loved the steep-pitched roof that shed winter snow onto children playing in the street. Children of Israel played with Gentiles as though nothing mattered other than who could make the best snowman. We would tumble inside with snow inside our collars, brushing aside customers, leaving muddy footprints on the tiled floor.

'Business is good.' My father spoke the words with satisfaction that matched the pride he took in his work.

Despite the poverty, my father's clients were never affected. They cared not which God we prayed to, only that Father could stitch the best waistcoats in Alsace.

One day, Father told me to take my brother to the woods by the river. He didn't allow him near the water because Ethan couldn't swim. We went anyway. Just enough breeze found its way through the trees to ripple the water. Shafts of sunlight pierced the canopy that swung its leaves to deny passage. One found its mark like a needle through leather, and the water threw back a million diamonds. We waited for a boat, then jumped forward to help with the lock gate, but calloused hands pushed us back. I watched the water sucked in from the upper level. Ethan asked how water trickles through his fingers, yet is solid enough to raise a barge to three times his height. Rolling on my back, I looked at the sky. The heat of the day was passing, and a pale moon had joined the dipping sun, rising from the Sarre whilst its sister quenched herself in the canal. It was time to go home.

I pushed open the arched door, expecting to smell fine cotton and heavy serge or the faint waft of leather from my father's order book. He filled the gold-embossed tome with numbers as neat as his stitching.

However, the shop was empty. Not knowing what it meant, I entered and my shoes crunched on shattered glass. Mother was whispering to Father in the back room.

'There will be another war; I feel it in my waters. They want Alsace back.'

Father nodded. 'The Germans still resent our land being returned to France after the Great War.'

'And if they invade?'

'They will conscript me into the German army.'

'You cannot! They will see you are Jewish!'

'As soon as I enter the shower.' My Father was not joking, his voice staccato, urgent and whispered.

She placed a hand on his shoulder. 'But what can you do?'

Father could not hold her gaze. 'Join the French Foreign Legion — we are still French.'

She turned from him, rejecting the proposal. He was right, but he was destroying the life he had built for us.

Mother turned back with tears in her eyes. 'What will I do? What about the children?'

He lifted her chin, forcing her to meet his gaze. 'You must leave. Go anywhere. Far from the German border. Take Mother, your sister, her daughter. I will join you when I am on leave.'

Ethan, wide-eyed, flipped his gaze from Mother to Father as they talked. 'Where are you going?'

Father squatted to look into my brother's eyes. 'Lyon.'

'Will there be tigers too?'

He looked at my mother for help. 'Lyon, not lion.'

'Can I come?'

Father took his hand. 'You are going on your own adventure. When I visit, you will tell me all about it.'

'Will you come?' I asked.

'Of course.'

He took me to one side. 'Your brother is young, so I look to you to help your mother through these difficult times.'

I did not understand how difficult things were to become, or how much help Mother would require.

Bodies packed the train, so I lifted Ethan onto the luggage rack and climbed up beside him.

'Daddy, come back! Daddy, come back! Daddy, come back!'

Ethan was singing himself to sleep, hypnotised by the train rhythm.

Brakes smelt acrid and metallic; sulphurous smoke pulled the air from our lungs each time the train entered a tunnel. Leather, wood, cracked varnish: these smells pinned me into the string luggage rack where Ethan was trying to sleep.

'Are we there yet?'

'No, my sweet. Go back to sleep.' Mother plucked words from the maelstrom of her own emotions.

Guards thrust us onto a dusty platform at Alençon. We crossed hot sleepers that leeched tar into our shoes.

Ethan took Mother's hand. 'Where are we going?'

She looked down at him, trying to convey confidence her frown told me she did not possess. 'To Madame Perec. She is a friend of your father.'

She was one of Father's wealthiest customers. Madame Naama Perec was a rich Jewess who fled Poland during the Great War and married well. She saw early which way the wind was blowing. Like many women of her age and belief, she was a worrier.

That she opened the door herself showed how low circumstances had brought her. The suitcases we clutched made the same statement. All the worldly possessions of a family of a once middle-class tailor.

She ushered us inside as if the streets already had ears. 'Germany will retake Alsace, and Belgium too. Your husband was right to send you away. You will be safe here — France is too large for Hitler to get to the west coast. Pierre Laval will never allow Paris to be taken.'

Mother bowed her head in deference to her husband's former patron. I recognised her disagreement, yet she held her peace. The pained expression showed how she hated to beg for favours. I hoped that Madame Perec had some rooms we could rent.

The old woman lifted her arms in supplication. 'I'm glad Abraham didn't live to see this. I bought the largest house my inheritance would allow, but it cannot house the entire diaspora. Let's see...' the old lady reckoned on gnarled fingers, 'there are you, your two children, your mother, and sister, and her daughter.'

Mother looked guilty when Madame Perec pulled a second hand from her sleeve to continue the reckoning. 'That will be six, eight when your husbands arrive.'

'My sister is a widow,' Mother whispered, 'and my husband will share my bed.'

'Your children will share your bed, and your niece must sleep with her mother. The grandmother can have her own.'

The room was large, but not for two families. For five years, our personal space was a musty blanket thrown across makeshift wooden frames.

Father would come home on leave and discuss politics in the manner of our people. As I played behind the curtain, the adults discussed the chaos of the French government in minute detail. The fortunes of the Socialist and Republican Union, the Popular Front, and the Radical Socialist Party ebbed and flowed. They whispered names like *Cagoulard* and other fascist groups, names hiding in the shadows.

Shadows waiting for the men to stop talking so they could creep up through the floorboards and devour us. To protect us from the slavering beast of fascism, the adults looked for advocates. Laval, Blum, Chautemps. All prioritised the downfall of political opponents before placing an axe at the root of the tree of fascism.

This tiny room was the political pressure cooker in which I grew up. By 1938, I was almost a woman. Father found time in between discussing politics to lie with Mother. By the time Benjamin was born, France had declared war on Germany. When Mother told me, I felt nothing, for nothing had changed in our tiny room. Beyond our walls, nothing happened either. The adults spoke of it as a phoney war. Then yet another government collapsed; Paul Reynaud formed an administration, and Germany invaded.

Mother took my hand. 'It has begun, the Germans have entered Paris, and the government has fled to Bordeaux.'

I tried to feel adult enough to be entrusted with this information, but did not. Instead, I pretended I had been following events. 'Has Prime Minister Reynaud gone to Bordeaux as well?'

Mother smiled but saw a child and not the woman I was fast becoming. 'Marechal Pétain has replaced Reynaud. He has gone to Compiègne to sign an armistice.'

I looked hopeful. 'Like Picardy after the Great War? Has the French army beaten the Germans?'

She held me to her. I could smell the clean apron she always wore, no matter how desperate our circumstances. She explained France had lost the war before it had even begun. Father was now stationed in Vichy France, and Alençon was in the occupied zone.

August 1941

A letter arrived from Father. I knew because Mother put on her best dress.

'I want to look my best when with your father.'

The letter included a document, a *laisser-passer*, allowing us to cross the demarcation line into Free France. She put down the letter. 'Your Father wants us to join him in Lyon.'

My heart sank. 'Lyon is far away. Benjamin is too young to travel that distance.'

Mother took my hand. 'We have no choice.'

She was crying. I already understood how hard it must have been for her to leave her mother and sister. Grandmother made her go. She was too smart to convince us to stay.

'Shall I pack our suitcases, Mother?'

She looked troubled. 'Wait a while, I have a toothache. I think it must be an abscess and I want to have the tooth removed before we leave.'

We waited. None of us wanted to go.

September

Finally, we packed our diminishing possessions into worn-out leatherette suitcases. Cardboard poked from the corners, and string replaced one handle, knotted and re-knotted like a bosun's lanyard.

Soldiers at the station were checking papers. I whispered to Mother, asking why they were doing this.

She whispered back. 'Because they can.'

Mother was clutching the identity papers and precious *laisser-passer* with the train tickets. One set to Bordeaux, another from Bordeaux to Lyon. They were under her shawl, away from the driving rain. Putting Benjamin down so she could present the papers, the toddler pushed one thumb in his mouth and the other into a hole he found in Mother's skirt.

There was a problem with the documents. Water dripped from the soldier's hat onto the paper. Drip, drip. His foot moved in time. Tap, tap. The swagger cane beat against a polished leather boot. Thwack, thwack. He turned to show the papers to his colleague. Benjamin turned around until it bandaged him into Mother's skirts, and neither could move.

The German held the precious papers as if they were contagious. 'They are not valid. Jews may no longer cross the demarcation line.'

Mother opened her mouth to speak, but no words came. The soldier extracted the laisser-passer from the sheaf of papers and tore it in half to emphasise his point. The pieces fell like tears. He returned the identity papers, clicking his heels in mock respect. The train tickets he kept. To show that the matter was closed, he turned and walked away.

This placed the others in some difficulty because they needed their papers approved before boarding the train. A menacing hiss from the giant beast urged the remaining passengers forward, pushing past Mother. Others feared the train's imminent departure, but Mother's anxiety rooted her to the spot. That and the straightjacket Benjamin had fashioned from her skirt.

My father's words came back. "Look after your mother."

I ran after the guard. 'Herr Commandant!' He turned, surprised to be addressed in German and flattered by his promotion. 'The train tickets, *bitte*.'

'You cannot go to Lyon.'

'To Bordeaux,' I said. 'We wish to go to Bordeaux.'

His eyes narrowed. 'Why do you wish to go to Bordeaux?'

What could I say? Turning away as other would-be passengers thrust their papers at him, he stopped and looked at me again, judging my age. I forced a smile.

'We are visiting my grandmother.' I blurted out the lie, asking for forgiveness.

He turned. 'The tickets for Bordeaux, *bitte*,' I repeated.

He looked at me, but I held his stare, feeling the weight of the smile I would not allow to fall. One thing I learnt when I was growing up in Alsace was that Germans are meticulous. The new directive required them to prevent Jews from travelling to Free France therefore, he had to destroy the *laisser-passer*. The tickets from Bordeaux to Lyon likewise. We could, however, travel within the occupied zone. Understanding this, he separated the tickets to Bordeaux and presented them to me with mock respect.

Angoulême was closer to the demarcation line, so we got off there. We reached our lodgings late, only to find it full of soldiers. Mother pushed us through the lobby where rationing had long overlaid the smell of wine and brandy with dust and fear. Upstairs, the odour of boot polish and hair cream insinuated its way into bedrooms where girls dispensed their hospitality. Our room had no key, so Mother wedged a chair under the door handle.

'In case someone mistakes their room,' she explains with tact. I am old enough to understand.

In the morning, the shadows under her eyes told me she had not slept. We set off on foot towards Torsac. The horizon was too low, the sky too large to hide a woman with two suitcases and three children. Ethan and I took a bag each, and Mother was carrying Benjamin when a farmer's cart overtook us.

'Adiu.' The driver raised a hand.

Our ignorance of Occitan meant we were uncertain whether he was greeting us or thanking us for letting him pass.

The cart stopped when Mother did not reply. Benjamin fed the horse some grass, forcing a smile from the man that had little warmth and fewer teeth.

'Why go you this way?'

Mother recognised Occitan but did not speak it. Was he asking where we were going?

Mother replied in French. 'We are going to Torsac - to visit relatives.'

A bushy eyebrow quivered, telling her he had understood, but the rest of his face remained expressionless. He turned his attention to Benjamin, showing him how to offer grass to the horse.

On so slight a character reference, Mother trusted him. 'I believe they live on the other side of the demarcation line.'

The man's smile changed. 'That is far; climb on the cart, and I will drop you more near.'

He added, 'The children can ride behind,' as if we were an afterthought.

Mother hesitated. She had taught us not to speak to strangers and not to accept invitations to ride with them, and yet she was doing both. I understand now that clandestine travel to Free France was not something she could manage without help.

We bumped along in the back of the cart, watching Mother's rigid back resist any movement of the wagon that would sway her towards him. Finally, we pulled into a farmyard, chickens scattering to evade the wheels.

The farmer raised a hand. 'Stay there!' he ordered, painting on his smile as an afterthought.

An inaudible conversation came from inside the barn. Crows on the ridge tiles tilted their heads, straining to catch the words. When they did, they bobbed in approval.

As he returned, Mother folded her arms and set her jaw, mirroring my mistrust.

His smile broadened, revealing rows of rotten teeth. 'The passeur will take you across the demarcation line for two hundred francs.'

I gasped. 'Mother, that would buy a kilo of roasting beef on the black market!'

She silenced me with a look, turned away to lift her skirt, and removed her purse.

When he saw the money, the farmer added, 'Two hundred I am giving to the passeur. Another one hundred is for my commission.'

Mother was used to driving bargains in our tailor's shop, but the fight had gone from her that day.

'I will give you one hundred. Two hundred I will give to the passeur.'

He gave a Gallic shrug, as if to cast off her impoliteness. 'As you wish. The fee for using of the barn is fifty.'

Our precious savings were slipping between Mother's fingers. 'We will sleep here.'

Another shrug. 'As you wish. Now I need to find a passeur.' When he had gone, his companion whistled as if calling his dog, then nodded towards a pile of hay.

All night, the crows kept their vigil. Soon after dawn, the passeur arrived. He looked so like the farmer that I wondered if they were brothers.

He thrust a cracked, calloused hand towards my mother. 'Where's the money?'

Our guide possessed all the pleasantry and charisma of his brother. Mother handed him a roll of francs.

He counted it. 'This two hundred is for me; I need another two hundred to bribe the border guards.'

Mother sobbed. 'I have no more.'

The passeur looked at her with a leer that made me wonder if he would lift her skirt to check.

Instead, he shrugged. 'If that is your situation, then you must stay here until dusk; we'll have to pass the woods at night.' Without another word, he left.

Ethan was worried. 'He has taken our money. What if he doesn't come back?'

Mother's face had found an expressionless place beyond desperation. 'He has to come back. He is French. We are French. He knows that, even if we have German accents.'

I said nothing. Some fascists who taunted me in Alençon were French.

At dusk, the passeur returned. I listened to the whispered instructions the man gave to Mother. Why was he not making eye contact?

Thin brambles trailed across unfrequented forest tracks like tripwires, shredding my shins. Benjamin cried and had to be carried. The passeur was always in front, seeming more concerned that we were following him than where he was taking us. He led us across a stretch felled by foresters. The trees, left where they had fallen, created extra obstacles in the darkness.

The ground steepened as we reached a track wide enough to take a cart.

He held out a hand. 'Stay hidden; I will check the path is clear.'

We ducked behind a fallen pine, resin oozing from its trunk and sticking to our hands. We waited while our guide crept onto the path, checking in both directions before beckoning us out of the undergrowth. I felt exposed on the track as the passeur ducked back.

Benjamin clung to our mother's hand. 'Where has he gone?'

Mother stooped and whispered in his ear. 'I think he has gone to relieve himself.'

I don't think it had occurred to Benjamin that adults urinated; it was such a constant topic of conversation when he was tiny, he assumed people just grew out of it. 'Why isn't he coming back?'

Even in the dark, I could see the panic in Mother's face. Her voice remained calm, however. 'Perhaps we have already crossed the border, and all we have to do is follow this path.'

Ethan frowned his scepticism. 'Which way?'

The only consensus was that we could not stay here. Before we had taken a dozen steps, we heard the sound we had all been dreading. Voices.

11

Nobody moved. Flight was useless.

'Pretend we don't speak German.' Mother couldn't think of any other advice. I doubted it would make the slightest difference.

Our captors were French *douaniers*. Their job was to police the border on behalf of the occupiers. Germans were not the only fascists — some French welcomed the invaders. The interrogation was short and pointless — they had caught us. The two hundred francs to bribe the border guards were the bounty for delivering us into their arms.

Benjamin looked up at the *douanier*. 'Where are we going?'

'Chateau de Mareuil.' To emphasise the point, the soldier prodded Benjamin with his rifle.

The castle walls were as cold and unyielding as our captors, gravel crunching under our feet like breaking bones. The smell of damp walls called out in response to our despair as they took Mother away.

In the cellar, straw mattresses made from hessian sacks offered the only concession to comfort. I dropped to the floor, too tired to notice the stench of human sweat that had long replaced the dusty smell of grain. Soon, Benjamin woke me. He had wet himself. It was not the first urine to soak the mattress, nor would it be the last.

A rough boot on my back woke me. Irrational feelings of guilt rose like bile. Ethan was curled into a ball, but Benjamin was crying. My father's words returned: "Look after your mother for me."

I shouted in German to the guard. 'Where is Mother?'

His only response was to point with his gun to show he wanted us to stand, then walk in front of him. In the next room, an officer sat at a desk, regarding us as an inconvenience to be disposed of as quickly as possible. *Saltpetre* spread like frost on the crumbling walls and onto the stone floor. Someone had taken my shoes, making the cold sting my feet. The officer, wrapped in a thick trench coat, was unsympathetic. I struggled to keep my voice steady, shivering from fear as much as cold.

'Where is Mother?'

The officer ignored me.

'Herr Commandant, where have you taken my mother?'

He finished writing before replying. 'Prison.'

Rocking the blotter over the paper, he passed it to a third soldier standing at his shoulder. 'Take them away.'

The soldier produced our last remaining suitcase. Mother had packed it with what few clothes we had left. Hidden in the lining of Ethan's jacket were a few francs mother had placed there for just such an emergency. The suitcase had no handle, so I wrapped my arms around it like a puppy, the last link to a life that was ending.

My next memory is of being at the mairie. In Alençon, the German swastika flew outside the mayor's office. Here the tricolour still hung, sporting a double-sided battleaxe in the middle panel. Indoors, behind a large desk, sat an even larger man, sweating inside a too-tight collar. Out of depth in his own inkwell, he stood when the Germans entered, trying to loosen his collar with a stubby finger.

The fat man spoke terrible German to the guards. I did not think it would help if I offered to interpret, especially as we were the subject of the conversation. The guards left, relieved to be rid of us.

Without falling in the inkwell, the man asked our names and wrote them in a ledger.

Too scared to talk to the mayor, Ethan asked me why the tricolour still flew.

The man smiled. 'Because we are in Free France.'

'It can't be that free if they arrested us. They took Mother away and we don't know where she is,' Ethan said.

I kicked him to make him stop. As the oldest, I made it my duty not to cry, but thinking of Mother made that difficult. Instead, I returned to the puzzle of the flag.

'The middle panel has a battleaxe,' I said.

The man smiled, congratulating me on my observation. 'That is the symbol of Marechal Pétain.'

Ethan resented being kicked and then me hijacking his flag conversation. 'I thought Free France was the Cross of Lorraine, you know, the red one with two crosspieces.'

The mayor checked the door was closed. 'That is the symbol of the resistance. We can't show that in the mayor's office. We are here to co-operate with our German cousins.'

To show the matter was closed, he continued, 'Now we must find you lodgings.' He took another ledger from the bookcase and consulted it.

'I have to take you back to the occupied zone. Madame Chalard will look after you.'

He saw my look of concern. 'Don't worry, it is not far; we are very close to the demarcation line. I have to send you back because of your illegal entry.'

Ethan cried. 'What about Mother?' I kicked him harder; I was only just holding myself together.

The man looked troubled. 'They took her to Libourne; they will release her if it is the first time.' He whispered the second half of the sentence to himself, then looking down at Benjamin, he smiled, took his hand and led us out of the office.

A rusty gate attempted to close the gap in the otherwise impenetrable hedge. Beyond, fig, pomegranate, and *pêche de vigne* fought a losing battle with the brambles. Despite appearances, the gate swung open at the mayor's touch, eliciting a slight sound that alerted the occupant.

Unsurprised by our arrival, a simple farmer's wife opened her door wide to usher us into a kitchen filled with the warm dampness of washing and cooking. It all scared me, but the smell set my gastric juices flowing. Beneath the smile of the farmer's wife, I abdicated my responsibility as head of the household and cried.

Madame Chalard found jobs for us. Ethan kept the fire going whilst I minded the cooking pots. One contained her husband's underwear; another, some kind of cabbage stew. She rummaged in a cupboard filled with shoes, returning with a selection, some of which fitted. She also had some wooden bobbins, which she gave to Benjamin to play with.

I cleared the table after supper, imagining my mother's soft smile of approval. Madame Chalard searched for paper and pencils and we wrote to say we were well. In my letter, Benjamin drew a picture of the house where we were staying. Ethan's had stickmen drawings of Madame Chalard handing us soup bowls.

The following two weeks were the best and worst of times. Madame Chalard found clothes for us, altering them if they did not fit. The beds were hard, but the sheets were clean. The soup was thin, but she baked her own bread. None of this, however, made up for not knowing our mother's fate. As the days passed, I got to know the woods, which helped me to drive maudlin thoughts from my head. I was no longer a child exploring as I had in Bassin de la Sarre. Now head of the family, my responsibility was to lead my brothers to freedom. I pulled off the boots Madame Chalard had found for me because one of them hurt; it being smaller than the other. After putting them on the boot rack as Mother had taught me, I went to see if Madame Chalard needed help with supper, unprepared for the surprise waiting for me.

'Mother!' I rushed to where she was sitting at the kitchen table with Benjamin on her lap.

Our joy was short-lived, however, as a bus was waiting outside. We had all been called to a tribunal in Bordeaux after she served her sentence. Our tearful farewell was marked by embraces that lingered a little too long.

Mother's watchful eye burned into my neck as I hugged Madame Chalard. 'Will you miss us?' I whispered, holding back tears.

She took my shoulders. 'No, for I have two girls coming to stay. They are not as fortunate as you.'

Ethan was waiting for his goodbye hug. 'Why are they not so lucky?'

Madame Chalard turned to him with a sad smile. 'They are

orphans.'

Mother told us her story as we travelled to Bordeaux.

'They took me in a sidecar to the prison in Libourne.'

'You are so lucky — I wish I could have a ride in a sidecar,' said Benjamin.

I pull him onto my lap to silence him.

'The conditions were worse than at the Chateau. Twenty-five women occupied a single room with nothing but a mattress and a communal slop bucket.'

I grew up in those weeks as head of the family. Mother did not acknowledge it — mothers never do, especially in our culture, but she needed to talk.

'I tried to chat to the other women, but they cut me short.'

'Was it because we are Jews?' Ethan asked.

'No, my sweet. Everyone was afraid of informers.'

Once a day, Mother could walk around the exercise yard. Nobody gave her any information about us or allowed her to write. They transferred her to a convent in Touriac, forcing her to take part in Catholic devotions despite being Jewish. For the entire period of her internment, they gave her two meals a day, comprising two slices of bread and a cup of coffee.

Bordeaux

Ethan's jaw dropped as he entered the building. High ceilings with antique chandeliers. Electric lights burned, impotent in bright sunshine. Madame Chalard had oil lamps, but no oil. The cold, tiled floor and sparseness of furniture exaggerated the room's immense size.

The officer read the report, unaccustomed to delivering good news.

'We will release you and you will return to Alençon. If you attempt to cross the demarcation line again, we will catch you and send you to a concentration camp.'

Alsace had youth camps before the war where they did running and swimming, but not for me, as I am a Jew.

'Mother, do they do sports in concentration camps?'

'My daughter wants to know where the centres are.'

Perhaps they are in Free France, and we could just leave and go in search of Father.

The German officer laughed. *'Mein liebe frau, ma chère madame. Vous ne semble pas realiser ce qu'est une camp de concentration!'*

With that, he waved us away. The soldier that brought us in had been studying Mother, looking behind to ensure nobody was watching. He led us down endless corridors before opening a door.

'In here.'

I smelt my mother's fear. What protection did she have among these men?

He jerked his head. 'Them too!'

Her apprehension changed to terror, eyes saying, "I beg you, not in front of the children!"

Smiling, he offered her a chair. 'Don't be afraid.'

Complimenting her on her German, he pulled our old battered suitcase out of a cupboard, then returned the money and jewellery.

'I believe these are yours.'

Mother, unable to believe what was happening, repacked our suitcase, closed the lid, struggling with the faulty catch, and looked at him. As she could find no words in her confusion, I stepped forward, offering gratitude my mother could not express. He smiled, so I extended my hand. He refused with the slightest of bows.

'We are not all monsters. Look after your mother.'

I have thought much about why he would not take my hand. He was offering fairness when I was offering friendship. I was too young to understand the difference.

This German soldier gave us something more than our confiscated possessions, more than the means to buy our way across the border. He gave my mother the courage to make a second attempt.

That was nine months ago. We entered our old apartment without a word. It had not changed, but we had. The smell was still damp even after the dry summer. Whilst the makeshift screens were still there, my cousin's dress hung over ours. She would have moved out of her mother's bed as soon as she could. Grandmother greeted us the way Jewish grandmothers always do, pleased to see us, and more so that we were not dead. In here, we were all waiting to die, so was it any wonder these experiences depressed us? Father's last letter made Mother cry, for it begged her to bring us to Free France. I read it when she was not looking.

They cannot tell us what happens to those taken to concentration camps, only that they do not return. Pétain will stop at nothing to appease the Nazis. He sets quotas higher than in Germany and criteria lower. To allege Jewish heritage without proof is enough.

I said this to my friend Eli. He is not much older than me but a real firebrand. Despite being hotheaded, he understood the futility of resistance.

'Fighting is useless. To give up is to wait your turn for the camps. Flight is the only option. Go!' he cried, with a hand gesture that betrayed his Jewish heritage.

We did not go, at least not immediately. Mother had been staying at home with Grandma for a while now whilst one of us queued for food. She could not stand the taunts, the bullying.

Ethan was growing up so offered to queue for her, but she would rather have taken the assault herself than see her son return bruised and bloody.

I touch Mother's arm. 'I'll go; it is not so bad for girls.'

Not so bad — it was worse. We crept like mice along the skirting boards of the pavement. Eyes down, silent, our only aim was the refuge of the food queues. There we pretended our tormentors meant the girl in front or behind. Until we reached the line, we were alone.

'Hey, *feuj*, Christ-killer, we're coming for you now!' they would call. They did not realise I was French and understood Verlan. *Feuj* was a pretty basic inversion of *juif*, whilst Christ-killer we have borne for millennia. When they were with their friends, the bullies refrained from coarse sexual references. It would not do to be caught contaminating their Aryan phallus with a Jewess. When they were alone, it was different.

Our little brother had no toys. The war had dragged Ethan and me beyond childhood, so we played to amuse Benjamin. I would pretend to be our mother, Ethan, our father, imitating our parents' mannerisms. It was too upsetting to think that we might never see Father again, or that Benjamin would never know him. Instead, we impersonated our father to give Benjamin a vicarious memory. One of the few things Father could not do was dance. To make Benjamin laugh, my cousin and I would sing *Hava Nagila*, whilst Ethan would attempt to dance the Hora with a passable imitation of Father's two left feet.

One day in June, I returned from the shopping ordeal with a single stale baguette. Not a sound came from the crowded apartment. Depression and hunger did that to us. Mother was reading a letter, sitting with her shawl wrapped close against the damp. Even in early summer, the apartment was cold, with no sunlight to drive out the dank smell of mildew.

With care, she placed each page in her lap as she read. Peering through ill-fitting spectacles, she had the inscrutable air of a schoolmistress.

Mother had written to Madame Chalard, enclosing photos, and thanking her again for looking after us. Now our foster mother had replied, saying she would love to see us again. Eli was visiting, paying unwelcome attention to my cousin Miriam. To deflect the rebuff, he turned his attention to our conversation about the letter.

'She is offering to help you cross the demarcation line!'

'It doesn't say that.'

'Of course not! The Germans read our letters. You must go.'

However, his remonstrations and Madame Chalard's offer were not enough to lift Mother from her depression. It was dragging us all down. The next day, tragedy propelled me into action.

Miriam came in, rosy-cheeked despite her shopping ordeal. One bully in the ration queue had said that he would never date a Jewess. There must have been something in the look he gave my cousin, for she unpicked her yellow star, left her papers behind, and walked out. When she did not return, my aunt was beside herself. She had lost her husband, and now her only daughter was gone. *'Ahh ve, ahh ve,* your children will be next!' she wailed.

She was correct; I was next. I left a note to Mother promising to return, took a little of our savings from behind Madame Chalard's letter, and slipped away.

It took weeks, but finally I found my way to Madame Chalard's door, not two kilometres from Free France. She pulled me inside with a gasp of surprise. Only my mother has ever kissed me like that. All the next week, she sent messages, made plans, and gave me instructions. By day, I renewed my acquaintance with the woods; at night, we plotted. I did not feel excitement, just fear.

'You have an excellent memory; we'll make a passeur of you yet,' my foster mother assured me.

When everything was ready and I was preparing to leave, she gave me that hug again that set me thinking.

'Do you have children of your own?'

'My Lord sends me all the children I need,' she whispered. 'May your God protect you.'

August - September 1942

Mother greeted me in the way only a Jewish mother can. Things were plummeting in Alençon. Grandmother and Aunt accepted their fate and refused to leave, saying that if the Germans took them, another would not die.

Eli was there. 'Most of us will die. Those who take their chances will survive. Which are you?'

Now I was back, Mother made no further delay in planning our departure. Her fight had returned, but she had aged.

The hotel in Angoulême smelt of stale Gitanes and damp carpets. Smaller than the previous one, it had an ill-fitting front door opening into an area filled with cane chairs and stained red-gingham tablecloths. The bar doubled as the hotel reception where one man checked us in, served drinks and apologised for the lack of food. Madame Chalard said we must not hide in our room, so instead, we sat in the corner of the cramped restaurant nursing one coffee and three glasses of water. The only difference was that one came in a cup, and the brackish water steamed. Mother fidgeted under the indifference of the German soldiers, her darting eyes betraying her guilt. We had no reason to be in Angoulême, so we concocted a story that we were visiting relatives in Saint Yrieix.

A girl came downstairs. She was not pretty, but drew men's eyes to her, although I couldn't see any skill she used to get a client. When I tried to spot how much money changed hands, it disappeared into some mysterious fold in her dress. The clock over the bar made it easy to calculate the time. Business was brisk.

A man weaving towards us drew away my attention. His straight-sided glass was cloudy and gave off a faint smell of anise, although the barman was more generous with the jug of water he held in his other hand. I turned away as the stranger put his drink on our table, took the thin tab from his mouth and put it behind his ear. Waiting for neither permission nor introduction, he sat half-turned away, voice low, without showing that he was talking to any of us. He described the Auberge, transport, and where to wait. Not checking to see if we had understood, he left and talked to the working girl. Without exchanging money, the two headed towards the stairs.

As instructed, Mother took Ethan and Benjamin up to our room. I followed, feeling the eyes of a soldier drinking alone in another corner of the bar. As a precaution, I put on a headscarf to hide my face before slipping back down, passing the soldier without attracting his attention. Only the working girl's eyes followed me as I left.

It was a long walk to the Auberge, but after checking it fitted the description, I went on to the woods. In the damp night, attentive trees monitored my every movement. Waning moonlight glinted on night creatures that scuttled away no matter how silently I walked. The boar grubbing in the leaf litter found wild garlic and other roots. Her favourite truffles must wait until autumn. Catching my scent in the damp air, she froze, then gathered her marcassins, ushering them away.

At the crossing point, I slipped off without the guard spotting me. By afternoon, I had returned to the hotel. Mother, as usual, was beside herself with worry, but she made no fuss, for an unfamiliar public building has porous walls. We did not know who might be in the next room. I had not slept, but we left straight away to keep our appointment with the bus. When it came, it bristled with soldiers.

12

The bus smelt of boot polish, exhaust fumes, and chickens. I was shocked to find it full of soldiers. Even the Germans must struggle with petrol shortages. These were regulars, travelling from lodgings to wherever their orders took them. They had none of the arrogance and hatred found in the faces of the officers, and but for the uniform, they could be factory workers on their way home. All the same, it would only take one to ask for our papers and he would uncover us.

A soldier stood to offer his seat to Mother, whilst another sat Benjamin on his lap. I remember watching him with my heart in my mouth. The soldier was trying to be friendly, asking my brother's name in broken French. Benjamin was terrified. Despite being born in Alençon, he had never left our lodgings, where we only spoke German. Today, he pretended not to understand, but I could see it petrified him. We got off as soon as the bus stopped, even though we weren't close to the Auberge.

'Did you see that?' I hissed at Mother.

She kept her eyes fixed on the road ahead. 'Maybe they were not looking for refugees but missing their own children.'

Finally, we reached the Auberge, but it did not reassure Ethan. 'Mother! It is as full of soldiers as the hotel in Angoulême!' His eyes were wide with fear.

Mother, plucking strength from an unknown depth within, smiled and strutted up to the bar. 'I am looking for employment. Is the house in need of a servant?'

She should have looked more disappointed when she got the expected negative response.

Returning to us, she whispered, 'I had to say something to explain our business. I told them Esther could work as a maid.'

'Anyone rich enough to employ a maid would have fled abroad before the war. You should have said I could harvest turnips.'

In the morning, we had to walk about eight kilometres to the crossing point. Benjamin was four years old, too young and too frightened to walk. The leaves rustled like a master of ceremonies shuffling his guest list, just in time to announce the rain's arrival. Nobody noticed the passing cyclist, even though he was conspicuous in his failure to acknowledge us as we ran for cover. The squall passed, so Mother picked up Benjamin. She had chosen this path, and must tread it whatever the consequences. Less than a minute later, we overtook the cyclist pumping up his tyre.

Whining his discontent, Benjamin swung from his mother's hand, lifting both feet, forcing her to take his weight. She had no grip on this limp sack of potatoes, so he slipped to the ground, complaining. Ethan picked him up, but didn't get far.

'On my back, Ben!' I said.

His trousers felt wet and gritty, redundant legs bobbed, too short to wrap around my waist. My own legs were empty from my all-night trek and soon I had to put him down. We had left the Auberge before breakfast to avoid questions, and my stomach was growling in protest.

Our Angoulême contact said to talk to nobody and not to stop until we reached the rendezvous. Benjamin was refusing to move unless one of us carried him. The cyclist passed us again.

Mother coaxed Benjamin to his feet. 'Just as far as that farm, my angel, then we will rest.'

I whispered to her, unable to disguise the urgency. 'We can't ask when we don't know who is there.'

In desperation, her eyes searched mine. 'What else can we do?'

'I don't know.' On the horizon, the moon, pulled too early from its sleep, hung red-rimmed, searching for victims. As soon as Mother knocked, the door opened, and a hand grabbed my wrist. Although rough from too many hours of in the fields, it bore no malice.

Benjamin's innocent face explored hers. 'Were you waiting for us?'

He may well ask, for we had not yet explained our business.

She smiled at him. 'We live close to the demarcation line, so an unexpected knock is to ask for shelter or search for fugitives. I saw you coming up the road.'

She added in a low voice that she had also seen the cyclist.

Benjamin stripped when he saw the fire, casting his wet clothes aside with petulant gestures. If Madame Mateau noticed his circumcision, she made no comment.

My damp skin clung to the rough cloth of my clothes as I pulled thin gruel into my welcoming stomach. Whilst I soaked up the dregs with warm bread, Mr Mateau saved his for later. He poured a generous splash of Bordeaux into the last of his soup, slurping it back with a noisy flourish. He wiped his moustache on his sleeve and smiled at our astonishment.

'En Périgord on n'a pas de pétrole, mais on fait chabròl.'

Mrs Mateau gave an indulgent smile as her husband cuts slivers of sausage with his clasp knife. Mother refused the slice he held out. She had heard the snuffling behind the wall. It took little imagination to identify the source of the next batch of charcuterie maison.

Our clothes steamed before the fire, vying with a wet dog to drown the savoury smell of soup. I went to check the weather and spotted a German patrol with the man on the bicycle, so I scuttled back to the safety of my co-conspirators.

Mother had no choice but to trust a stranger for the second time. 'We are trying to reach Madame Chalard, but Benjamin is too young to walk the whole way.'

Madame Mateau led me out the back door. We returned with two bicycles and a wooden handcart. 'I will collect them from my friend next time I visit.'

'Mother, let Madame Chalard know we are on our way. Ethan and I will tie the handcart to the back of the second bike,' I told her.

With Benjamin in the cart, we took turns, one on the bike, one steering and pushing Benjamin. The rain had stopped, the sun had set, and the moon had lost its red halo. Full stomachs, a change of weather, and our satisfaction at giving Mother a brief respite combined to lighten our mood. Benjamin was enjoying his ride in the cart and I swung it from side to side to make him squeal. Another cyclist appeared round the bend in front of us, giving us no time to hide.

In an instant, Benjamin curled up on the cart's bottom. Soup rose into my mouth as I recognised the border guard who arrested us last time. I lowered my head and swallowed my supper again.

Ethan, on the bike, raised his hand, calling *'Bonsoir!'* in a passable *sud ouest* accent.

Thankfully, the guard did not recognise us.

My tongue, glued to my palette with bile, flooded with relief. I turned away from Benjamin and spat, cursing myself for turning a desperate bid for freedom into a game.

When we arrived, two women were sitting at the scrubbed chestnut table, heads bowed, talking in whispers. One I had loved all my life, the other for two short weeks.

My foster mother beckoned me to the table, friendly but a little distant. She had stepped up and become our mother when we needed one, but she was taking a back seat now our actual mother had returned.

'I've chosen a little-used crossing point. We stationed two of our men within sight of the checkpoint. You must find somewhere near to wait. As soon as the checkpoint is unmanned, one man will signal. You just have to jump over the barrier. You will be in Free France, but the nearest safe house is in Saint Etienne, thirteen kilometres away. They search all the houses closer to the demarcation line.'

Young as I was, she was entrusting the survival of our family to me. She did it because I had proved my worth. It mattered not that I was a girl. This woman's faith overwhelmed me. She was risking her life to help. Mother hid what little money she had left behind the clock, but Madame Chalard retrieved it and pressed it back into Mother's hand, saying nothing.

The time had come for us to leave. Unable to find words, I hugged Madame Chalard, grateful to be a child again. The brief embrace could not hide her emotion. She had no children of her own, but I knew a mother's embrace. We separated, confused yet comforted, each eager to hide our tears. Mother noticed but said nothing.

Inhospitable dampness dragged at our feet. The woods near the track begrudged our intrusion as we forced ourselves into our hiding place. To pass the time, I traced in my head the directions down little-used forest tracks that Madame Chalard had taught me. Our aim was Saint Etienne and the house on the square with a balcony. Like an actor learning his lines, I muttered the safe-house password: *Les grues partent tard cette année.*

At last someone came to find us. 'Jump the barrier, then run and keep running.'

With that, he pushed us onto the track, whispered, *'Bonne chance!'* and was gone.

Benjamin looked up at me. 'Are we there yet?'

We could not tell him we had to walk another thirteen kilometres, so took turns carrying him. I don't know which was worse, awake and squirming, or asleep and a dead weight. Darkness returned, and with it, the rain. In the gloaming, woodland creatures listened, then as night fell, a more malevolent force shifted the paths. Shadows drew forth ghosts from the damp litter, rising like fungi, scrambling our brains. Somewhere we took a wrong turn, exhaustion moving us beyond reality into the spirits that circled us. They waited for us to cast aside our living mantle and join them in timeless sleep.

Mother staggered and slipped to the ground as gently as she would into a warm bed. I leapt forward and caught her — if she slept, she would never wake.

She raised a hand to me. 'Take your brothers. Give my love to Father. Tell him I thought of him at the end.'

I sink to my knees beside her. 'NO! You must not go where I cannot follow! I am not ready. I promised Father I would look after you.'

Benjamin was now awake and crying, so Ethan took his hand. I put my arms around Mother to give her the strength I no longer possessed.

As the rain returned, we crept forward, detached from the living world, to join the wraiths who encircled us. In this half world, departed souls sensed our imminent arrival. Time no longer existed.

Dawn broke into the world we were leaving but did not reach our consciousness, illuminating only the farm building. Mother did not see the figure approaching, and for me, he was another wraith coming to take us to the next world.

To Ethan, he was just a man.

'Help!'

A single arm lifted Mother. Relieved of my duties, I collapsed.

Later, I learned the man was Jean. He looked back over his shoulder. 'Stand up! Follow me!'

He held a sack over Mother's head and frog-marched her along the main track.

As light grew, the earth, careless of the follies of her freight, turned again towards the sun. The path became more manageable, and his guiding arm stronger. It must have given Mother an inner reserve she thought long spent. Only the driving rain conspired against us.

A wooden barrier blocked the track, made more threatening by the shed at the side of the road. Guards huddled inside, sheltering from the rain.

Jean looked back at me. 'Give the baby to your mother and hold her skirt. Keep your heads down.'

As we approached, Jean called out to the guards, 'Raise the barrier; the doctor's wife needs to pass.'

Mother staggered forward, Benjamin in her arms, her face hidden by the sack. Inside, a guard slapped another card on the table whilst his colleague lifted the barrier just enough for us to duck under.

Jean did not turn back. Instead, he put Benjamin on his shoulders and urged us towards the village.

Just as my terror subsided, a crack split the air. Spinning round, I saw Ethan flat on his face, arm stretched out towards me. The guards had left their hut and levelled their weapons.

So many things happen when time stops. Jean almost threw Benjamin off his shoulders. There would be a second whilst my baby brother registered the indignity and prepared his lungs for protest. Mother was staring at the guard who, having felled her son, aimed at her. Fear rooted her to the spot, a silent scream branded on her face. She seemed to be willing the soldier to kill her as if the sacrifice would somehow return her son.

Jean bundled her to the ground, giving me a second to launch myself back towards Ethan. The passeur's shoulder hit the back of my legs, throwing me to the ground, his forearm on my back preventing me from scrambling to my feet. A bristly jowl hissed in my ear.

'Your brother is dead. Should your mother lose two children on the same day?'

Ethan was twitching, the outstretched hand clasping and unclasping as his eyes found mine. Jean, meanwhile, was assessing his minimal options. Impenetrable forest bordered the track down which the guards were now running. Gorse filled the spaces between the trees. When he spotted a gap no larger than a dog, he dragged me towards it.

At his insistence, I crawled on all fours into the thorny tunnel. He turned his attention towards our mother and Benjamin, who was screaming his opinion of being dumped. Mother reacted as all mothers do and tried to pick him up, so Jean pushed the two of them into the tunnel. He had no weapon, but backed himself into the gap, guarding the entrance and sizing up the enemy.

I imagined the two soldiers pausing by Ethan's body, but could not bear to think what they would do. Instead, I pushed forward, feeling Mother following and Benjamin between us. I knew where we were. During my time with Madame Chalard, I came across similar boar runs in the woods. They were the only creatures powerful enough to force a way through this thorny undergrowth. I steered clear of them. A wild boar is a dangerous beast, and this was his territory.

To my relief, I heard Jean following us. We entered a clearing away from the track.

'Don't move, and stay silent!' he ordered. The adrenalin ebbed away, and my skin burned from a thousand scratches. Jean dived back into the tunnel.

Soon he returned. 'They are not following us.'

'I have to go back to my son.'

Jean put his hand on her arm, both in comfort and to restrain her. 'I will retrieve his body, but not today. We must get you to the safe house.'

I frowned. 'How will you do that?'

'Saint Etienne is not far now. The mayor will make a formal

complaint tomorrow after we make sure you are safe.'

'The mayor?'

'He is one of us. I told the guards you were the doctor's wife. Since they have not caught you, they cannot refute this. The mayor will say the guards fired on the doctor's wife as she was treating sick children, and that they killed one of her patients. The least they can do is return the body. I will make sure he has a Christian burial.'

'We are Jews,' Mother whispered.

13

I'm tucked away in the shadows. There are reasons I cannot appear. Francine puts down the sheaf of papers. Each paragraph she has read and then retold in English. My poor Benjamin — it's too much for him. My heart aches to see him so old. He has given the breathers the first part of my story. He doesn't know what happened when he and Mother left me behind. When John drove off the road, he witnessed the end, although I am not sure he understood. Peter wants to know the middle, so he asks what happened next, putting his hand up, like in school.

His own story absorbed my little brother for more than an hour. Now he looks at Peter as if he has only just seen him.

'Jean was as good as his word. The mayor had my brother's body returned. We were lucky they did not strip him.'

Peter looked puzzled, so he explained. 'They would have seen he was Jewish. The authorities do not return the corpses of my people.'

'Was he given a Jewish burial?' John asks.

Benjamin smiled through his tears. 'No. They gave him something that gave us more hope.'

Francine hands him a handkerchief and waits for him to continue.

'The doctor had indeed been visiting a family whose children had glandular fever. When the boy died, the parents allowed the mayor to

94

say that the Germans shot him. He also claimed it was the doctor's wife that had been escorting them across the border.'

The breathers are fortunate. If they had lived during the war, that could have been Peter.

'That was very kind,' John whispers.

Benjamin's voice drops. 'They did much more than that.'

Complete silence shrouded the room as we waited for him to continue.

'Soldiers delivered Ethan's body to the farm; the family identified him as their own son. We sealed the corpses in the same coffin. Ethan lies in this churchyard beside a Gentile he never knew. Another name is on the headstone.'

Now it's Francine's turn to cry. 'That is so sad.'

Benjamin looks at her. 'Do you think so? I think it is wonderful.'

Benjamin looks at Peter. Ethan was about his age.

'Because a Jew and a Gentile lie together. They were strangers in life, but at peace in death. It gives me hope.'

'What happened after that?'

'Mother and I went to Lyon. There we met Father. After the war, we returned to Bassin de la Sarre. I grew up, met Leah, and we married.'

Peter frowns. 'What about your big sister?'

Benjamin takes the precious sheets from Francine and gives them to his wife. 'Esther stayed. She fell in love.'

He was only a toddler, but he knew. Maybe our mother told him when he was old enough to ask questions.

'What happened to your sister after you left?'

Benjamin smiles at John. 'I am here to find out. I was hoping there would be people here who would remember.' His voice trails off. 'It was all so long ago.'

Francine takes his hand. 'Jean died in the war. He went to meet an allied plane and we think someone ambushed the landing party. I'm guessing your sister was one of the casualties. There are stories of a refugee from Alsace joining the resistance. Speaking German would have been very useful.'

I can't take any more. Flying back to the loft, I scatter Benjamin's precious papers.

Peter finds me crying.

'Esther, your little brother is downstairs. Say hello to him.'

I can't!

'Why not? You showed yourself to me in the woods.'

I am not used to having arguments with a breather and let out another sob. *It's the gibbous moon; it's dark.*

'I don't understand,' says Peter.

The moon was almost full when they shot us. Every month from sunset to sunrise, we carry those injuries.

Peter shuffles in irritation. 'I can't see what difference it would make. You are as dead as when we chatted in the sunshine this morning.'

Pierre, you did not find our bodies; you have not seen what happens when they shoot someone in the head at point-blank range.

He shrugs. 'So show me.'

Not a chance. I will come back when I'm pretty again.

Peter stomps down the stairs. He is right. I follow him and find my living self talking to Benjamin.

'I'm sorry to bring you the news about your sister's death.'

Benjamin looks up at her. 'That's alright. I guessed she died. If they had to die, I am glad they died together. It would have been what they wanted.'

Leah stands. 'Thank you so much for your hospitality; the food was delicious. I am afraid Benjamin gets rather tired these days.'

Benjamin looks at her with an expression that says, oh, are we going?

Francine shows them to the door as if she was in her own house. Jean and the English spy are having one of those arguments they used to have where neither spoke. In my grief, I take some comfort that, as John and Cathy, little has changed. Cathy is collecting glasses and empty nibble bowls, banging them together the way I remember the English spy doing when she was cross.

At the door, Benjamin turns to Francine. 'Esther and Jean, were they...?'

Francine smiles. 'I believe they were.'

'And was Jean a Gentile?'

'I believe so.'

'Pity. Still, Esther loved Jean. That's the important thing.' He smiles. 'Thank you for a lovely evening. I hope I haven't bored you too much.'

John and Cathy remember their manners and see their visitors out to the car. I materialise behind Francine, taking care to hide my head.

Age has wearied him. They grow old as we do not. We will remember them.

Francine hears. She turns, but cannot see me.

Peter comes back from saying goodbye to Benjamin. 'Are you alright, Francine?'

She jumps, then pulls her cardigan close to her. 'It is pretty emotional meeting someone still alive with such a personal link to local history.'

'I don't believe you! Esther was here. She talked to you; you heard her.'

John also comes back. 'Are you alright, Francine?'

She repeats what she said to Peter.

Unlike John and Peter, Cathy doesn't care whether Francine is alright. 'Yes, well, it was fascinating. Thank you so much for introducing him to John and me. Will you stay longer?'

Francine is French, but speaks enough English to recognise "go away" however said, so she makes her excuses and leaves.

John and Cathy are going to argue. I feel an unhealthy satisfaction when I listen. My fear is not that the English spy will change her mind about moving to France, but that if she stays in England, John will abandon his project to reclaim this house. If that happens, I will never reunite him with Francine.

14

John, December 2004

We are back for Christmas. They've done loads of work: fixed the roof, insulated, changed all the wires, and made a bathroom. That's the bit Cathy moaned about. The new doorway will connect the kitchen to the little house at the front. It means Peter can get to his bedroom without walking round the outside of the house. I go in first so I can see the new doorway, although it's not new at all. The bit over the top is an old beam, and the sides are stone, just like the other doors. It must have been there before and bricked up. Someone is standing in the doorway. It's Peter's ghost, Esther, the one he calls Resistance Girl.

For the first time, I get a proper look at her. 'Hello!'

She doesn't answer, but I'm sure she sees me. Maybe she is answering, and I can't hear her. Unlike Peter, I've not had much practice talking to ghosts.

He comes in just then, carrying his teddy-bear, and asks me what I am looking at.

I shake my head like I am changing the pattern on a kaleidoscope. 'The door; you can get to your room now.'

He gives me one of his looks. 'Liar! You saw Resistance Girl.'

I give the kaleidoscope another twist while I think about what to say. 'I'm not sure it was a girl; she had boy's clothes. Maybe it was a pretty boy.'

Peter drops Pooh on his head. 'Ha! You saw her!'

The ghost scatters as she pushes past me, like someone kicking through dried leaves. The kaleidoscope explodes and disappears.

There's a thump behind us. 'Ta for helping with the bags.'

Cathy makes a point of struggling up the steps with two suitcases. She looks tired after such a long journey. If she is thinking it's far from England and Richard, that was the idea.

'I'll light the boiler.'

'I'll come too.' Peter puts Pooh on the table and runs after me.

'I hope it wasn't a mistake to come here in the winter,' I say. 'Maybe if I can get some heat into the house, it will feel cosier.'

He takes my hand. 'You're right, but we will be here all year round when we move.'

Not for the first time, I wonder who is the adult, and who is the child.

The boiler won't light, so we go upstairs and make a wood fire in the living room.

Over the next couple of days, we get used to country living. Cathy gets into the Christmas spirit and drags greenery in from the woods. There's still no kitchen, so I make curry for Christmas dinner using camping stoves. Francine got us a load of logs for the fire, which gives Cathy something to moan about. This time I'm not having it.

'She wants to help, same as Lee.'

'What, the old git that keeps lending us the gardening stuff?'

'Exactly. He's only doing it because he fancies you.'

'I've clocked that, John, but there's no way I'll show my appreciation, at least not the way he wants!'

'Nor I with Francine.'

'Glad to hear it!'

It's New Year's Eve, and we have finished the Monopoly game. Peter is in bed, and with refilled glasses, we are staring into the flames. Alcohol has mellowed to forgetfulness the sniping about Lee and Francine. Cathy leans into me, so I put my arm around her. For the first time in years, I feel the ghost of Richard recede, and I believe Cathy will keep her promise to leave him and move to France.

'I can't believe it's been two years since we agreed to move,' I say 'We are almost there.'

Cathy leans into me and takes a sip from her glass. 'Apart from the kitchen.'

'I've booked the kitchen fitters for the New Year. We've got the floor tiles, so they'll finish by Easter. I reckon if I put in a couple of months after that, we could move in next summer.'

Cathy doesn't answer. Now that it's come to it, will she leave Richard? He may not allow it. If only I could make her see he is gaslighting her.

She snuggles closer, so I give her a squeeze.

'If you come down after Easter, you'll have to come on yer own. Peter's got exams.'

Is she thinking that one last fling with Richard will get him out of her system? The alternative is too awful to think about. Craig's parents have divorced and I don't want Peter to go through that.

'I'm not sure I'll manage two months without you to keep me in order,' I tell her.

'Nonsense! Your French is coming along grand, and you've made friends. You don't need me to look after you.'

I don't feel reassured. She said it with a bit too much confidence. I check on Peter before we go to bed. He's talking to himself again.

Esther

I am waiting for Peter to come to bed.

Hello Peter.

'Hello Esther. What's that?'

I hold out a book. *Your Christmas present. It's the next part of the story.*

'The one with the airman?'

No, that came first. That one your mother wrote.

He nods. 'But you wrote the one about escaping. The one you gave to your little brother.'

Yes, but that stopped when we arrived. He went away with that part, but I carried on writing.

'Is it the bit where someone killed you?'

Don't be silly. No, it's another operation about when we captured the informer.

'Why didn't you write about being killed?'

Because I was dead.

'OK, but I want to know how you met Jean.'

I've already told you, he found us when we were crossing the line.

'Yes, that is in Benjamin's story. He said you fell in love with him; I want to hear about that.'

You are too young.

'You are as bad as Mummy and Daddy. I'm confused because Mummy's book says the English spy was in love with Jean, and your brother said you were.'

It's complicated.

'Only to grown-ups.' He plonks himself down on his bed in a huff.

'So, tell me what happened when your family went to Lyon and you stayed.'

That was November 1942. It's in the book.

The diary of Esther Fröhlich Part 2. Dordogne, 1943

Mother wanted me to go to Lyon. Losing Ethan was hard for her. At the funeral of the boy with glandular fever, we waited at the back until everyone had gone. Mother knelt and placed a tiny dried olive branch on the fresh earth.

'Where did you get that?' I whispered.

'The Rabbi gave it to us before we left Bassin de la Sarre. He said it came from Mount Sinai. He prayed that after the war they would give the Jews back their homeland, and he would return.'

'Will he?'

'No. They arrested him because he stayed too long.'

'And you kept it through all our travels?'

'Sewn into the hem of my skirt.'

She stands and brushes the earth from her hand. 'For all the good it did us.'

I cannot bear to see her like this. 'But Mother, we made it,' I tell her. 'You can take Benjamin to find Father now.'

'And you? He has lost a son; is he to lose a daughter too?'

'No, Mother. He is fighting for our country. I must fight too.'

She says nothing for a long time. 'Jean is a fortunate man.'

I flush despite the autumn chill.

'Don't look so coy,' she says. 'I've seen how you look at each other.'

'Mother! He is married!'

'He is not married. I checked,' she adds after a pause.

'Who is that woman with him?'

'She is an English spy they parachuted in about a year ago.'

'Since you seem to know so much, are they in love?'

'He seems to love her.'

'That is not what I asked.'

'He is her trophy.'

She takes my hand. 'Esther, when I met your father, he was engaged to the daughter of Madame Perec. Monsieur Perec offered a substantial dowry that would have bought Father his first shop, but he left her for a poor seamstress. We sewed together in an attic by the light of a single candle and sold lace gloves from a handcart.'

She is crying, so I take her hand.

'Esther, I will not make you come with me, but promise me this. Marry him, and after the war, bring me my grandson.'

'Mother, he is a Gentile.'

'And you are a Jew. Your children will be Jews.'

The Informer

Herr Schneider sits at the large oak dining table. Last November they renamed Free France the southern zone, under direct German control. He no longer has to pretend to be there at the invitation of the Vichy government. Schneider had exceeded his authority when he killed the airman, and he persuaded the mayor that French guards shot the boy with the doctor's wife. Now that it's official that German soldiers are in command, he intends to tighten his grip.

The resistance is active in the area and poses a constant threat to the *oberleutnant*'s troops. It's a threat he faces with ruthless efficiency. Summary executions are frequent and public. They shoot malefactors where they catch them. Unlike most of his troops, Herr Schneider is Nazi by conviction. He exploits nationalism, feeding the cannons with the blood of his own men. For this, he exacts retribution from the French with ruthless Germanic efficiency.

Ricardo rents the old schoolmaster's house attached to Louis' farm house. Before the war, when he arrived from Torano, an experienced stonemason was always welcome. Today, the locals view him with suspicion.

He opens his front door, checks the square is empty and slips down the path beside the barn. At the Templar house, the guard makes no move to acknowledge or challenge. Ricardo passes under the Maltese cross and into the room where the *oberleutnant* is working. A few moments later, he leaves empty-handed. Payment is by results.

Herr Schneider barks an order. An *unteroffizier* with two *soldats* salutes and marches out. They turn away from the village towards Blazon Noir, the isolated home to Joeliyn and Amia. The women lost their husbands in the Great War but continued to work on the pig farm.

Yesterday, these women handed over two beasts to the Germans but concealed the third, which they slaughtered this morning. They are burying it when, too late, they hear jackboots. Two shots crack, sending a flock of birds skyward before the *soldats* put their guns back in their holsters. The *unteroffizier* pushes the corpses into the hole that was being dug to conceal the pig. He then motions to his two subordinates to pick up the animal before the three of them leave. They have completed another routine assignment.

Ricardo hears the shots. He will return tomorrow for payment.

'You are certain of this?'

Louis is questioning the English spy. The facts of the execution are undisputed, but Louis wants proof of Ricardo's role before he orders his own judicial killing.

'He told me himself,' Jenny said.

Louis stands. 'Then he dies. I want a volunteer to carry out the execution.'

The spy raises her hand.

'Not this time, Jenny. I do not want you to get into the habit of murdering your lovers.' He glances at Jean, concealing a smile.

'That guard was not my lover.'

'No, he died before he got the chance.'

They seem to talk in code about an incident that happened before I arrived.

'I'll do it.'

Jean's offer prevents an argument breaking out between Louis and the spy.

I am waiting by the well with Pierre and Jean. Ricardo moves to pass us, but we step to block his passage. Together we bundle the Italian up the track. Pierre produces a rope to tie Ricardo's hands.

I hand Jean the airman's revolver. 'Take him further into the woods. I'll take Pierre home. He is too young to witness an execution.'

Back in the village square, there is no synagogue, so I take him into the church. I don't want Jean to kill Ricardo, but then I think of the old pig farmers. Maybe I want the Italian dead after all. I pray to my God; the conversation is brief. 'He deserves to die.'

Many deserve death.

'The old ladies at the pig farm did not deserve to die.'

God is silent. In the distance, a shot rings out. I came to confess my love for a Gentile. Instead, I questioned God for allowing the innocent to die and the guilty to go unpunished. I leave, taking Pierre with me.

'Where are we going?'

'To Ricardo's house; I want to look for information before the Germans arrive.'

The kitchen stove is still burning, and the parlour is a mess. If the Italian keeps secrets, they will not be in the casual disorder of a bachelor's living room, so we go up to the bedroom.

'I'll check the loft.' Pierre climbs the second flight.

I am still searching the bedroom when I hear a noise downstairs. I pray Pierre stays in the loft because there's no other way out. Hearing a step on the stair, I pull the bedroom door open, pressing myself against the wall behind it to provide some cover. Someone is muttering in Italian, causing beads of sweat to form on my brow. My soul freezes. Between soul and forehead, my mind struggles to process the information, eyes straining through a crack in the door. The Italian takes a knife from his pocket, folds back the carpet, and finds a loose floorboard. Prising it up, he pulls out a wad of banknotes which he stuffs into a bag. Turning, he looks straight at the door that I am holding to stop it swinging closed.

Suspicious, he reaches for the handle. Suddenly, footsteps clatter on the stairs from the loft. He must suspect a trap, for Ricardo hurls himself down the stairs, giving me just enough time to grab the boy before he descends in pursuit.

Pierre works it out. 'Ricardo is alive, so Jean must be dead.'

Seeing me crying, the younger man takes control. 'I'll tell Jenny.'

'I'll stay here and see what I can find.'

'Don't stay too long; the Boche will be here soon.' With that, he is gone.

Unlike me, Jenny does not hide her relationship with Jean. Is it because I am Jewish and he Christian? It doesn't matter now. If Ricardo is alive, then Jean is dead. I curl into the foetal position and wait for the Germans to arrive.

Boards creak on the stairs. Unprepared for death without seeing Jean's body, I slip into the room next door, using the French windows and balcony.

Footsteps cross the room I have just vacated. I am no longer afraid. When a tall figure appears in the French window, I turn to face my executioner.

My relief is so profound I would have given myself to Jean right there on the balcony. Instead, he kisses me. It's clear that is what he wants as well. The kiss becomes a promise.

'What happened?' I ask when I can speak again.

'I crossed the square towards Ricardo's house, glancing up at the balcony to check he wasn't waiting for me. That's when I noticed the French window was closed. I guessed Ricardo would return to his house before fleeing. In the woods, I could not kill him in cold blood, but innocent lives are at risk while Ricardo lives. When I opened the bedroom door, the French window was open. Someone was in the next room listening. I had no gun, and there are only so many times a man can cheat death, so I stepped through the window to keep my appointment.'

'I thought it was me that was going to die.'

'We are both alive,' he smiles, and kisses me again. This time I die of happiness.

When I can talk again, I ask what happened after we left him.

'There was such hatred in Ricardo's eyes. We walked in silence until we were deep in the woods. There, I made him kneel. I don't think fighting was ever the Italian's preferred option. Perhaps he considered flight, then remembered the gun. I untied his hands.'

'Why did you do that?'

'I don't know. I knew I could not kill him in cold blood, so was looking for another solution.'

'What was that?'

'I told him we had found him guilty of passing information, and the penalty was death.'

'What did he say?'

'That I should shoot him now. Either he wanted to get it over with, or was calling my bluff.'

'I heard a shot, but then he came to the house just before you, so I thought he had shot you,' I say.

'If he had killed Joeliyn and Amia himself, I might have been able to do it, but I answer to a Higher Authority.'

'What does that mean?'

'I had to show him that the French were better than the fascists. I gave him three choices. He could run. I would say he overpowered me, took the gun and escaped. The second option was to shoot me. His chance of escape would have been greater.'

'What did he say to that?'

'He said, "What makes you think I will not kill you?".'

'He had a point. What made you think he wouldn't kill you?'

'I had spared his life. The spark of decency I saw in him told me he would not repay my clemency with murder.'

'You were taking an enormous risk.'

'Maybe. But I could not see another way to do it.'

'What was his third option?'

'To take his own life. It is the only one he had the moral right to end.'

'But he didn't. You are both alive. What happens now?'

Emboldened by his kiss, I unbutton his shirt.

'Not that,' he whispers. 'Not yet.'

15

Esther, June 2005

Did you like my story? I'm awake again, which means John is coming back. I long for him to hear me as Peter can. He heard me in the doorway, which has always been our special place. That doorway has existed for almost two hundred and fifty years. When I sleep, the house tells me its history.

Mallet rings on chisel, carving an anvil on the lintel above the door. The mason adds the date: 1776. John, the dashing *sans-culotte*, is building a house and dreaming of the rise of the Third Estate. Before the Revolution, the door looked down on an empty churchyard. Strong arms reach out to save a girl from falling into the street below. That was our first kiss in that doorway. Like most of the *sans-culottes*, they killed him in the Terror.

France survived the Revolution and the ghosts who walked the corridors were reborn and reclaimed the house looking for lost loved ones. One such, more than a century later, sits next to a distinguished gentleman. 'Monsieur Fauré, while you rest, I will visit the abandoned farmhouse yonder.'
John is now the musician's protégé and reclaims the house he built when he was a *sans-culotte*. He adds the façade and seals the doorway.

Another mason carves 1911 above the new front door. Within, Fauré's cello concerto drifts from the new room. My previous self, Francesca, waits for him to return from Verdun. Her portrait is in the bedroom. She is the girl in the *belle époque* dress, hand-painted on the wallpaper.

By 1941, the music room is dancing to a different tune. Ricardo, the Italian informer, gathers intelligence to sell to Herr Schneider, the German *oberleutnant*. Louis makes salami on the other side of the wall. His back door opens, and John, the fearless passeur, pushes me into the kitchen.

Last year, yet another builder chipped away, removing rubble and restoring our doorway. Now Peter can have Ricardo's room as his bedroom and access the kitchen. That is where my living self must take John. If she kisses him there, the ghosts of our previous selves will combine to bless the union.

Today, John is back. He wasn't always called John, but the same heart beats beneath, whatever name he answers to.

Peter is not with him, so I have no interpreter. Do you remember when I first met Peter in the loft? I gave him the diary of the English spy and asked him to give it to Cathy. Last Christmas I told Peter the story of the Italian informer. He is too young for me to tell him of my love affair with Jean, but his father is here now. It's time to give John the next instalment, so I leave my diary on the kitchen table.

One thing ghosts have is time. Time to think. I have no love for the English spy. You know that. John, however, loves her. That hurts, but I have to understand why he feels as he does. If not, how can I prise him away from her and reunite him with my living self?

We never met after death. Maybe there's a heaven for Jews and another for Gentiles. I could not exist beyond the veil without dissipating, like the water in a glass when the container shatters. With souls, the process is much slower. As my body became more diaphanous, I looked amongst the breathers for newborn babies with Jean's eyes. Years slipped by. It scared me he might have been reborn and be growing up whilst I still waited. Eventually, I chose local parents, and Francine was born. This gave me a portal back into this world, where I came to wait for Jean.

He was reborn in England, like the English spy. I hoped she had survived the war and was today too old to interest his next incarnation. What hold did she have on him that made him choose England when our history rooted us to this region, to this house?

I know why Jean fell for her charms when Cathy came here as Jenny, the English spy. She was foreign, exotic, very good at what she did. She seduced men — a valuable skill for a spy. To stand a chance against her, I had to prove I deserved his admiration and affection.

Today, the English spy has again got to our lover first. I feel no guilt at taking him away from her. Theirs was a wartime romance that has spilt into the current incarnation. Ours is a love conceived when the world was young.

I follow John to the library and see that he is holding my diary.

'Hello, Francine.'

He hesitates, looking around for inspiration.

Francine's face lights up. 'What is it I can do for you?'

She looks towards the exercise book in his hand.

He looks too, remembering why he is here. 'Peter found this in the loft. It seems to be some sort of journal, but I cannot read the handwriting.'

'May I regard it?'

'If you're not too busy.'

'Not at all. Shall we look together?'

YES! There's a squeak, like a bicycle brake that needs oiling. That's me.

Sitting down together with the diary open, my living self translates. There's no skin contact, but their arms are close enough for him to feel her warmth. I waft her scent towards him. He says nothing, but I watch him inhale while she flips the first few pages back and forth.

'This seems to be the diary of someone who lived in your house during the war.'

Feeling his eyes on her, Francine holds his gaze for a second too long before returning to the book. His arm is very close to hers, hairs on his arm touching, sending out an electric shock.

She pulls her arm away. 'Look, this says November 1942.'

He nods. Dates are easy to pick out. 'Who is the author?' he asks.

'I think it's the eldest child of the Jewish family. Do you remember an old man came to visit you? He said his elder sister kept a diary, which she passed to him when they left for Lyon.'

Francine points to my fine handwriting. I have written in French, not German. I hoped that, when the war was over, Jean and I would have the leisure to read it together.

John's hand hovers over the words where her fingers rest. He wants to touch them, too, or perhaps her fingers.

'Yes, her name was Esther. She stayed and joined the resistance.'

I shiver as he says my name. My living self mirrors me, rubbing her arm and smoothing the fine hairs standing on end.

'I am sorry, John, but I have work to do. I'm sure it's the same for you.'

He jumps as if she has hit him. 'Of course. I just felt this journal wanted me to find it. Does that sound silly?'

'Not at all. I am sure it is so. I love things like this. May I borrow it? I could translate it into English for you.'

'Please do. I want to borrow some library books; perhaps we could look at this again when I return them.'

Their fingers touch as Francine takes the diary. 'Of course. Now, what sort of books would you like to borrow?'

That night you are writing in your diary, Francine.

John is back on his own. He brought a notebook, but I am not sure he realises its importance — an original primary source written by a member of the resistance. I offered to translate it for him. When we looked at it together, he sat so near, I would swear he fancied me. It's hard to tell with Englishmen, but anyway, he can't — he's married and I don't date married men.

I thought this would be easy. I do not understand why neither of them can hear me when Peter can. Tonight, John tosses his half-eaten pizza in the bin, finishes the beer and pours himself a whiskey. I worry he drinks too much. During the war, the Germans took most of the wine. He takes the glass to the bedroom. I'm glad they have not painted over the picture of Francesca. When I was alive, that picture spoke to me. Now it's silent.

John talks into his glass. 'She seemed pleased with the diary. Why did I show it to her? I was not hitting on her. Maybe she wanted me to — it's hard to tell with French girls. Anyway, she can't — I am married. I made that very clear from the start. And yet...'

Who is he talking to? Not me. The *belle époque* girl in the wallpaper offers no opinion.

A week later, he is back at the library.

My living self skips round to the front of the desk. 'John, I was hoping you would come today. The journal is fascinating!'

His face lights up. He wants to please her, so that is an excellent start. 'What does it say?' he asks, edging closer.

Francine glances towards the assistant. 'Jules, if anyone else comes into the library, will you look after them?'

She leads John into the office and closes the door. 'There are important things in that diary. For the moment, I would rather people did not know.'

He looks surprised. 'People?'

'It concerns events some in the district will still remember.'

Sitting beside her, he draws his chair a little closer. 'It is seventy years old. Who will remember?'

'Benjamin to start with.'

John nods. 'That was a strange evening. I don't think it thrilled Cathy that I invited him.'

She stares into space, as if remembering, then looks straight into John's eyes.

'Do you think someone is haunting your house?'

He holds her stare. 'Peter does. He's met her several times; he even talks to her.'

'What about you? What do you feel?'

Her eyes tell him she is no longer talking about ghosts.

'I've seen her twice, but she has never talked to me. Peter is much younger.'

'I also am young.'

He lets his eyes wander over your face. You do not blush or look away.

He whispers, as if trying to solve a puzzle. 'Yes, you are younger than me but much older than Peter.'

When she looks at his hand on the book, his small finger crooks into his palm.

In the merest whisper, she says, 'The ghost talked to me.'

He shoots her a look. 'What did she say?'

Her eyes focus on an imagined horizon. '*Age has wearied him. They grow old as we do not. We will remember them.* The ghost was talking about Benjamin.'

'It sounds like the memorial poem read on Armistice Day but flipped round.'

As she places her hand over his, he flinches but does not withdraw it.

Only a ghost can see the smallest movement in Francine's fingers. 'Nobody has flipped it round if you are a ghost.'

John wakes as if from a dream and withdraws his hand, placing the other over it. A bandage to prevent her touch from escaping.

'Where did you find the journal?' she asks.

He looks at the desk, then at my living self. 'On the kitchen table, but Peter found it in the loft. He says the ghost gave it to him.'

'I believe the ghost put it where you would find it,' she says, unable to look him in the eye.

There's a hesitant knock. 'Yes, Jules?'

'*Il est treize heures.* The library has closed. I have to go home.'

'Thank you, Jules. You go; I will lock up.'

Jean stands too. 'I have kept you too long. We didn't even start on translating the book.'

Francine pulls out a sheaf of papers from a drawer. 'It is done, so we can look this afternoon.'

'But the library is closed.'

'At the lake. It is sad to waste such a beautiful day.'

'I have no lunch.'

'There is a *guinguette*. How do you say that? A snack bar. There are picnic tables and trees for shade, but maybe you don't want to come.'

Francine insists on eating her chips at the guinguette and wiping the picnic table before producing the journal. Since the bench is more suited to sitting close, John has pressed his arm against hers. Neither of them acknowledge the intimacy and instead, discuss my diary. It tells how I used Ethan's clothes to disguise myself as a boy. I would read it to you, but I think you are more interested in what is happening between my living self and John. They stay crouched together over the journal, ignoring the incidental touch of flesh. John goes back to the snack bar for beers. The sun dips, sending children back for their supper and jewels of sunlight towards you.

'Another beer?'

You hold up a hand. 'No, thanks. Let's go for a swim instead.'

He looks up, his surprise mixed with apprehension. 'I don't have a swimming costume.'

Her smile is mischievous. 'Wear underpants — if you have to', she adds as an afterthought.

John looks down. 'I'll stick with the beer, if you don't mind.'

Francine skips away from the picnic bench and calls out, 'It's as you wish,' over her shoulder.

As she dances towards the water, she pulls at her dress, kicks off her sandals and plunges into the water, scattering the diamonds.

You're in there.

John looks up. A man in a scrum cap towers over him, four pints of beer in his hands.

John's jaw drops. He must have drunk too much to see the vision of his best friend from the rugby club.

'Tree! What the fuck are you doing here?'

'I could ask you the same question.' Tree deposits the glasses with reverence. 'Happy Hour', he explains. 'Quite appropriate in the circumstances.'

John pouts. 'I don't know what you are talking about.'

He has moved the journal and translation off the table just in time.

'Does Cathy know?'

John looks guilty. 'Know what?'

'Come off it, John. I'm your best mate. Remember Toulouse?'

'What goes on tour, stays on tour,' John says as he stares into his beer.

'You took the words out of my mouth, so what's happening on this tour?'

John has downed one pint in a single breath and picked up

another.

'Nothing.'

He puts down the second glass, half-empty, with a twinkle that suggests otherwise.

'That's more like you. I want a full report afterwards.'

John picks up the glass again. 'Not a fucking chance.'

My living self has left the water and is walking towards us, scooping up sandals and her frock as she does so. With no sign of the friend, John pulls off his T-shirt and hands it over for her to dry her face. Francine dabs off most of the water and wriggles the cotton shift over her damp body.

Later, alone in her flat, Francine is writing.

Dear Diary.

I have finished the translation written by the ghost in John's house and shown it to John. Since the library closed early, we went to the lake. I have never got so wet sitting next to a man. Just my luck for him to be married! I know he should be off limits, but his wife was bitchy when I went to their house. There's gossip that she's cheating on him. That's why I suggested skinny dipping. He said no, but I went anyway. I thought I saw someone bring him beers while I was swimming. Nobody was there when I came out of the water, and he said the beers were for me. He gave me his T-shirt to dry myself on, so I drank my beers and ogled. I didn't know older men looked so hot.

Back at the house, John is talking to the wallpaper again.

'I couldn't believe it when Francine went skinny dipping. Maybe I should have gone too; I would have got a better view. The wet dress left little to the imagination. I'm trying not to overthink about Cathy. First off, because I know she is with Richard, an extended hen night before settling down to our new life in France.'

The picture does not reply.

'And then Tree turning up. I must have imagined him. Too many beers. Still, he is right: what goes on tour stays on tour. If I don't give it a shot, I will always regret it.'

From this angle, the figure seems to have turned away. Gentlemen did not conduct courtships like this a century ago.

'I'll cook a meal to thank Francine for all her work. It'll just be a meal between friends. I'm sure it's all it will be; we haven't even kissed.'

Francesca's lips curve in a mysterious smile, enigmatic as the Mona Lisa.

16

John, June 2005

One thing living with Cathy does is ground me in reality. I'm in a place that I don't like, yet lack the willpower to change it. Moving to France was supposed to do that, and I felt a sense of destiny as I made my first life-changing decision. Of course, I needed Cathy on board to carry it off, and now here I am, on the cusp of doing so. Without her, the grounding has gone. I am not sure whether releasing the mooring rope has cast me adrift or set me free.

'Watch her, she fancies you.' Cathy's words were a warning, but after I drop the mooring rope, I see it as an instruction followed by an observation. I am watching her, and yes, she fancies me. Even on its own, that is a revelation. More so is a truth I am trying to avoid. Do I fancy her? I am not yet ready to answer, so I change the question. Is she attractive? No contest. I collect the library books and head out.

Peter and Cathy are the reason we are emigrating, but I am pleased I came to France on my own. Meeting Francine has changed everything. For two years she has been a friend kept at arm's length. The other day at the *guinguette*, was that a date? Is she now more than a friend? Finishing the house is the keystone of the bridge between my two lives. Who will cross that bridge to join me?

'*Bonjour Francine. Tout va bien?*' I try to make it as casual as possible.

She jumps up, unable to disguise the light in her eyes. '*Coucou, Jean.*

Comment va tu?'

As she brushes my cheeks in the traditional French greeting, each touch is a second longer than necessary. 'What can I make for you?'

All the words I rehearsed evaporate.

'I mean, do for you. My English is not good.'

I make not-at-all noises, then show her the books. 'I'm bringing these back.'

'Ah, did you enjoy?'

My stomach turns to water as the blood rushes to my head. 'No. Er, I don't know.'

'You don't know if you enjoyed zem?'

How can her inability to pronounce a digraph chase all thoughts from my head? 'Of course, I mean, er, I haven't read them.'

'So, why return zem?'

'The library is closed tomorrow, and I have finished my kitchen.'

Now it is Francine's turn to look lost.

I continue. 'As it is your day off, I was wondering if you would help me christen it.'

'I don't understand.'

'I am making my first meal in the new kitchen and I would like you to share it.'

There, I've done it. For the first time since meeting Cathy, I have asked another girl out on a date. Calling it just a meal between friends is bullshit, and we both know it. A page marker slips from the book, so I stoop to pick it up so I can avoid her eye.

'Ah, *bien sûr*. But the library is not closed tomorrow.'

I feel dizzy. Before standing, I take in a long breath and persuade myself it's just as well.

Francine is smiling. '*Quand même*, I would love to join you.'

The sun shines again. 'Brilliant, thank you. About seven?'

'Perfect. See you tomorrow.'

As I reach the door, she calls to me. '*Et Jean...*' I turn back. '*Merci.*'

I leave whilst my legs can still carry me.

It's still daylight, but the full moon is so bright, so close I can smell it. A shining silver franc hanging in the sky. It reminds me of Francine returning from her swim, swaying her hips like the girl on the coin. Even the dress made her look like Marianne. Is this a date? I am married, but for Francine, I will make this a special meal. As Tree said, 'what goes on tour, stays on tour'.

All the next day, I pour over my cookery books. The kitchen is redolent with fresh herbs. I want to impress but not scare her off. The crisis of conscience after the trip to the lake has gone. Cathy is also planning a meal with Richard, although her preparations will be courtesy of the Raj and their takeaway service. She is in no position to take the moral high ground.

To stop myself from thinking of Francine, I concentrate on the recipe. A splash of white wine to cut through the heaviness of the oils. Tarragon or thyme? I add both, keeping the best leaves back to garnish.

Starter and dessert are in the fridge. I've laid the table. No candles, this is a simple meal between friends. If she doesn't bring wine, I have some in the cellar.

The main course smells cooked, so I turn off the oven and check the clock. Ten to seven. Just time to get changed. There's a low throb in the square. Francine's car is as big as she is petite. I finish dressing, resisting the impulse to go out to greet her. Back in the kitchen, I check everything that doesn't need checking because I have done it a thousand times already. It's now ten past seven. All afternoon I was wondering if she would turn up. She arrived almost a quarter of an hour ago, so she must be waiting in the car. Is she having second thoughts? I run my eyes over the meal I have prepared with such care, and wonder if she will just drive off again. The doorbell rings. I jump, despite expecting it for the last twenty minutes.

She stands in the doorway in a simple frock that runs like mercury over her tiny body. The silk shimmers like moonlight. Its soft grey patterns allow the bright radiance of her face to shine, sunshine behind clouds, eyes flashing like sunbeams.

I stoop to greet her, try to do the French two-cheek kiss, get it wrong, and our lips meet. 'I'm so sorry!'

She smiles. 'Ah non, don't say sorry. It was nice,' she adds with a smile.

Not knowing where to put the smile, I invite her in. Francine hesitates, then puts the wine on the table. It looks expensive, and the dress is perfect.

Helped by the wine, the evening passes, and with it, the awkwardness. Francine asks to use the bathroom, leaving me adrift in my emotions. It's not the wine that has intoxicated me, but Francine. I need her more than I ever needed Cathy.

When Francine returns, she moves her chair next to mine. Deliberately, she rests her hand on my thigh, so light it might have been a butterfly.

'The meal was perfect. You spent a lot of time on it.'

Fleetingly, my hand hovers over hers. To rest it there would be to say I share her feelings. She knows, yet acknowledging it would set us off on an irreversible journey. I pull her coffee cup towards us.

'Thank you.'

In the silence, she raises the cup to her lips. My hand is on top of hers. The journey has begun. 'Esther was brave to choose to stay and join the resistance instead of going with her family,' I say.

She gives my thigh a slight squeeze. 'Was she? Love is a powerful thing.'

I respond by doing the same to her hand. 'Is it?'

She smiles. Fleetingly, I wonder if it's her first time, but can find no words. She is not wearing perfume, so I move closer to smell her skin.

Francine takes a deep breath. 'You smell of cooking.'

Her comment makes me jerk away. There would have been time to shower before she arrived.

'I don't mean cooking fat. The herbs and spices make me want to eat you.'

My insides turn to water at the thought. 'You are brave too.'

'How so?'

'Well, we are dining alone in my house. I might do anything.'

'You mean something I don't want you to do? How do you know I wouldn't want it?'

'I don't, except that I am married. You don't seem to welcome the attention of married men.'

'I do not. That I am prepared to make an exception should flatter you.'

I'm sure I don't look flattered. The fact is, I am struggling with my conscience more than she seems to be.

'Kiss me.'

Her look is earnest. 'Isn't that what you don't want?' I ask.

'Not anymore, but it is considerate of you to check first.'

I lean into her. This is going to be one of those awkward kisses, not knowing where to put my hands.

'Not here.'

She goes to stand on the step. The one where Esther stood when I arrived with Peter and Cathy.

Like this, we are almost the same height. Francine smiles and puts her arms around my neck. 'Thank you for this marvellous soiree.'

What is she doing? Is she saying goodbye? She leans into me, breathing her warmth into my face. Her eyes are open, staring into mine. Our lips touch, hers parted, warm, imploring. We close our eyes, and the other senses take over. Lips touch, tongues taste, I smell her skin. With a slow deliberate movement, she kisses, then waits for a response. My hands slide over the silk of her dress, then her bare arms, fine hairs quivering in response.

As I slip my hand into the small of her back, I mirror her kiss, pulling her against me until my bulge presses into her stomach. Her hand leaves my shoulder and moves to stroke me through my trousers. I respond with a hand on her breast, her nipple as hard as my cock.

At last, our lips part. 'Do you have to go?' I whisper.

Her eyes never leave mine. '*Pas du tout.*'

'Then stay.'

The smile on her still moist lips reaches her eyes. 'That would please me very much.'

I let her lead me across the living room towards the bedroom.

She looks like a sparrow beside me. Who was the singer they called the sparrow? Edith Piaf. I scoop Francine in my arms and carry her over the threshold. *Non, rien de rien,* I whisper to myself, *Je ne regrette rien.* She smiles up at me from the bed while I push her hair away from her face, swimming in her soul. Holding my gaze, she returns it with a smile. It blazes like the sun, constant yet ever-changing.

Breaking the spell at last, she sits up, bouncing the hem of her dress from under her. Grabbing the frock, she lets the light material float down onto the pillow. The same pale gold that tumbles about her face nestles in her armpits. I bend, letting the light down caress my cheek, releasing her fragrance. Every sense is now assaulted by her presence. She removes her last piece of clothing while I stand, taking in her nakedness.

Placing a finger on my cock, she whispers. 'Your turn.'

When she inclines her head downwards, I push her away. I do not want it to end, and if she does that, it will. She falls back, legs still bent over the side of the bed. I kneel between them to do what I just prevented her from doing.

She is lying with her head on my chest. I thought I had bought this house to start a new life with Cathy. Was I buying it for Francine? What will the future bring? Does the house know, and if it does, will it tell? Will it tell me false stories, the ones I want to hear? Are there two futures, and like Schrödinger's cat, I will be dead with Cathy and alive with Francine? I shake my head, as if dislodging the thoughts. I don't want to waste the experience of holding Francine in my arms.

Finally, I release her so I can look into her eyes. 'I thought you would not come.'

A tuft of hair falls, caressing the hollow of her neck. 'Why have you thought this thing?'

I lift it away, tracing a finger on her collarbone. 'You sat in the car for twenty minutes.'

She laughs. 'English is so unsuited to love that it is a wonder you British reproduce. I was too soon.'

I do not lift my finger from her skin, watching the sensation send shivers through her and into her breasts, pulling at her nipples until they stand erect. It tells me she already wants me again, but my body is not ready. She can tell, so removes my hand.

I put it back. 'Only a couple of minutes — I saw you arrive.'

'It is called *le quart d'heure Perigordin*. If someone says seven, you must not arrive before seven-fifteen.'

I continue to trace patterns on her skin. 'That's silly.'

This time she does not stop the steady advance of my finger. 'Not at all,' she continues. 'Suppose I had arrived at seven and you were still cooking. I would have embarrassed you. This is not polite.'

The digit is getting closer. I pretend my finger is not following the conversation. 'If I know you will not arrive until seven-fifteen, then I will try to be ready for seven-fifteen. You, of course, know this so cannot arrive until seven-thirty in case I am not ready for seven-fifteen, which is the time you should arrive if I say seven.'

My finger has reached her nipple and is circling it. She reaches between my legs, holding my flaccid penis in her hand.

'Now, perhaps you will let me have a turn,' she whispers.

I laugh and roll onto my back. '*Bonne chance!*'

She gives it her best shot, but her previous performance was so effective she has no success. The effort, however, pushes her to the edge.

I sense her excitement and roll on to my side. 'You are backing the wrong horse.'

She makes a face. 'There is only one horse for me to bet on.'

I smile. 'Yes, but there is a filly.' I guide her hand between her legs.

She strokes, then whispers, 'I would rather it was you.'

'Then show me how you like it.'

She does; I mimic her actions, adding the tongue movements I used earlier. Suddenly, her legs shake. Instead of stopping, I speed up and tickle her. The shaking intensifies until she is screaming. 'John, *non! Arrete!*'

When I stop, she is a sweat-drenched bag of jelly.

I collapse beside her, laughing.

She punches me and laughs, too. 'I said stop!'

'Did you? Someone was screaming in my ear so I couldn't hear.'

I stop laughing. 'Why did you kiss me?'

For a second, she looks puzzled. 'When?'

'In the kitchen — I thought you were leaving.'

She smiles. 'To see what would happen.'

'Did you like what happened?'

A trace of playfulness crosses her smile. 'What is it you think? You know. You just want to hear me say it.'

'True.'

'Well, John Cartwright, I did like it. I liked it very much. Your turn.'

'Francine Lefèvre, I liked it too. I like you too. So much it scares me.'

I cannot say the words even in the post-coital glow where lovers only utter truths.

17

Esther

I have just watched my living self and our lover make love for the first time. For Jean and me, the world was different, and we were much younger. It's a story I did not want to tell Peter because he is too young. It's in the diary Francine translated — the one they read together at the picnic. You, gentle reader, seemed more interested in our living incarnations than my dusty story, but I will tell you now. If I say that this was the mission where I lost my virginity, then perhaps you will read the whole chapter!

January 1943

They have accepted me into the resistance, but I have not yet seen active service. The Maquis does three things. They help families like mine to cross the demarcation line, they gather intelligence to pass to the Allies, and they blow things up. Since the Germans took direct control of Vichy France, the demarcation line has become symbolic. We are no longer in a region worth escaping to.

Jean was a passeur. Now he is searching for a new role within the group, choosing sabotage rather than assassination. Jenny, the English spy, continues to gather evidence. I do not agree with her methods, but she says the end justifies the means. Louis respects her because she killed a guard, and he likes the information he can pass to London.

I must prove my worth to my brothers in arms, and to one in particular. Jean looks at me, his eyes lingering when he thinks I am not looking. He says nothing because he feels Jenny's eyes on him. That is so unfair when she has other lovers. I have let no one touch me in that way. The ruffians in Alençon were nothing short of rapists. Here in Dordogne, the boys look at me, but I am keeping my first time for Jean. Talk whispers around the meal table about Georges Guingouin. They refer to him as the first maquis. He who took resistance out of the cities into the countryside. Louis doesn't like him because he is a communist.

'The communists didn't even condemn the German occupation. They said Hitler and Stalin had signed a non-aggression pact.'

Jean unfolds his pocket knife. 'That was in 1940. Guingouin never agreed with that policy and now he pretty much runs his own show up in Limousin.'

I soak in all this local gossip. Jenny, too, pays close attention. A spy needs to know any potential divisions within the unit. She has to make sure there's no mole, and tell her handlers who they can trust.

'He's hiding in the woods now. How much can he do when he is living in a rabbit hole?'

Jean pares off another slice of sausage. 'They are very effective. They have blown up the main railway line. If the war turns against the Germans, that is the way they will bring up their troops to defend the north.'

'They have already repaired that. They just use trucks instead.'

'Then we must render them useless too — blow up the fuel depots.'

Louis gives an irritable shrug. 'They defend them much too well. We are a resistance group, not an army.'

'Then we attack where they are less well defended, but we can still do damage,' Jean says.

'Where do you suggest?' I say it to show I have been listening, but more to make Jean look at me.

'The rubber factory near Limoges. Trucks need tyres.'

Louis puffs out his irritation. The young spot opportunity, the old difficulty. 'Where would we get enough explosive to destroy a whole factory?'

Now it's Jenny's turn. 'I heard talk of a new dynamite — dynamite-gomme. It is like putty and you can mould it around the part you want to destroy, so you need less of it.'

He waves his knife in a sarcastic imitation of an aeroplane. 'Maybe you could get one of your fly-boys to drop some, assuming it doesn't go off when it hits the ground.'

Why is Louis being so negative? Perhaps it's because Georges is FTPF and Louis AS.

Franc-tireurs et partisans français and *Armée Secrète* have always been rivals, even though both are fighting the Germans.

Jenny ignores the dig. 'There's no need. There is a depot near Saint-Léonard. You know the tungsten mine at Puy-les-Vignes?'

She has got Louis' attention. 'How do you know they store explosives there?'

'A carpenter told me the Germans made him install a lightweight roof.'

He works it out. 'If it goes off, the roof lifts off, and the blast goes straight up. If it was a proper roof, the walls would blow out and do much more damage.'

He stands as he always does when he is about to give his verdict. 'We don't do the rubber factory. We leave that to Georges, but I will tell him our cell is prepared to help by supplying the explosives.'

Jenny raises a finger to speak. 'Shall I ask the carpenter to brief you?'

'No, I need to know the operational routine. Madame Villachou's son works at the mine. I know I can trust that family.'

Four days later, a nervous young man is standing in the kitchen, wringing his beret with calloused hands and reciting as if he were in school.

'The dynamite is in a powder magazine two hundred metres from the extraction centre.'

'What kind of building is it?'

'It comprises a masonry building pierced by mesh openings.'

'How do you get in?'

'To enter, one passes through a double door. On the one inside, they have fixed a device which triggers an alarm signal in the guard's apartment, placed at about eighty metres.'

'What about outside?'

'A large embankment surrounds the powder magazine, then a three-metre high fence. At night, the guards make regular rounds.'

The plan is to wait until the patrol has passed, then clip enough fence to slide underneath. The Germans guard the door too well, so once inside the perimeter fence, we will head to the rear of the building. Using a grappling iron on the grilles, my job is to climb onto the roof. I volunteered for this because the roof would not take the weight of a man. I must remove a roof panel and drop into the room containing the explosives. Jean is going to climb onto the top of the wall and pull up the boxes through the hole I make in the roof. He will then lower them down to Pierre, who must take them back to the gap we have cut in the fence. Others will wait outside the fence to take them down to the cart waiting in the woods.

The day arrives, or rather the night. Jean, Pierre, and I huddle under a tarpaulin in the back of the cart whilst a grim-faced farmer eggs his horse on, pulling us through the damp woods. The operation goes as planned, with Pierre ferrying five boxes to the waiting cart. Jean is gesturing for me to climb back up because the rope is fraying as it passes over the parapet. I weigh less than the boxes, so I give a 'one more' signal and tie another. The last part of the lift is awkward. It swings under the hole I made in the roof, requiring Jean to lean in to get it over the lip. I watch him struggling, regretting my greediness. It slips from his grasp, and I brace myself to take the strain. The rope goes taut, then snaps. In the two seconds it takes for the box to fall, I make my peace with my father and apologise to my mother for not giving her a grandchild. I then send a message to Ethan that I will soon join him. Finally, I tell Jean that I love him, and that I don't want to die a virgin.

The box breaks, spilling its contents around me, breaking the silence. Jean's distraught face turns to alarm as the inner door opens. A siren sounds, and he makes a frantic gesture behind him, telling Pierre to run. The German advances towards me. I consider picking up a packet of explosives to threaten him with. Since it survived being dropped from the roof, I doubt that hurling it at him will be of much use.

With the utmost care, he picks his way through the detritus, motioning with his gun that I must leave by the door he has just entered through. I have just passed the second door with a gun muzzle in the small of my back. It slams with such power into the face of my captor that it knocks him backwards. Wrenching it open again, Jean leaps through and onto the guard, pinning his head to the ground with a garrotting wire. I stand frozen, watching the man bleed out as the veins in Jean's neck pulse in a determination that this man should no longer be a threat to me.

Desperate times lead to strange declarations of love. Jean, who could not fire a gun at a convicted informer, was killing a guard with his bare hands just to protect me. Finally, he stands, places the bloody wire in his pocket, and embraces me. Our lives still hang by a thread, but in his arms I feel safe. He does not allow the feeling to last.

'We must go.'

He pushes me towards the gap in the fence.

'Where's Pierre?'

'Gone with the farmer. And the explosives,' he adds as an afterthought.

We are now outside the perimeter fence and in the relative safety of the woods.

Puy-les-Vignes was a long way from St Etienne. 'How are we going to get home?'

'Walk.' I look up at him in disbelief. 'But not tonight. We will find a barn to sleep in.'

Sleeping is not on either of our minds. In the barn, Jean pushes a cow out of the way and loosens the hay for me to lie on. She does not seem to mind giving us her bed, and the straw is warm from where she had been resting. We lie together, both wide awake, my body responding to Jean's nearness. As he shifts position, I can tell that he, too, is ready.

'I don't mind,' I say, then curse myself for making such an insipid comment.

Every fibre of my being aches to feel his naked flesh against mine, for him to make this girl into a woman. I want it even though I do not know how my body can accommodate what is now pressed against my leg. Why could I not say all that instead?

He raises himself on one elbow. 'I don't want to make love to a boy.'

In reply to my questioning look, he fingers the lapel of my brother's jacket. I put my hand on the top button, but he pushes it away.

With infinite care, he releases my body from its chrysalis until the butterfly lies before him, damp, crumpled, and bewildered. He gazes down at me until I feel comfortable beneath his stare and I can look into his eyes.

'It's not fair,' I say.

'What is not fair, my love?'

I thrill at the last two words. He has never called me that.

'I want to see you, too.'

He undresses with almost as much care. I want to look into his smiling eyes, yet something else draws mine downwards. Never have I seen an uncircumcised penis, but that is not what concerns me. I want him inside me, but looking at him, I cannot see how it's possible.

'It is my first time.'

'I know. Don't worry, I will not hurt you.'

He lies on top of me with his cock pressed against my stomach. Our bodies are on fire, the hay is warm, the barn dry, but it's still January and I am glad of his warmth. For a long time, the unfamiliar sensation is all the emotion I can bear. The touch of his skin against mine, and the smell of his torso as I bury my face in his chest.

Finally, I move so I can speak. 'Kiss me.'

He slides down until his face is close, then rubs his nose against mine in the manner of the Inuit. My eyes close as I feel his lips on every part of my face, finally brushing my own. I part my lips, feeling the most intimate part of me part too. His lips on mine, he explores my mouth with his tongue penetrating me, as I know he will do elsewhere. Instinctively, I part my legs. He slides until my face is once more against his chest.

Then it happens. As if he were coaxing a wild animal to eat from his hand, he presses his cock into me, allowing me to open. I wait for the pain. My gift to him, to endure for the sake of our love. There's none, only fulfilment. He pushes a little more; I open a little more. Finally, he is resting with his full weight on my pelvis. Sliding my hand between us, I touch my stomach. Fingers brushing my flat belly, feel the slight rise in the skin, pushed up by his organ deep inside me, motionless. I am crying, but they are tears of happiness. He half withdraws and, with infinite care, thrusts in again so my hand feels the bulge through my skin. I'm fascinated by the sensation as his movements become more rhythmic. At last, he thrusts deeper than before and stops. The pulsating of his cock thrills as his seed fills me. My muscles contract, holding him inside. When I wake, he is still on top. His penis has slipped from me, but it doesn't matter. I have given my first time to him, and did not disappoint him.

Do you see now why I did not tell this story to Peter? I see from watching my living self that sex is different today. Both girls and boys experience a *jouissance*. Francine more intensely than John. Am I jealous? No, I am happy for her. Girls in the forties did not have orgasms. If they did, they did not talk about it.

18

June 2005

My living self has read about our first time. Do you realise you are reading about yourself in a former life? I watch you creep out of bed and fetch your car keys. John stirs, his arm reaching towards an empty pillow where he breathes, burying his face into where yours had been.

Half an hour later, there's a car with a low-pitched purr, the door clunks, and a stair creaks. 'Bonjour! Breakfast is served!'

You are holding out a brown paper bag. 'Café is brewing.'

He pats the bed, but you shake your head. 'I cannot rest. I am a working girl, remember?'

You scoop up your knickers from the floor. 'Better take these — I wouldn't want your wife to find them!'

With that, you are gone. If I had been as confident in 1943 as you are today, would things have ended differently? John breathes in the smell of you on his own skin.

He is on his back, staring at the ceiling. Outside, the throbbing of your car engine fades into memory, returning in another rhythm at the back of the house.

He leaps out of bed and hurries barefoot into the kitchen, pulling on shorts and a T-shirt before bumping into a man in overalls.

'Sorry, I forgot you were coming. There is a snagging list

somewhere.'

The carpenter follows John's gaze. An uncleared dining table is not the place to look. John goes through the list from memory. The musky warmth of your lovemaking still fills the bedroom. The man ignores this as studiously as he did the unwashed dishes.

When he is gone, John drives to the florist, then the library, where he produces a bunch of flowers from behind his back.

You let out a cry of surprise. 'Why have you done this thing?'

'Because I love you.'

John has said what he could not last night.

You lower your voice. 'I know, and now the whole town knows it.'

'I don't care.'

'Are you sure? Cathy might think differently. I don't mind. As soon as I parked my car overnight at your house, I knew people would brand me as the other woman.'

A customer enters.

'Let's talk later, at the ice cream shop,' you whisper, turning to the next customer.

You are ten years younger than John, and half his size, yet you have the measure of the situation.

'I am going to start by saying that I love you,' you say. 'Last night must have proved that. I have loved you for longer than you know.'

He stares at you.

'How long?'

'Since the day you first showed me the house. You feel as I do. I felt that last night, too, but I remember why you came to Périgord.'

When he opens his mouth, you put a finger to his lips.

'You have come because you love your wife and you wish to save her from — Sorry, I do not remember his name.'

'Richard.'

'Before you say that now you love me, I will remind you I know. That changes nothing.'

John looks at you with round puppy eyes. 'It changes everything.'

'You say that because you think you cannot love two women. Why? Before we met, you loved Peter and Cathy. You still do. It is possible to love two people.'

John is tearing the paper napkin into strips. 'One is my wife; one is my son. They are different loves.'

You take the shredded napkin from his hand and put it aside. 'And now you love Cathy and you love me. One is your wife, and the other is your mistress. They too are different loves.'

Without the napkin to play with, he reaches for your hand. 'And you are OK with that?'

'Yes, because I don't aspire to be your wife.'

He pulls his hand away. 'Thanks very much!'

'Like this, we stay free. I don't intend to be tied, even to you. Go back to England and bring your wife and son to the home you have prepared for them.'

His eyes are filling with tears. 'And you?'

'You have accorded me the honour of not marrying you. Our love will be on the wing with the birds.'

'What will I do without you?'

His phone rings. 'I will not reply to this question. You will not be without me. Now, answer that call.'

'It's the plumber; he is at the house. I forgot. I have to go.'

What are you doing? All the years I have waited. Finally, I find our lover and he makes love to you. Why are you turning him away?

'Another coffee?' Ariane picks up the empty cup. You nod. She returns with her own and sits in front of you.

'John and I made love.' You tell her. 'Have I done the right thing?'

'Why do you ask?'

'You understand Englishmen. You married one.'

The older woman reaches out a reassuring hand. 'You did nothing; you both did it.'

'I took the lead; he is timid.'

'He invited you to supper when his wife and son were away.'

You raise an eyebrow. 'You know that? It was only yesterday!'

'This is rural France; news like that travels fast.'

'*Oui, mais quand meme!*' First laughing, now serious. 'How can I help him? I have made his life hard.'

Ariane puts her hand on yours. 'John must do this on his own. I think it will be Cathy who decides. You told me she has a boyfriend in England. Let's see whether she leaves him.'

'She must! John has moved mountains to get her back.'

'If she changes her mind, it will leave him free to marry you.'

'I don't want to marry him! Look how unhappy being married has made him!'

'Then don't. Life will be simpler for him. He is not the only man who is not very good at infidelity.'

I go back to the house. John is packing. A cold fog of reality creeps down from the forests, consuming the trees as efficiently as wildfire. Maudlin thoughts swirl like mist. He is talking to himself. *I will have to give up Francine. That way, I will make the same sacrifice as Cathy.* Hunched shoulders manoeuvre an empty trailer towards John's car. The coupling drops into place with a resigned clunk. Ferry tickets are on the passenger seat.

John continues to mutter, rehearsing what to say to you. *I'm going back to England. When I return, it will be with my wife and son.* His furrowed brow rejects that opening and tries another. *Making love to you was the most beautiful thing.*

The car stops outside the library. I am scared that he has decided that when he comes back, there won't be any more John and Francine. If he says that, it will make that night a one-night stand.

The man behind the computer looks up.

John strides forward with a resoluteness at odds with his countenance. 'Bonjour. I am looking for Francine.'

'Bonjour. She is not here.' He has returned his attention to the monitor.

'When will she be back?'

'I don't know. Francine went home early, saying she was unwell.'

The colour drains from John's cheeks. 'Can you tell her I called in to say goodbye?'

'What name?'

'John. John Cartwright.'

He nods.

Turning to go, he hesitates, and turns back. 'Tell her I will write.'

Another nod. Finally, the man looks up and confirms he will pass on the message. Tears running down his face, John goes back to the car and turns the key.

I follow him. Rain mottles the oncoming headlights. While the storm whips up outside, I watch another rage inside his head.

He talks into the void. 'The man might not relay the message.'

A car behind flashes its headlights. 'She will think that the meal and what followed means nothing to me.'

He pulls back into the nearside lane. 'Maybe this is for the best. If she thinks I do not love her, she will cease to love me. It's the only way to make my new life with Cathy work.'

He almost misses the slip road and swerves. 'I don't understand Francine's talk of loving two people. She can be a mistress; Cathy can take a lover. I cannot.'

A lorry blasts its opinion of John's driving. 'I wanted to tell her that last Friday was not just a one-night stand. Had she been at the library, and I ended it, that is exactly what it would say. It's the least I can do if Cathy leaves Richard.'

Cathy, England

Something happened. I tune in to John's emotions even when he is not there. The bonds that tie us are pretty elastic. God knows I've stretched them often enough. I don't hear him when I'm with Richard. Those times are emotional taekwondo, but when I am alone and I've washed Richard out of me, the bush telegraph hums and I connect with John. But this last week, nothing. I never phone him because he always phones me, like he's checking up on me. At first, I was thankful to be spared the 'I miss you. You're going to love the house' updates. When it all stopped, it's like when I can't hear Peter and his friend playing. I know they're up to something. It's the same with John.

The door opens.

'Hiya, y'alright?' I try to sound casual.

He doesn't answer, so I go up and give him a kiss. Poor lamb, he looks washed out. 'Everything alright?'

This time he focuses. 'What? Oh yes, I'm just shattered. It's a long drive.'

'I've not cooked — I didn't know what time you would be back.' He doesn't answer. 'Shall I get a takeaway?'

'What? No, I ate at the services. Get something for you and Peter if you like.'

'Peter's at football — Craig's mum is picking him up so they'll get a burger.'

I'm drowning in all this trivia. What fucking happened? I want to scream it at him but hand him a can of beer and shut up.

'Kitchen's done.'

'You said.'

'Looks fantastic.'

'Good.'

I go back to my wine.

'Cat, I'm shattered. Do you mind if I just go up?'

'Peter's not back yet.' He sits down again and goes back to reading the beer label. I relent. 'You go. I'll send him up. He missed you.'

'I missed him.'

He goes upstairs without kissing me. He didn't miss me.

You need to let him go.

It's the same voice I heard after the parents' evening. The one who was trying to warn me about Richard.

'Who are you? Why can't I see you?'

I'm your previous self.

'Are you one of Peter's ghosts?'

I wouldn't say I was Peter's. I thought I was Jean's, but I was not.

The shower runs, then John is back downstairs like he forgot something.

'Was Sir Evelyn OK about you handing in your notice?'

Shit.

'It's only a month's notice. We don't need to be in France till school goes back,' I say.

'We could have gone as soon as he broke up,' says John.

Now it's my turn to hide something. 'We need to get this house ready to rent.' I avoid his eye.

He comes back from wherever his mind has taken him. 'Everything OK?' he asks.

I smile. 'It is now you're back.'

John

We are in bed. The sex is perfunctory; the completion of a ritual we always perform after we have spent time apart. This time, both minds are elsewhere.

Now Cathy is sleeping, but I am still wide awake. Slipping downstairs and into the study, I open my laptop, and then remember that she checks my emails. What did people do before computers? Closing the lid, I open the drawer and pull out a pale blue Basildon Bond writing pad.

The paper and fountain pen with its broad italic nib belonged to my mother. Tonight, I miss her innocent wisdom. Perhaps by using her pen and paper, some of it will find its way on to the page. When I finish, I address the envelope, insert the letter and place it in my jacket pocket.

Cathy

I'm up first, which means everybody is late. Peter bundles down the stairs, checking his watch. I shoo him out of the door, but he bounces back. 'Dinner money.'

John's wallet is in his jacket pocket, so I pull it out and hand Peter a banknote.

'Thanks, Mummy.' He gives a wave and is gone.

I spot the letter when I return the wallet. Upstairs, someone is crashing about in the bathroom. 'Where's the shower gel?'

'Where it always is.'

The room turns. I never pass out, at least not when I'm sober. I grab the bookcase to steady myself and a book falls down. It's the one Peter gave me and I never finished. I stare at it, willing myself not to faint. Concentrate. Think of something, anything. I grab the book and open it at random. I've not read this bit.

Dordogne 1943

'Il n'y a que Maille qui m'aille!'

The German soldier has drunk too much. Mademoiselle Maille was the name the resistance had given to Jenny. The Maille family made their money from mustard before the Great War, much in the way Coleman had done in England.

The German had taken a shine to Jenny on a previous visit. He found it hilarious that the jar of mustard shared its name with the server, little guessing that she was an heiress to the Dijon company.

Jenny was late for work and the maître d' looked about him for help.

'Il n'y a que Maille qui m'aille!' Only Maille pleases me, he repeated, pointing to the slogan on the jar.

Things were getting difficult as Jenny entered, adjusting her apron.

'I am sorry to be late. Is there something I can help with?'

'Yes, you can take this gentleman's order. His drinks will be free, and I will take it out of your wages.'

Jenny accepted the censure, then put her arm across the German's shoulder and smiled her sweetest smile.

As the soldier removed his jacket, an envelope fell to the floor.

'Verzeichnis,' he explained, not expecting the girl to understand. She did. A list of people being deported. It would compromise her if she stole the envelope. They had sealed it, so borrowing and returning was not an option either. She poured him another drink and flirted before asking the officer how they selected people. He recounted with pride the meticulous process. It required several triages before they sent the last list to Touriac to be checked against those loaded on the cattle trucks.

'What happens to all the draft lists?' she asked.

'We throw them away.'

'That seems a waste of paper.'

'We have lots of paper.'

This went a long way to explaining why nobody else did.

After work, Jenny shared this information with Louis.

'We can't steal the final draft without blowing your cover, but we can look for discarded ones. I'll get Pierre to go through the rubbish heap.'

Cathy 2005

I slip the envelope back into John's pocket. I know who he has written to because Francine's name is on the envelope, but I do not know what he wrote.

The story I have just read gives me an idea. I spot the screwed-up notepaper in John's waste bin. Instead of emptying it, I hide it behind the bushes, and as soon as John has left for work, I retrieve it.

Francine, France

Jules always arrives at the library before me. He collects the post, and then the returned books, before waiting, admonishing me with silence when I am late.

Today there's a blue envelope with my name and *strictement privé* handwritten in blue ink.

Jules, beside himself with curiosity, is hovering.

'Aren't you going to open it?'

'Later, we should have started work.'

Disappointed, he picks up a pile of books and slouches off. As soon as he has gone, I rip open the letter. I've tried so hard to improve my English, but John's handwriting is so bad I can't read it. Deciding to ask Ariane to help me decipher his scrawl, I slip the letter into my pocket.

Ariane has no other customers and is glad to have an excuse to sit down. 'Are you sure you want me to read it? It might be very personal.'

'If you please, we have no secrets, and otherwise I cannot read John's handwriting, so how do I know if it is personal?'

Ariane opens the letter. 'He starts by saying he loves you, that he is despondent, and that he made you think the opposite. He says that it is his fault.'

I nod. 'John is gone without saying goodbye. Jules said he called at the library, but I had already left.'

Ariane nods. 'Gosh, he is head over heels in love with you. He talks about the song you shared, saying he could not have written it. He says you and he are very different. You were talking to Peter about priests wanting bigger spires!'

I giggle. 'Priests like to have churches with large steeples the way men like to have large penises.'

'I will not ask how you came to have that conversation! He doesn't understand how you can be OK with being a mistress, even though his wife is mistress to another man.'

'*Je sais.*'

'He says for you, wives and mistresses, existing side by side is normal. For him, he sees being a mistress as temporary. Either they get fed up with each other, or the man leaves his wife and marries his mistress.'

'*M'enfin! Il ne manques pas de culot!* What about the other way round? When it is the wife quitting her husband and marrying her lover?'

Ariane shrugs. 'He says the affair between Cathy and Richard has been going on too long. If Cathy was going to do that, she would have done so by now. I think John means she doesn't have to leave him because he didn't make a fuss. She can have the best of both worlds.'

I push my cup away, slopping coffee on the saucer. 'This is what I was proposing to him. It is clear he still loves Cathy. I can't change that. Nor can I stop loving him. I just want him to love me. When we made love, I was a strong, confident woman. Now I am a little girl asking to be loved.'

Ariane takes my hand. 'I think he still loves her. Her affair with Richard has not changed this. I think it changed after he met you. He says that when he bought the house, he loved Cathy with all his heart. Now he says that he has given part of his heart to you. He admits you are right, and he is mistaken; it is possible to love two people. He talks about his love for Cathy. Are you OK for me to read it?'

I nod. 'I need to know everything.'

Ariane looks back at the letter. 'His love for Cathy is recognition of the life they have shared and his concern for her welfare. He says that is the way a husband loves his wife, but that the night you spent with him is the way a man loves his mistress.'

'Maybe he will come back, and we could again be lovers.'

'I'm afraid not. John tries to explain why he cannot leave Cathy in England with Richard and come to France and live with you. It's not uncommon. Many people need to convince themselves that their ex is happy so they can move on to their next partner.'

Ariane returns to the letter. 'This is interesting. John says, I cannot leave the woman I once loved. That is a Freudian slip. He has not yet admitted to himself that he no longer loves her. Maybe he pretends out of duty, or he is clinging to the past when they did love each other.'

'Why can't he leave her?'

Ariane is silent for some time, then puts her hand to her mouth.

'What have you just read?'

She traces the words with a finger to ensure she has read them correctly. 'Richard is controlling Cathy. John can see it, but Cathy does not. John thinks Cathy will be under Richard's spell.'

Now it's my turn to put my hand to my mouth. *'Mon Dieu!'*

Ariane scans the rest of the letter for some mitigation, but finds none. 'He finishes by saying that he has to bring Cathy to France to break the spell. Once here, he will have to give all his love to her, but he says the love you shared he will hold for all eternity. He calls it a testament to what might have been.'

I am crushed. 'He loves me.'

'Yes.'

'He does not love her.'

Ariane reaches for my hand. 'John feels a duty towards Cathy as a doctor might to a patient.'

We weep silent tears. In another corner of the cafe, a girl dressed in boy's clothes also cries.

Ariane takes me in her arms and whispers, 'Francine, I am so, so sorry.'

I dry my eyes. 'We can't leave it like this. I'll write back, although I do not know what to say, and even less how to get it to him without Cathy seeing it.'

Ariane pats my hand. 'Write the letter. I'll get it to him.'

19

Cathy, England

'You said you would do it last week.'

I can't be having this. John's had his leg over in France, then comes home giving it all that about me not handing in my notice. What's the point? Does he still want me to go? If he fancies a threesome, he can stuff that. But I can't say any of this because he doesn't know I know.

'Well, I haven't, alright?'

John storms out. As soon as he's gone, I pick up the phone. I'll get the fucker.

Sandie from the office is doing one of them *women wot lunch* things with me.

I hand the menu back with a smile and turn to her. 'I'm fucking fuming.'

She says nothing, so I tell her about the letter. She knows about Richard because she was one of the few people here when we got the Cheung Kong contract. If I'd wanted sympathy, I would have picked someone else to dump on. Sandie disapproves, but she keeps her mouth shut.

I look at her again. 'No, don't judge me! He set up this whole going to France thing just so he can shag his French tart.'

She orders, letting my words echo in my head while she doesn't reply.

'You agreed to the move before John met her.'

'That's splitting hairs. As soon as he found a house, he wanted her to see it. Peter told me. Then he invites those Germans to talk about living there in the war.'

'French.'

'Are you sure? They were talking in German.'

She gives me a patronising smile. 'They came from Alsace.'

I can always slap her later, so I point to her glass. The server pours. 'That's Germany, isn't it? I don't know; it doesn't matter. He invited her to our house. I dunno why she came.'

Sandie unfolds her napkin like a teacher opening my report. 'She translated the story for you.'

I give her my look that says "whose side are you on?" 'OK, but why her?'

That's how lunches with Sandie work — I talk, she listens, I pay.

She chose an expensive wine, so I get my money's worth. 'I need to take some time out. Richard's blagged the use of a holiday cottage in Dartmouth. I was going to say no, but I changed my mind because of the letter. I have to tell John, but he won't say anything, even if he guesses. Well, he can't now, can he?'

Sandie smiles and takes another sip of wine.

I go home with a plan that involves pretending to be nice to John.

He comes in, dumping his briefcase in the way.

I call down the hall. 'Hiya, y'alright?'

He kicks the bag and pulls out his wallet. 'No, I've got to pay for the taxi.'

He disappears, comes back, gives his bag another kick and slumps into the sofa.

'You said you would pick me up at the station,' he sulked.

'You said you would phone to tell me which train you were on.'

'I did — it was engaged, so I left a message.'

Flippin' eck, I'm not his ma. 'I never checked me messages.'

Now he's looking at me like he wants me to jump up and fetch him a beer. Stuff that.

'Have you handed it in?' he asks.

Not that again.

'Sir Evelyn wasn't in today.'

John may be naïve, but he isn't stupid.

'Why didn't you give it to HR?'

If he's picking a fight, he won't win. 'Sir E. would go ballistic if I'd done that.'

It looks like he bought it, so now I'm thinking about the weekend with Richard. 'Sir Evelyn wants me to go on a business trip with him.'

'You just said he wasn't in.'

Shit! 'Er, he sent me a text.'

'Where are you going?'

I look round for inspiration. 'Dubai.'

Dubai? Fucking Dubai? Why did I say that? He'll never buy it. I wish he would just say he knows I'm going away with Richard, then I can throw that fucking letter in his face. We eat in silence and go to bed. There's no sex. Not surprising — why would he want to? He's traded me in for a newer model. As soon as John is out of the house, I retrieve the discarded drafts of his letter to Francine and pack them in my overnight bag.

Devon

The sun has just set over the Dart. Rippling water sparkles, turning from rose gold to platinum in the moonlight. Richard dangles himself in front of me, as elusive as the breeze. I long to fill my jib and let him pull me to dangerous waters.

I'm forty-one, but can still boss a red lace thong. The shop didn't have the bra my size, so I'm letting them all hang out. Richard's always been a tit man. He looks ridiculous in those Bermudas and a floral shirt which he leaves open to show his hairy chest.

'I like a nice manly chest,' I simper.

'Mutton dressed as lamb. Put them away. I've only just had supper!'

When he talks like that, it can hurt, even when I know it's just to keep me on my toes.

I jiggle them at him. 'Then you can have a mouthful of these for afters!'

Taking the bait, he comes to sit astride me, smelling of coconut from the sunblock and some knock-off aftershave he got at the pound shop. He can afford the real McCoy, but is too much of a tight arse.

I push him off. 'John's been playing away from home. He shagged that tart from the library.'

It's the first time I've caught Richard off guard. He looks surprised, so I fetch the letters. I don't like that he looks at them and not my tits. I gyrate a bit whilst I sip the champagne.

He shuffles the sheets and reads another one. 'I never knew the old dog had it in him!'

Not the reaction I wanted. 'I'll show that French midget who's the better lover,' I say.

'If you want to do that, then make love to your husband, not me.'

After I make breakfast the next day, I lower myself onto the seat with care. I'm sure he is getting rougher. Why do men enjoy doing that?

Shifting my weight to the other buttock, I pick up the papers John discarded. 'What should I do?'

'It's obvious. We've been waiting for this. Now you can divorce John and get maintenance.'

'I wasn't thinking of going that far. It's not fair to Peter.'

Richard jabs a finger at me. 'You stupid fucking cow! That was the whole point. John would have got custody if you had asked earlier. Now you can make John the guilty party.'

I'm lost. If I say so, he will get angry, so I turn on the waterworks. He must love me if he's OK with me keeping Peter. It means he is prepared to take me on with a sprog.

'Don't you fucking go soft on me! We've got him by the balls, and we'll squeeze them till his eyes pop out.'

I don't understand why he is so agitated. What's in it for him? He can already have me whenever he wants. Now he is tearing his croissant apart and waving it at me.

'If John had filed for divorce, you wouldn't have got any maintenance. He didn't because he never had the balls.'

I give in — I have to when he is like this. 'You're right. You see things so much clearer.'

All at once, he flips and comes to sit next to me. 'That's my baby.

Sit tight. You were a clever girl to get the letter.'

I smile, grateful he has stopped his verbal assault.

'Tell John that you've handed in your notice, but it is six months, not one.'

'What difference will that make?'

'Oh, you stupid fucking cow! You want to keep Peter, right? He will have to start secondary school in England. That will boost your custody claim.'

I am too scared to say I still don't understand.

'Persuade John to go to France first. I'll try to go, too — I may get proof John's been playing away from home. It'll show desertion.'

I feel terrible about tearing Peter away from his dad, but at least Richard is OK for Peter to stay with us. I don't know how I will sell the plan to John.

He says nothing when I get home. He doesn't ask about Dubai, just left my passport on the coffee table. The nearest he gets to an argument is letting me know he knows. It's worse than a screaming crockery-throwing session. I've known both men since uni and still can't work out either of them. For starters, John has found someone else. It's clear he loves her, but he is preparing to take me to France. Why? The only reason I can think of is that he still loves me. He loves me despite me being unfaithful. He loves me, despite finding someone far better for him than me. I don't deserve him. I deserve a total arsehole like Richard.

Supper was a peace offering. OK, I drove to the Tandoori and sneaked a quick pint, waiting for the order.

'I can't go to France until Christmas,' I tell John when I get back. 'My boss changed my contract, so I have to give six months' notice.'

'That's fine for you, but Peter needs to start school in France.'

I thought he might say that.

'Peter can start secondary here. I'll bring him out at Christmas.'

I'm sure he does not know it's giving me time to start divorce proceedings.

Peter has paused the game he is playing, so I turn to him. 'You're OK with staying here with yer mam until Christmas, aren't you, pet?'

Peter puts the controller down but doesn't turn to look at us. 'No, I want to go to France with Daddy.'

'I know it's hard for you to understand, but you need to let the grown-ups decide what's best.'

John says nothing. Peter slams down the controller.

'It's easy,' he shouts. 'Daddy wants us all to move to France, so you stop seeing Richard.'

'Bloody hell, John. What have you been saying to him?'

Before John can answer, Peter deals a killer blow. 'Nothing. He doesn't have to. Daddy, I want to go to France with you as soon as we break up. Mummy, I want you to quit your job like you promised and follow us as soon as you can.'

'It's not as simple as that.'

Peter jumps up, pushing away the games console. 'YES, IT IS!'

He storms out. John goes to find him and calm him down.

I scribble a note. *Gone out. Don't wait up.*

Richard leaps up, tipping over the coffee table. He kicks it out of the way and bears down on me, the torrent of abuse finally subsiding into words that might have some meaning.

'Are you sure John doesn't know we know about him and Francine?'

My eyes dart around the room like a cornered rabbit. 'No. I mean, yeah, I'm pretty sure he doesn't know we know. I'm sorry.'

'Sorry for what? That he doesn't know we know?'

He gets worse when I cry, but I can't help it. 'Richard, please stop. You're confusing me.'

He calms down a bit and goes back to pacing. 'Let John take Peter to France, give it a month or two, then we'll file for divorce.'

'It's come to that, then?'

I'm not sure he hears me. It's better that he doesn't. He is too busy listening to the sound of his own voice.

'Desertion, infidelity, child abduction. The fucker won't know what hit him!'

He turns on me. 'Has he ever hit you?'

I flinch. 'No,' I say in an inaudible whisper, before adding, 'you're the only one to do that.'

I hate Richard when he's like this. Maybe a slow death from

suffocation beneath John's love is better than being mauled by the tiger pacing in front of me.

I turn to pick up the car keys. 'I should go. John will wonder where I am.'

'If he wonders that, he's even more stupid than I thought.'

When he raises his hand, something snaps inside me.

'If you fucking hit me again, I'm out of here. I'll leave for France tomorrow if I have to.'

He crumples. 'I'm sorry, pussycat. I shouldn't have called John stupid. It's just that I'm afraid of losing you.'

He is pretending to cry. I'm a gullible bitch, so I put my arms around him.

'Just a quickie, but I'm not staying.'

I tiptoe into the house. Richard's behaviour has put John's in perspective. He has served his sentence. Slipping into bed and moving close to him, I still don't know what I will do.

John, two weeks later

I am at the rugby club, helping Tree with his U13 training.

'You should bring Peter - he's a natural.'

'I'm afraid he's only into soccer.'

He looks over his shoulder as if I had betrayed state secrets, then leans forward with a mock conspiratorial whisper. 'I feel yer shame. Yer secret's safe with me.'

I laugh despite myself and offer to get the next round.

Tree rummages in his kitbag. 'Speaking o' secrets, I've a letter for thee.'

'Is this one of your practical jokes?'

My name is written in Francine's handwriting, the address written by someone else.

'It's from Francine.'

Tree rolls his eyes. 'John, I may be a forward, but I had worked that out. Haven't you guys heard of email?'

'Cathy and I share the same email address.'

Tree taps his nose. 'Schoolboy error.'

Ignoring him, I rip open the letter. He pulls his chair closer and is trying to read. 'Well?'

'Well, what?'

'Christ, John, what does she say?'

'Blah blah blah, when do we arrive? Missed school open day. Peter's teacher wants to see me. Blah blah, do we want more wood?'

Tree leans back, testing the chair to its limits. 'Sounds like a letter from the wife.'

I sigh. 'No such luck.'

The unconsidered response hangs between us.

'Why send it to me?'

'Francine wants to talk.'

Tree smiles. 'Yeah, women are like that. Scares the shit out o' me when Lena says it.'

'Francine's right — we need to talk. I was a real bastard. I'll write back.'

'What ye gonna say?'

'I'll just say when we will arrive. Cathy is staying here to work her notice. I'll invite Francine over when Peter's not about.'

'Careful, look what happened last time.'

Tree calls after me as I turn to leave. 'I still want to know how the letter got to me.'

Turning, I spin a rugby ball in his direction. 'I don't have the foggiest.'

Cathy is reading a book when I get home. It's the one written by the English spy. I left the diary of the Jewish refugee with Francine.

20

When I signed up, I wanted to join the SIS, but Dad said the Special Intelligence Service are chauvinists and he didn't want his daughter used as a honey trap. He got his way. I asked, and they told me they were not recruiting women. I fared little better with the Special Operations Executive. 'Do your First Aid and we'll send you out as a FANY. You might get to do a bit of courier work behind enemy lines if you are a good girl.'

First Aid Nursing was never my thing. They gave me the courier work without the First Aid certificate, but refusing to return has landed me in trouble. I need to get results or face a court marshal. Maybe Ricardo is the coup I need.

They think women can't be spies. I'm here to prove them wrong. I am also young, attractive, and damned if I'm going to let the war steal that from me. Jean was my first conquest, the airman my first heartbreak. I am still not sure whether that was because he died, or because he stayed faithful to his fiancée.

That leaves Ricardo. The Germans at *Le P'tit Chou* are ugly, and drink too much. I flirt with them, get them drunk and remember the conversations. Ricardo is different — maybe it's the Italian accent. I got through to him by pretending to support Laval. Ricardo was over the moon when he returned to power. He was saying the Germans occupying the whole of France was the best way to deal with the Americans joining the allies. I just rubbed his chest and pretended to agree with him. My mind told me he was the enemy, my body said differently. Espionage gave me the excuse to surrender to his Latin lovemaking and pretend it was for the war effort. It felt dangerous. With Jean, it felt safe. I don't know how else to describe it.

Jean and Louis pulled me in to talk about Ricardo. Jean is worried I am getting too involved.

'I'm not getting involved. We have sex.'

Louis noticed the flash in Jean's eyes. I don't like Louis, but his job is to keep the cell united. I respect that. The most likely thing to compromise an intelligence network is an affair. Even if my training hardened me to the Italian, Louis would consider Jean a weak point if he disapproved of my liaisons with Ricardo. It's now clear that he does.

I'm not saying Louis encouraged Jean's relationship with Esther, but he considered it less risky. In the currency of war, an English spy is worth more than a Jewish refugee. Jean could have Esther; Ricardo could have me. Everyone wins. Such was the simplistic logic of a man long married. There is no reason, other than Louis, why I can't have Jean and Ricardo.

Turning to Louis, I hold his stare. 'I am not married to Jean. He has no right to object to my methods.'

Louis's slight nod to Jean seemed to say, 'She's right.'

He turns back to me. 'If you are going to play this dangerous game, then we need to up the stakes. At present, you are getting the same information he gives the Germans. All that does is level one tiny part of the playing field.'

'What are you suggesting?'

'Feed him inconsequential things like black market traders. Once the Germans have confidence in the quality of his information, you can start giving him false intelligence.'

Jean puts his hand on Louis' arm. 'We can't just ask Jenny to hand over fake secrets. He's going to want to know where she got them.'

'What happened to your hand?' I ask. He has strapped two fingers together.

He pulls it away and looks cross. 'I broke it tying bundles of wood. One slipped, trapping my little finger.'

'You should get it seen to or it will set crooked,' I say.

'What, are you my mother now?'

With that simple comment, I know I have lost him. He is right about handing over fake secrets. I'm supposed to be a farm girl from Dunkirk waiting tables at a restaurant.

Louis turns to me. 'How well do you know Ricardo?'

'He's fascist, adores Laval, thought Pétain was going soft on the resistance. He's convinced Hitler and Mussolini will win, and France is better off being on the winning side.'

Louis nods. 'Does he still think he is on the winning side?'

I hesitate. 'Things are going well for the Allies in North Africa. There is talk of an invasion in Normandy. If he thought Germany would lose, he would change.'

'Can you turn him?'

'Only by revealing myself as an SOE operative. He's certainly devious enough to be a double agent.'

Jean stands. 'He's not devious, he's an arsehole. An opportunistic carpet bagger only interested in himself.'

Wow! He's jealous! Maybe Jean does still love me. He would if I could get rid of Esther.

Louis also stands to impose his authority and show that the meeting has gone on too long.

'Jenny, you are not to recruit Ricardo. Under no circumstances must he know your real purpose in France. In the meantime, keep feeding him the black-market stuff. We can pull him in and put the frighteners on him. That might be enough to turn him without blowing your cover.'

That was it. Female spies are not clever enough to recruit enemy agents. I could feed him crumbs like Joeliyn and Amia supplying pork to the black market, but even that I got wrong. I did not know the Germans would shoot them. There was no time for a warning. I think it even shocked Ricardo. That upped the stakes. Either we do nothing, in which case the two old ladies died for nothing, or we pull him in and deal with Ricardo as an accessory to murder. In these hard times, that means summary execution.

As the informer, the original information compromised me, and I could not take part in the arrest. That way, if it went wrong and Ricardo survived, I could act shocked and claim no knowledge.

The day unravelled. At first, I thought Ricardo was dead, then I thought Jean was. Finally, I find out Ricardo escaped and Jean was back in Esther's arms.

That hurts. I'm taking the long way home from work. The empty woods give me time to think.

'*Ciao bella.*'

'Fuck me Ricardo, you scared me! I thought you had run away.'

'Call it relocation.'

He nodded towards an abandoned hunter's shack. '*Voglia di un cazzo per amore dei vecchi tempi?*'

I don't speak Italian, but with the look he gives me, I don't need to. For once, it's easy to say no.

'A nice offer, but I think I'll decline.'

'Oh, I don't think you will.' He grabs my arm. In these deserted woods, I have limited options.

'Oh Ricardo, you are so forceful,' I simper, fluttering my eyelashes.

The inside of the hut is sparse. There're some sacks of maize the hunters used to feed the boar, one chair, a mattress, and an upturned wine crate. On the crate is half a sausage and a bottle.

He closes and locks the door. With a sack over the only window, it's almost completely dark. Sunbeams slice through the dusty air like swords. Caught in the sunbeams, dust dances to escape the oppressive odour of a man left too long alone with his thoughts.

He sits, pulls a clasp knife from his pocket, and cleans his nails. 'It was very obliging of you to tell me about the two dykes selling pork.'

To illustrate his point, he picks up the sausage and peels off thin slices. One he offers to me. I shake my head.

'Sit down.' He jabs the knife towards the mattress.

'I'll stand, thanks.'

He shrugs. 'I've been wondering how the maquis knew I was the informer.'

'Process of elimination?'

He waves the knife. 'That would take some time. They were waiting for me the next morning. If I didn't know better, I would say there was an informer in this room.'

I say nothing. He would not see the irony. Instead, I try to be seductive. Difficult in near total darkness.

'I was worried about you.'

There's the slightest pause as he puts down the knife. 'You don't look worried.'

'How can you tell?' I ask. 'It's dark.'

He pulls down the sack. A beam of light picks me out, a singer in a darkened concert hall. I don't know the words.

When he stands, body pressed against mine, I put my hands on his hips.

'That's better,' he smirks.

In a world that deals all the cards to men, I have played my only trump. He slams the ace on top of it, and with his arm in the small of my back, forces his tongue down my throat. I cannot allow him to rape me. That would surrender my little remaining control over the situation. I remember the cyanide capsule, carried with me every day since leaving England. With one hand on the back of his head, I feel for the cyanide with the other, slipping the pill into the bottle of wine before he pushes me to the bed. The sex is short and brutal. My one remaining card is to pretend I enjoyed it and want to do it again. Even Italian lovers require a brief interval. I am relying on him drinking while he waits.

'If it wasn't you who told Jean, how did he know?'

'I may have told a friend that they better buy soon because the supply might dry up.'

'Who?'

I give him a name.

'That can't be it. How would that link to me?'

I pick up the bottle and offer it to him. 'They asked how I knew, so I said Ricardo knows everything that goes on in the village.'

He gives the bottle back. 'You first.'

I pretend to drink, then hand it over. He takes a long draught. I hold my breath. Nothing happens. I take the bottle from him, pretend again, then hand it back, hoping he will drink more. He does. Still nothing.

Is there nothing the spivs in London will not do to make money from this war? That pill was big enough to kill an elephant. The supplier must have cut it with salt to save money. I pray they have left enough active ingredient.

He pulls my face towards his groin. Jean has never asked, and I have always refused Ricardo, but this time I oblige. I can think of no other way to play for time. Hard again, he takes one last swig of wine and pushes me face down on the mattress.

'Not that way!'

Rough hessian muffles my protests. I cry out in pain, praying for the cyanide to take effect. Stimulated by my cries, he pushes harder. Amongst the grunts of effort, I detect other sounds. He pulls out, and drops to the floor, retching.

Grabbing my clothes, I find the key, open the door, and run naked into the woods. Only when I am sure he is not following, do I stop and dress. For a moment, I regret giving him that name. It does not matter, he can't tell anyone. I have done what Jean could not. I hope Ricardo's death is slow and painful.

21

It's moving day at last. Peter got his way and is coming down with me. Tree's brother-in-law Jakub and his mate Filip are doing it on the cheap, but their Luton is nowhere near big enough. We put the furniture in the van and garden stuff in the trailer, but there are still loads of boxes. I rented a Transit for Cathy. She can drive back empty tomorrow.

'I'll drive it.'

Richard is here to see us off. I smell a rat.

'No need. Cathy has to come back, anyway.'

She chips in. 'I can't be having something that big.'

'You take the car; I'll drive the van.'

'It's got the trailer; ye know I don't enjoy towing. Anyway, Richard's offered.'

'Richard's always offering, usually babysitting.'

'Look, he said he would do it! He wants to help. What's your problem with him?'

Apart from you two having sex? Of course, I don't say that — she might change her mind. Peter is sitting in the car, crying. I go to find out what the matter is.

'I want to live with you if you and Mummy divorce.'

'That will not happen, big fella.'

He doesn't look big, and at this rate, the signs are not good. He looks up at me with wide, tear-filled eyes.

'That means going to stay with Mummy on weekends. It will be like Craig, except he lives with his mum and sees his dad every other weekend. If I live in France and Mummy stays in England, I will spend term-time with you and holidays with Mummy. England is a rubbish place for holidays. France is much better.'

I can't remember Peter stringing so many sentences together. He must have been thinking about it.

'Peter, we are going to get the house ready for Mummy to come down for Christmas. She is going to come because she promised.'

I wished I sounded more convincing.

It takes forever to drive through France. Richard wants Peter to take turns doing one bit in the car and one in the Transit, but he refuses outright to go in the van.

When we get there, Jakub and Filip have already slung the furniture in the garage and gone, so we leave everything in the car and go for something to eat. Richard is getting up my nose. He keeps asking questions, all innocent, like he is trying to find something out. What? Cathy tells him everything. I wonder if he has found out about Francine? Tree is the only one who knows. He would never say, especially to Richard.

I take Peter home. The poor boy is asleep on his feet.

Richard and Peter are still asleep when I wake, so I go to get croissants. Peter is up when I get back and cross that I didn't take him with me. I need to get Peter to the library, as Francine has news about his school. I thought Richard would stay and rest, but no such luck.

Peter says he wants to surprise Francine and runs on ahead. This is not how I wanted the first meeting to be, and not with Richard in tow. I keep as close to Peter as I can without running, but Richard is just behind. When we arrive, Francine is putting books away. When she sees me, the one she is holding slips to the floor. I want to rush into her arms, but Peter is watching. She doesn't see him, so comes up and hugs me. All the emotions flood back. All my resolve evaporates.

Feeling two sets of eyes on me, every pore on my skin fights the urge to kiss her. Richard has the look of a wolf that has finally cornered its prey and is drinking in the fear before gorging on the blood.

Then Peter does something extraordinary. He pushes in between us. 'What about my hug?'

I'm stunned. They get on well, but he has never asked for that before.

Francine turns to him. 'Peter! It is so beautiful to see you.'

She brushes his cheek the way the French always do, then he grabs her, giving her a hug like she did to me. Francine looks surprised, but hugs him back.

He turns to Richard. 'Everyone says hello like that in France. That's why I want to live here.' He winks at me.

Francine looks lost. We are the only ones in the library apart from the pretty young girl in the history section with a tall, posh looking friend who is looking at sheet music.

'Francine, I'd like you to meet Richard.'

I emphasise the name. B minus for originality and A plus for effort. Like a pro, Francine turns to Richard, hand outstretched.

'Enchanté.'

The Lefèvre's and the Cartwrights forge a Franco-British alliance in the face of a common enemy.

'He is going back tomorrow.'

I say the words through gritted teeth. We've got the van for four days, but there's no way I'm letting Richard sniff around that long.

Francine turns to him. 'Well, come chez moi this evening for apéro. Say dix-neuf heures?'

Richard looks at Peter, then Francine, then me. It has become a game, and for once, Richard is the kid at school who's had his book nicked and the others are passing it around and laughing.

I promise to meet Peter's teacher, then we go back to unpack.

At Francine's flat, Peter whispers as he grabs my hand.

'Richard looks like Tigger when he swallowed a mouthful of thistles,' he giggles.

Tigger pours himself another glass of wine and takes it into a corner.

Peter spots his chance. 'Can I have some wine?'

Before I can open my mouth, Francine answers. *'Pourquoi pas?'*

She half fills a glass with wine and tops it up with water. Seeing my disapproving look, she turns to me. 'If he will live en France, he must learn to drink wine. It's how we teach our children.'

When she looks across at Richard, he looks away. 'Maybe I was too rude to Richard. I'll put some water in my wine.'

Picking up her glass and the bottle, she crosses the room and chats with him.

Peter is sipping his wine like a pro. 'What did she mean? She only put water in my glass.'

'She thinks she was too hard on him. *Mettre de l'eau dans son vin* means "tone it down".'

'I don't think she was being hard,' he says.

It's morning. Judging from Peter's unsteady path to the bathroom, I think he might have his first hangover. That will not endear Francine to Cathy, but to be honest, it's the least of my problems.

Richard makes an early start. Our neighbour comes out as he is getting into the van. When people don't speak the same language, they point and wave. I guess she is telling him that Francine stayed the night. That's all I need.

We are late for the teacher's appointment. She is worried Peter will struggle until he learns French and suggests extra language lessons.

'The library has details of teachers who will do this,' she tells me.

When I get there, Peter is already behind the desk with Francine.

'Francine is going to teach me to speak French! I left it to you, Daddy, to tell her the bit about moving in so we can do it every day.'

What? I shut the door. 'Peter, that is enough! I'm sorry, Francine. His teacher was saying he needs help learning French. She suggested you might know someone.'

He grins. 'No, she didn't. She said Francine would be an excellent teacher. She also said that I need to speak French at home.'

'Peter, I am serious. Francine and I need to talk.' He opens his mouth. 'Alone.'

'Then invite her to supper, and I'll put myself to bed.'

'We have just moved in — I can't move, let alone cook.'

'We passed a pizza kiosk on the way from the school.'

I hesitate and turn to Francine. 'We need to talk. Are you free tonight?'

'*Bien sûr*. You sort out the house. I will command the pizzas. Vegetarian, no?'

I give in. 'I'm not sure we have wine. Are you OK with beer?'

'Of course. The French drink other things than the wine.'

'Good. I brought my homebrew with me.'

Francine frowns. 'Homebrew?'

'Homemade beer. It is a hobby of mine.'

'*Vraiment?* I wonder what else I will find out about you.'

We sit on boxes eating pizza with our fingers and drinking homebrew.

Francine puts her bottle down. 'Peter, I would love to teach you French, but your father and I have to speak. When you are in your pyjamas, I have a little surprise for you.'

'What?'

'Pyjamas first!'

He goes without another word. I'm impressed!

When he comes back, Francine pulls a book from her handbag. 'It's only a book of the library, but if you work hard on your French, I will buy you your own copy.'

'It's Winnie the Pooh in French! Wow, thank you, Francine!'

He rushes up to her and gives her a hug and a kiss. 'Are you going to read it to me?'

'No, Daddy will. That is his work. I will correct his pronunciation. He must also learn the French!'

'OK, Francine, but not tonight. You two need to talk.'

He kisses her again, then comes to kiss me. 'Goodnight, Francine; goodnight, Daddy.'

I wait for the door to close. 'Is he matchmaking?'

Francine chinks my bottle. 'What do you think?'

She takes mine out of my hand, looking serious, and forcing me to meet her gaze. 'Peter says that he thinks not that his mother comes to France.'

'She said she would, but I'm not sure. She thinks Richard makes her happy, but he doesn't. Peter deserves two parents.'

Francine stares at the floor. A tear wells up before trickling down her cheek. 'It doesn't matter how I love you and Peter, it is not enough for you to leave your wife, not enough for Peter to call me Mamy.'

'Francine, I'm so sorry. I have made you unhappy.'

'Stop trying to make other people happy.'

'What's the matter with making other people happy? Do I make you happy, apart from just now, of course?'

She leans forward and kisses me. 'Yes, you do. But you should think of yourself too. You render me happy, but that is not your job — it is my work. Cathy too, it is her responsibility to look after herself.'

'I am her husband. It is my job to look after her.'

'No, John, she is not an infant. She must look after herself.'

'What if she can't?'

'Well, she must learn. Did Cathy ever take responsibility for her own happiness?'

'Yes. She has always done whatever made her happy.'

'And is that rendering you happy?'

I avoid her gaze. 'No. Sometimes it hurts a lot.'

She puts her hand under my chin to force me to look at her. 'When did it hurt?'

'When she made love to other men.'

She takes my hand, smoothing the fingers against her palm. My little finger folds under its neighbour, emerging beneath her caress, then slipping back like a shy toddler behind his mother's skirt.

'Is that hurting?'

I take my hand away. 'No, it's always been like that.'

'If it hurt you so much, why have you let it happen?'

'Because I loved her.'

'Is it you love her now?'

'Not anymore,' I whisper.

'If she leaves Richard and comes to France, could you love her anew?'

'I would have to.'

'Why? Because she is your wife? Because you thought she was "The One"? Has she merited your love, your fidelity?'

'No, she hasn't. I wanted her to, but she couldn't.'

She puts her hand to my cheek, wiping away a tear. 'I would merit your love. I want it because it makes me happy. When we made love, you thought only of what would satisfy me. Tonight, I want you to only think of how I can turn you on. Take me. It does not matter what.'

'And if I ask for something you don't want?'

She takes her hand away. 'I will say no. It is just as likely I will ask you for something you don't want to give.'

October 2005

The weeks pass. Already, life with Francine seems more real than it ever did with Cathy. Tonight, I'm reading Winnie the Pooh in French to Peter. He is not saying anything.

'Everything alright, big fella?'

'I'm trying not to think about Mummy.'

'It's OK to miss her.'

He gives me a hug. 'I know.' He looks up at me. 'She will not leave Richard, will she?'

'I don't know. Let's wait and see. It's nearly half term. You can see her then.'

'I don't want to.' His whisper is so quiet that I wonder if I misheard. 'The move to France was so exciting, but I hoped she would try harder to stop me if she was not coming too.'

'She hasn't said that she is not coming. Let's wait and see.'

Francine is on the computer when I go through to the living room.

'There are two emails from Cathy. One says *For Peter - Private.*'

'That's odd. Maybe it is about Christmas presents. Have you read it?'

'Of course not. I'll print it and give it to him. He's still awake, right?'

'Yes.'

While she is in with Peter, I open the other email.

Hi John, I'm not moving to France. It shocked me to hear from Richard that you saw someone behind my back. You haven't even had the decency to hide it from our son. Richard told me Francine kissed you in front of Peter. She had the nerve to kiss Peter as well. Then she invited Richard for drinks at her house with you and Peter as if you were already a couple.

I was even more shocked to hear that she tried to get Peter drunk. He's not yet eleven! Your neighbour told Richard that a woman stayed the night with you. In our house!

I have to protect our son from this corrupting influence. Please arrange for him to return to England.

You will hear from my solicitor regarding my sole custody and maintenance payments. I will have to switch to working part-time now you have abandoned us. Raising Peter as a single mother will be expensive.

Francine comes back. 'Everything OK?'

I tilt the screen so she can read.

There's a long silence. 'I wondered whether she would come, but I can't believe she would write something like that.'

'She didn't. That is Richard. He's won.'

'John, she is not a trophy to fight over.'

'That's not what I meant. I can't protect her from his gaslighting if I am not there.'

'John, let go. She's not your responsibility anymore. She never was.'

Francine is right. I think of the other email.

'We should check Peter is OK.'

He is sitting up in bed with the printout on his lap.

'Mummy wants me to live in England with her and Smarmypants.'

Francine sits on the bed. 'You should not call Richard that. I don't know what it means, but it doesn't sound very polite.'

'It's not supposed to; I don't like him.'

'Lots of people don't like their new mummy or daddy,' I say.

'I like Francine, but I don't want Richard to be my new daddy.'

Francine takes his hand. 'Do you want me to be your new mummy?'

'Of course.' He gives her a hug to prove it.

'Can I have two mummies?'

'Of course.'

He smiles. 'Good. Francine, you can be my other mummy, but I am going to call you Francine, or Daddy will get muddled.'

'OK, then when you go to visit Mummy in England, Richard will be your other daddy, but you can call him Richard.'

Peter folds his arms. 'Aren't you listening? I'm not going to England.'

'But how will you see Mummy?'

'She will have to come here. Without Smarmypants. Promise you won't send me back to England.'

'If that's what you want, I promise.'

22

I'm watching John help Peter with his homework. Such a young boy shouldn't have to go through this. It's unforgivable that Cathy sent that letter. John saying Richard wrote it's no excuse. She's his mother. His welfare is her responsibility. I try to say this to John, but my English is not good enough yet.

'She really loves him. That makes her act strangely, especially when Richard is about.'

I don't like it when he defends her. Cathy could turn up, say she's dumped Richard, and want John back. Then there's Peter. He is adamant he will not go back to England whilst Richard is there. Is there something he is not telling us?

'Do you mind if I invite Eimear for supper?'

John looks bemused by the apparent change in tack. 'Who's Eimear?'

'My best friend. She's a retired counsellor. She used to work with children mostly, but understands relationships better than anyone.'

'Do we need relationship counselling?' He has crossed his arms.

'No. The time to get it is before we need it. You said some pretty heavy things about your feelings for Cathy. I'm flattered that you could, but I felt out of my depth. Anyway,' I kiss his forehead, 'it would be for Peter. To help him make the right choice.'

He looks down to avoid my eyes. 'I want him to stay here.'

'I know you do, and so do I. He knows that. It is a lot of pressure on an eleven-year-old.'

'And you think Eimear could help?'

'I know she could.'

'OK, find out when she is free. I'll make supper.'

'*Fáilte!*'

A thousand smiles crease her weathered skin, yet Galway drips from her lips as if she is a young lass fresh up from Oranmore. She can be any age she chooses. Eimear wears the wise old woman from Lough Corrib cloak because it suits her, but can lose her accent when it gets in the way.

She holds out her hand. 'You must be Peter. I am Eimear, a friend of Francine.'

Peter takes it. 'That makes you English. The French are always kissing. Not that I mind,' he adds, shooting a mischievous look towards me.

Eimear smiles. 'Irish actually, Peter, but I know what you are trying to say.'

He does not ask to be excused and retreat to his bedroom. Instead, we sit round the kitchen table and chat like she's known John and Peter all her life. Eimear says very little but always draws Peter in. Nobody knows how it happened, but the conversation turns to Winnie the Pooh.

'Those are my favourite stories. Do you read them to your dad?'

Peter pulls a face. 'Of course not. He reads to me.'

She feigns surprise. 'Why? You can read, can't you?'

Peter gives her one of his looks. 'You know I can. French and English.'

'Then you can read your bedtime story to me. I'll let you choose the language.'

We've moved to the living room when Eimear returns. 'Peter would like you to say goodnight.'

I am sitting on the floor in front of John with my head on his lap.

'Coffee?'

'No, thank you, but a herb tea if you have it.'

'There's some mint in the garden.'

'Perfect.'

John puts the kettle on and follows me into Peter's bedroom. 'Did Eimear like the story?'

Peter is sitting up in bed. 'She loved it. She knows all the Pooh stories but has never heard one in French.'

'Did you talk about anything else?'

'Me not going back to England.'

'What did she say?'

Peter looks at his father and makes the nose tapping gesture I've seen John use on him. 'It's confidential. She will tell you.'

Back in the living room, I smile at my old friend. 'Eimear, is it normal that an eleven-year-old boy still asks for bedtime stories?'

'Unusual, but perfectly normal. He has an exceptionally close bond with his father, one that was established at a very young age. He was aware of the tensions in his parents' marriage, but remembers how it was before.'

She turns to John. 'Are you OK to talk about Cathy's relationship with Richard? It must have been hard for you when you found out.'

John squeezes my hand for support. 'Not really. We all hung out together at university. I knew she was seeing both of us. I suppose I convinced myself that I was the one she was serious about.'

'What made you think that?'

'Well, we shared digs to start with. When I graduated, I proposed, and she said yes.'

Eimear inclines her head. 'That sounds reasonable. How did Richard take it?'

'He left. Went to work abroad. We lost touch for a bit but would still get Christmas cards.'

'When was that?'

'When Peter was a baby. He'd just started school when Cathy got a letter saying Richard was returning to the UK and wanted to see us again.'

'You or just Cathy?'

'Oh, he said "you" meaning "you two" but, well...' He trails off.

Eimear puts a sympathetic hand on his knee. 'And Cathy picked up where she left off at university.'

John looks at her. 'How did you know?'

Eimear smiles again. 'I read the signs. It is what I do.'

I change the subject. 'You were talking about his obsession with Winnie the Pooh.'

Eimear frowns. 'Obsession is rather a strong word. His make-believe world helps him make sense of this one. His subconscious puts the answers to his questions into the mouths of Pooh and Piglet.'

'Should we stop him?' John asks.

Eimear looks shocked by the idea. 'Goodness no!'

'So his conversations with Pooh and Piglet help him?'

'Of course.'

John looks worried. 'That is fascinating, but I am no closer to knowing how to reply to Cathy's letter.'

'Has Peter made his feelings known?'

'Abundantly.'

'Will you look after him properly if he stays here?'

'Absolutely.'

'Then there is nothing to discuss. You can explain that Peter's problem is not with his mother, but her boyfriend, but if she has an ounce of sense, she will know that.'

John stands. 'You have given us a lot to think about. Thank you so much for helping Peter.'

Eimear finishes her tea. 'All I have done is eat your excellent food and allow your charming son to read me a story. I would love to spend more time with him. May I come back next week? My turn to cook.'

Eimear has gone. Each of us lost in our thoughts, we weave around each other like Baucis and Philemon. 'What now?' I ask.

He kisses the curl he has been playing with. 'It's still early. There's an open bottle of wine on the table. I'll fetch it.'

I stare at the carpet, tracing the pattern. 'My English is still not good.'

'Why do you say that?'

'Because when I said "what now?" I meant, what is going to happen to us? You thought, "what now?" meant shall we finish the wine or get an early night?'

He turns. 'Your English is excellent. "What now?" can mean either. I have to answer those emails. It's pretty clear Richard wrote them.'

'Wasn't it from her account?'

He has gone into the kitchen to fetch the wine, so calls back over his shoulder. 'Yes, but he dictated it. Cathy is a secretary.'

'That's a horrible thing to say.'

John comes back with two glasses of wine. 'What do you mean?'

'*Je ne sais pas*, it was the dismissive way you said "only a secretary".'

John sits down, offering the glass. I ignore it.

'I said "secretary", not "only a secretary".'

Taking the glass, I shrug. 'Things have changed. I was happy to be your mistress. Now I've moved in, next Cathy will want a divorce. I was happy to take joint responsibility for Peter's welfare, but now...'

'Now you don't?'

I shoot him a warning look. 'Of course I do, but this is hard.'

'It's harder for Peter.'

I put my head on his shoulders. 'I know.'

We drink in silence while I wonder if this is our first argument, and what we are arguing about.

'Give me time to think about what to say to Cathy and I'll answer the email tomorrow.'

I stroke his hair. 'I'm sorry I was cross, but you have to sort this out face to face.'

He pulls a face. 'That means flying back to England.'

Has everything happened too fast? When I moved in, it seemed so natural. Peter was almost begging me to stay. Now we are harvesting what we have sown. Cathy has misbehaved, but she is losing her son. John has to tell her *personnellement*. I kiss him to show I am not cross, and understand this is hard for him.

'She will not like it when I say Peter doesn't want to go back.'

'You could take her a letter from him.'

'That's an idea. I'll help him write it.'

'No, John, Cathy will accuse you of putting words in his mouth. If he wants to write, Eimear will help.'

He takes my hand. 'If Peter won't go to England, we are going to have to invite her here.'

I hadn't thought about that. 'Will she want to come?'

'Peter's her son. She loves him.'

My stomach twists, wringing a tear from deep inside. 'Of course she does. Invite her for Christmas.'

He studies my face. 'Are you sure?'

'Yes.' I wipe away the tear. 'As long as she doesn't bring Richard.'

He hugs me. 'What is it?' he asks.

'I don't know. I imagined it like we first said. You the dutiful husband, me the mistress, making you happy.'

'You make me happy, happier than I ever thought possible.'

'But I am no longer your mistress. Cathy staying in England makes me your wife. Now, being your mistress is not enough. Like Julia Roberts in Pretty Woman, I want the fairy tale.'

'Then marry me.'

'You are already married.'

He looks hurt, so I give him a hug. 'I will, when the time is right. Everything has happened so fast that there are parts of your old life that need to catch up and find their place.'

'Like Peter?'

'Peter has already found his place. I was thinking of Cathy.'

'I don't love her anymore, but I don't hate her. She had a tough childhood.'

'I don't hate her either, and I promise I'll do everything I can to make Christmas work.'

'Thank you.'

23

Peter

Eimear's here for supper again. She's going to read my bedtime story. I've chosen the one where Tigger lives with Kanga and steals Roo's medicine. Eimear hasn't noticed that Kanga is the only female in the hundred-acre wood. I think it's because A. A. Milne didn't believe women mattered. Tigger goes to live with Kanga and Roo, so that is why I chose that story. Kanga looks after him even though she is not his mummy.

Eimear puts Piglet on her lap. 'Is Kanga good at being Tigger's mummy?'

I hold Pooh's hand, so he is not jealous. 'It's hard to say. A. A. Milne doesn't write much about mothers. She's not bad, but she is also about as different to Tigger as you can get. They are both wacky, but in different ways.'

Eimear is playing with Piglet's ears. He doesn't like people doing that, but because it's Eimear, he lets her.

'Does that make it harder to get along?'

I put Pooh down so I can explain.

'Think of a jigsaw where each bit is a perfect square. Every piece fits every other part, but that makes the jigsaw harder. You think they get on, but they don't stay together. In a real jigsaw you match a sticky-out piece to a sticky-in one. They are opposite, but they stay together just like Daddy and Francine, who are very different but fit together. I think Mummy and Daddy held together once, but Richard changed it. He wanted Mummy to match up with him, so he changed her. After he broke her, she stayed with him because if you force two bits of the jigsaw that don't fit, they get stuck. Daddy tried to pull them apart. He couldn't do it. Even if he did, Richard broke Mummy, and Daddy didn't fit anymore.'

Eimear gives me a hug. When I calm down, I show her Mummy's email. I think she will know what to do.

My Darling Peter,

I am missing you so much. It was very naughty for Daddy to make you go to France. It must be very hard going to school where nobody speaks English. I have been talking to the headteacher of Nine Elms. He will try to get you in with Craig. I know that is what you want.

Richard told me that Daddy has a girlfriend in France. That explains why he wanted to move. I cried when Daddy left us both just to be with her. He doesn't love you, or he would not have done it. I have written to him to ask him to bring you home. Richard and I love you very much and will look after you.

Don't worry, my darling, you will be home soon. Richard has a surprise for you. Don't say I told you, but it's a new games console. You are growing up, so we both think you are ready. It has much better games than the baby ones on your old one.

Looking forward to seeing you soon.

Lots of love,

Mummy xxx

I put the letter on the bed. 'I haven't shown it to Daddy or Francine because they will be upset. Here's the letter I wrote back.'

Dear Mummy,

I miss you too. You are lying about Daddy. He loves me, and so does Francine. Do you think I don't know why Daddy wanted us to move to France? It's because you and Richard were having sex. Daddy would never have seen Francine if you had come to France with us. It's all your fault, so don't blame Daddy.

That's not right. It's not your fault; it's Richard. He made you do it. He makes people do things they don't want to. I don't know why you love him. He is horrible.

I don't want to go back to England. I can't see you because Richard will be there. Come and see me on your own. I never want to see Richard again. All this is his fault.

Lots of love,

Peter.

P.S. Francine will be here. Get used to it like Daddy had to with you and Richard. I don't know why he did. I would have just punched Richard in the nose.

P.P.S. Bring the games console.

Lots of love,

Peter xxx

Eimear thinks it's an excellent letter. She puts Piglet down, and he scuttles over to Pooh, where he leans against him to stop his ears twitching.

'If Mummy and Richard split up, would that make a difference?'

'Yes. It means I could go to visit Mummy.'

'Would you like Mummy and Daddy to get back together?'

'I used to; now I don't know. Daddy is so happy with Francine. I don't think he was happy like that with Mummy. I want to live with Daddy and Francine and Mummy.'

Eimear smiles. 'Would that work?'

I laugh. 'Not in a million years. Mummy would be jealous. I'm not sure whether Francine would be jealous because she sees things differently.'

I think about it and decide Francine will not because she knows Daddy loves her more than Mummy and that is why Mummy would be.

Grown-ups make their relationships complicated; that's why they find them hard. It takes a child to sort it out. Even Eimear needs help sometimes. I explain it so even a grown-up can understand.

'One, Richard goes away and never comes back. Two, Francine and Daddy, stay here and look after me. Three, Mummy comes to France and lives close enough to visit. Four, Mummy stops having boyfriends.'

Eimear gives me a hug. 'Mummy might be lonely.'

I pull away so I can look at her. 'She wouldn't, because she would have me. Oh, you mean Mummy has to have sex! She could have a girlfriend like Auntie Jan. They have sex. I know because they came for Christmas and slept together. Auntie Jan is Mummy's sister, and she's a lesbian.'

'Peter, it doesn't work like that! I think your letter is very good. Daddy is going to go back to England and sort everything out with Mummy.'

'Face to face?'

She nods.

'Wow.'

Daddy has gone to England. Francine is acting weird. Maybe she thinks he won't come back, but that's silly. I'm late for school.

'Can I have a packed lunch?'

I should have asked earlier — the school bus is due in ten minutes.

'I thought you were having school dinner,' Francine says.

'School trip. Didn't I say?'

'No.'

'Sorry.'

'There's no time to make lunch, so take half that baguette and an apple from the fruit bowl.'

She cuts a generous chunk of cheese and fetches a tomato and a bottle of water from the fridge.

'Here, put these in this bag and go or you will miss the bus.'

'Love you,' I shout as I clatter down the stairs.

'Love you, too,' she calls as I slam the door.

The trip is to Oradour. The Germans destroyed Oradour-sur-Glane during the war. They massacred the entire village. I was ill while we were there. Not a tummy bug or anything like that. I had a fit. They have called Francine to come and get me.

I am in the coach park by the visitor's centre with a teacher who stayed behind with me. I think she is cross. Francine's car does a cool skid when it stops.

The teacher stands up. 'You should have written on the permission slip that Peter had a medical condition.'

Francine is standing with her legs apart and arms crossed. 'He doesn't, and I dislike being greeted in that way. Perhaps you would like to tell me what happened.'

'After the presentation in the visitor's centre, we allowed the students to explore on their own. The friend that was with him said they were walking back from the church towards the garage. Peter suddenly started shaking uncontrollably and fell. We called the pompiers when we called you. By the time they arrived, he was sitting up and said he was feeling better. They gave him a thorough examination but could find nothing wrong. As you were on your way, there was no point in him going back on the bus. The coach has only just left.'

Francine turns to me. 'How are you feeling, darling?'

I give her a watery smile. 'I'll be OK. Can we go? This place gives me the creeps.'

'Of course.'

She bundles me into the car, helped by the teacher, and prepares to leave.

'I'm sorry to ask...'

The teacher doesn't sound cross any more. I think I scared her and she thought the school would get into trouble for not looking after me. 'It's just that the coach has left and...'

'You want a lift back to the school?'

'That would be most kind.'

Francine drives in silence until we have dropped the teacher. When we are alone, she asks me again what I think happened.

'I don't know. I just had this really strong feeling when we got to the village that I'd been there before. The more we walked about, the more scared I became, like I knew something bad was going to happen. The church was the worst. I told Gifford I wanted to go back to the coach. As we were going, I felt there was someone behind me. That's silly because there were loads of school parties, and there were people everywhere. This was different, though, like when Esther was in the room, but the feeling with Esther was nice. This felt really, really awful, like an electric shock. Once, Daddy and I were fixing my lamp, and he forgot to unplug it. It was like that, but on my back. The next thing I remember was the teacher asking if I was alright.'

It's early when we get back, but I'm so tired I ask if I can have supper in bed. Esther is waiting for me in the bedroom.

Hello, Peter. Are you alright?

'Hello, Esther. I'm fine, thank you. Just shaken.'

I've brought a friend to meet you. I'd like you to meet Pierre.

A spirit materialises that could be my older brother.

I sit up in bed. 'Who are you?'

The ghost smiles. *I am you, or should I say, who you were.*

Esther interrupts. *Pierre died in 1944, so I never knew what happened to him. He came back with you and this is the first time we've met since we died. I want to know what happened to him. After today's incident, I think you should know, too.*

24

Pierre, 1944

My mother died in childbirth in 1932. France squabbled its way closer to fascism. My father christened me Pierre, handed me to my ten-year-old brother, Jean, to raise, and turned his attention to the farm.

Five years later, the invasion of Poland convinced France that Germany and not Russia were the enemy. My father abandoned the farm to the care of his teenage son and enlisted. The Saar offensive was a disaster. France was supposed to invade Germany whilst the Germans were busy invading Poland. The Poles surrendered almost at once. This enabled the returning German soldiers to launch a counteroffensive. Father died.

Jean and I were now orphans. Louis was the leader of the maquis cell in Saint Etienne, which became our new family. As big brothers do, Jean fell in love. First with the charismatic English spy, then with Esther, the vulnerable teenager he found trying to cross the demarcation line. Jean and Esther's death in 1943 orphaned me for a second time. Louis had neither the patience nor the empathy to add a twelve-year-old boy to his many responsibilities.

The legendary Georges Guingouin led the resistance cell to the north. I packed a small rucksack and walked towards the vast Limousin forests.

By chance, or divine intervention, I stumbled upon a camp. Only my years of mushroom gathering alerted me to its presence. Leaves strewn on the ground to hide a mushroom site sit differently than those that have fallen unaided from the tree. This was too large a patch to be mushrooms, and the tracks too well concealed to be done by one man and his dog. The leaves hid pine trees, cut too early for the sawmill, but too late to serve as fence posts. Set close, ends supported by a stone wall not half a metre high, they formed a roof at ground level. I traced the oval wall until I found what looked like an opening.

A crack, a sharp pain, then darkness. When I woke, a group of dirty, shirtless men in their twenties surrounded me. Introducing myself as Jean's younger brother was enough to pass the entrance exam. Eight young men shared the hideout. It would have seemed like a summer holiday, but for the grim faces.

The nearest town was Oradour-sur-Vayres, where our sectional commander owned a small knife factory. It did not take me long to settle into my new life. Theirs is my kind of resistance work. Not smuggling and hiding refugees the way my brother did. Not wheedling intelligence from soldiers like the English spy. Blowing things up was much more exciting. Georges Guingouin gave an order to the Oradour-sur-Vayres cell. They had the job of disrupting the movement of Germans travelling from the South to repel the D-Day invasion.

Le Lay gathered his men about him. I sat at the back, hoping nobody would ask why I was there. Most were only about ten years older than me, and almost all had younger siblings.

'We are not large enough to attack troop trains,' Le Lay said. 'We let this one pass.' He stared at each one, daring them to challenge his decision.

Someone took up the gauntlet. 'If we do that, more Germans will be in position to drive back the Allies.'

'They will have only the guns they carry. All the equipment is following. If we blow up the troop train, we will knock down a wasp's nest and they will overwhelm us. Even if we survive, they will re-route the following goods train. We need those arms for ourselves. It is not just about taking them out of German hands.'

The next day, we placed a tree across the track.

'Won't the driver see it and just stop?' I asked.

'That's the idea. If we derail it, we will have to carry everything several kilometres,' André explained.

The driver spotted the obstruction and stopped, just as he predicted. The ambushers dealt with those sent to remove it and tossed their bodies down the embankment.

Peter's eyes widened when he heard this. 'You look my age. Didn't it upset you to see people being killed?'

The ghost shrugged. 'My father, brother, and best friend Esther were all dead. The madness had to stop. It's like burning a section of forest to create a firebreak. All the same, I did not take part in the killing, and was glad when it ended.'

All the carriages were freight wagons except one. We crept aboard, not knowing how many would be inside. A middle-aged man in a full dress uniform sat at an inlaid table. He was inspecting the papers that covered it as if nothing had happened.

'My name is Major Helmut Kämpfe. I surrender. I trust the FTPF have enough military training to understand their obligations regarding the treatment of prisoners.'

Our leader, Bernard, narrowed his eyes. 'You captured my predecessor. When you returned his body, he had no tongue or fingernails. You covered his body with cigarette burns, and he died from multiple bayonet wounds.'

The major shrugged. 'You make it sound as if I carried out the interrogation personally. I am sure that if he had cooperated, he would have been unharmed.'

'If he had cooperated, we would all be dead.'

The major raised a glass to acknowledge the point.

'Forgive me. A glass of wine? We passed through Bergerac. I am told the wines are as good as Bordeaux.'

Bernard snapped, swiping at the major's outstretched hand. This sent the crystal goblet flying across the carriage to smash against the window.

'I am aware of the Geneva Convention. It does not extend to allowing prisoners to keep their loot. I am locking the door and placing a guard on the other side.'

'As you wish, but since you will soon suffer the fate of your predecessor, let me tell you this. We got some information out of him. We know about the knife factory in Oradour. I had a word with General Lammerding. He has ordered my dear friend Major Adolf Diekmann to oversee a thorough search. I assure you that if they find so much as a razor blade, the Glane will run with the blood of your compatriots.'

Outside, the ambushers held a hurried debate.

'They know about the monnerie. We must warn them. The Germans are sending a Panzer division to search the town.'

'Unloading more arms for them to hide will increase the risk. Do you know how they found out?'

'He said Phillipe talked.'

'Hard to believe. What did the German actually say?'

'If they find so much as a razor blade, the Glane will run with blood.'

Bernard laughed. 'Phillipe is sending them to Oradour-sur-Glane. They don't operate a black market, let alone maquis. When the SS find nothing, they will leave with their tails between their legs.'

'Maybe. Clever of Phillipe to lie by altering the truth just enough to keep it believable, but we should warn our near namesakes.'

Bernard slapped him on the back. 'Leave it. If they put the frighteners on them, it will make it easier for us to recruit. I'd like a cell on the tram route to Limoges.'

'I hope you are right. OK, we unload the cargo at Oradour-sur-Vayres as planned, then continue north until we can hand over Kämpfe to the Allies for questioning.'

Bernard had removed the papers from the old crew so we could bluff our way through the checkpoints. Inside the major's compartment, Helmut Kämpfe was busy writing messages on the back of his papers. He slipped one out of the window whenever the train passed through a checkpoint.

Eventually, a soldier had the initiative to pick one up and give it to his commanding officer. He telegraphed Breuilaufa, north of Oradour-sur-Glane.

Bernard knew the game was up as soon as he approached the checkpoint, bristling with soldiers. He had two objectives: save me, then kill Kämpfe.

'Go to Oradour-sur-Glane and warn them the Germans are coming to search the village.'

We slowed, then he pushed me off the footplate.

The sun rose into a clear sky on the tenth of June. I guessed Bernard had seen the fight coming at the checkpoint and wanted to get rid of me. I walked until noon. Though the region was unfamiliar, I had inherited my brother's navigating skills.

'Rivers always flow downhill. The sun rises over Brive and sets over La Rochelle. The pole star always points north.'

Remembering my brother's words, I checked for the sun. 'Jean, if you are watching me, I will make you proud.'

The Germans had already thrown a cordon round the town. Even in full daylight, I had taken to the road to make better time. Now I had to dive into the woods and track back.

Approaching the town from the North East about two in the afternoon, I found soldiers were rounding people up and sending them to the main square. Nobody was panicking, it just seemed to be an identity check. I had no papers. Creeping past the boys' school and tram station, I tried to keep behind the soldiers and out of sight.

The opportunity had passed. The sensible course would have been to abort the mission and start the thirty-five-kilometre walk to the other Oradour. Breaking through the cordon as the Germans were setting it up had been hard enough. Now the trap had snapped shut. My best hope would be to avoid detection until the Germans had run all the ID checks, done their house-to-house weapon search, and left.

The soldiers in the boys' school I had just passed were herding children towards the town square where the adults were waiting. Since I was not much older than some of them, I allowed myself to be swept along with the group.

By the time we got there, they were dividing the crowd into men, women, and children. I was the only one that seemed to feel panic. Having rounded everybody up, I sensed a growing annoyance that nothing was happening. People wanted to show their ID and go back to work.

The next part of the story I did not find out until later when I reached the Other Side. I put it here as it explains what happened later.

Just outside Oradour, Major Dickmann set up his field command.

'Someone will die this afternoon, Captain. Perfect weather for it, no? We will find the knife factory, then kill the proprietor and all who work there.'

'And if the factory does not exist, Major?'

'Then I personally will kill the informer who said it did.'

Captain Kahn pointed out that they had extracted the intelligence under torture and that the subject was already dead. The major was about to receive even more upsetting news. A motor-cycle courier came in, saluted and handed an envelope to him.

'An urgent message from Breuilaufa, Major.' He saluted again and left.

The major opened the envelope and stared in disbelief. Turning bright scarlet, he crushed the paper in his fist and slammed it into the desk.

'Kahn, get Barth in here now!'

Captain Kahn escorted Second Lieutenant Barth into the room.

'Kill them all! Kill every fucking one,' the major bellowed.

'What about the women and children, sir?'

'Kill them too. Burn them. Let them all burn in hell.'

Barth turned to Kahn as they left. 'What happened?'

Khan lowered his voice. 'The Oradour chapter of the FTPF has assassinated Major Helmut Kampfe. He and Major Diekmann were at the Eastern front together.'

It annoyed me that the Germans put me with the women and children. According to the traditions of warfare, this should increase my chance of survival. However, here in Oradour-sur-Glane, the Germans abandoned all such conventions. After hours of waiting, they marched the women and children towards the church. This was not a place of greater safety. Once inside, it would trap us.

In the menacing silence, someone detonated a grenade. At this signal, all the machine guns they had set up in front of the men fired. Even the most disciplined soldiers herding the women and children into the church looked over their shoulders.

Having lingered my way towards the back of the group, I took advantage of the distraction, turned and ran past the soldiers up the street towards the screams. I had reached the bakery when a line of pain seared through my back and I pitched forward into the next world.

25

Francine, Autumn 2005

John is back from England. I needed him to be here to support me over the Oradour incident. Furious, I phoned the school and got the 'never happened before' excuse, then a long lecture on the importance of local patrimony in the curriculum. The teacher said if I wished to make a formal complaint, it would have to be made by Peter's mother or father. I put down the phone and cried.

As if she knew I needed her, Eimear came into the library.

'We're closing soon.'

'Good, then nobody will disturb us.'

She locked the door and came to sit beside me, reaching for my hand when I stopped crying.

'Are you cross with the school for taking him, or Esther for introducing him to Pierre?'

'Both. Mostly the school. Being cross with Esther feels like being cross with myself.'

'Indeed.'

'You and Pierre were very close. Jean was older than you, so you looked up to him. It is not surprising that you fell in love, but Jean was also very close to his little brother.'

She is talking about the war.

'You needed to know what happened to Pierre after you died and

186

he has told you.'

'You mean Esther needed to know?'

'It is the same thing.'

I'm not ready to buy this group reincarnation story.

'It's obvious what this is. He goes on that bloody school trip, and they fill his head full of nonsense, then he comes back home to his imaginary friend, and makes up this story.'

'What makes you think he made it up?'

'It's obvious, isn't it?'

'Not to me.'

'But it must be. He got the basic story from the school trip, then made up names and details to fill in the gaps.'

'Francine, when I went to see him, he repeated the story exactly. He made me write everything down, especially the names. These were his brothers in arms at Oradour sur Vayres. The school did not go there. All that remains is a memorial opposite a petrol station. Look. She shows me a photo on her phone. They are the names Pierre remembers. The munitions factory he called the monnerie. The only record is German intelligence saying they suspected there was something at Oradour-sur-Glane. Nobody knows why a routine search and ID check would turn into a massacre. Peter has provided the answer. He remembered Major Helmut Kämpfe was the high-ranking officer on the train. He remembered the SS officer who ordered the massacre was Major Adolf Diekmann. It is possible that Peter heard that name during the school trip, but not Kämpfe, he is unrelated to the story. Historians would need to do a lot of digging to find that Kämpfe and Diekmann were friends.'

I hold up my hand. 'OK, I accept Peter is remembering his past life. The question is, what to do about it? I can't imagine a more traumatic incident to recover from.'

'Can you not? You are lucky. Give him a holiday away from St Etienne. It will help him reconnect with the present.'

'I will. We were wondering what to do at half term.'

'Ah yes, half term. Did John speak to Cathy?'

'I would hope so. That is why he flew to England.'

'She knows Peter's not going back for the autumn break?'

'Yes.'

'Does she understand why?'

'I imagine so. I wasn't there. Sometimes I just have to trust him.'

'Indeed.'

I make supper and put the plates in front of my men. 'Shall we go away at half term?'

John nods. 'What a good idea! The forecast is dry.'

'What about a camping and cycling holiday?' Peter asks.

'That's a fantastic idea. We could take the *voie verte*.'

John doesn't look so sure. 'Why don't you and Peter cycle together while I carry the tent to the next campsite?'

I love the idea of cycling with Peter, but want to spend time with John as well.

'We could cycle every second day so we can be a family in the days between.'

Cathy, England

I snap off the radio. There's a forced levity to the DJ, which is worse than the oppressive silence of breakfasting alone. Richard was supposed to move in once John left for France, but he keeps making excuses. God, I miss Peter.

At least John had the balls to come and tell me to my face that Peter was not coming back. The letter he wrote is on the table. I'm not angry. Peter does not deserve it, Richard will not accept it, and I cannot bear it. Richard fulfils many needs, but comfort is not one. I never asked him for that before because whenever I needed it, John was there, almost begging to be allowed to provide it. That was before he met Francine. Since driving him away, Richard is all I have left.

I pick up the phone. 'Peter's not coming back.'

For once, I have Richard's attention. 'Like fuck he's not! How do you know?'

'John came to tell me.'

The phone cuts off before I finish the sentence. I'm still trying to work out what this means when I hear the key in the door.

Richard comes in like an SAS hit squad, scanning the room. He spots Peter's letter, picks it up and reads it. A chessboard is on the coffee table. White has already lost his queen, so Black expects him to concede. White has moved a pawn to place the black king in check.

Richard stares at it before sweeping the pieces onto the floor. 'Get your knickers on. We're going.'

I refold my tissue, looking for a dry corner. 'Where?'

'To get Peter.' He stuffs the letter in his pocket.

Francine, France

Peter is feeling unwell. I would have liked to have made it all the way to the coast, but there's no point if he is not enjoying it.

John checks the weather forecast. 'There's a storm coming.'

'That settles it. We'll stay here tonight, then head home in the morning.'

The next day, in driving rain, we pull up in front of the house, a lazy week cycling and sightseeing in autumn sunshine undone in a day.

John cuts the engine. 'No point in all of us getting wet, especially with Peter feeling rough. I'll get umbrellas.'

He gets out while I lean over to the nest on the back seat. 'How are you feeling, darling?'

Peter looks up, bleary-eyed. 'I'll be OK.'

John doesn't come back. The rain has eased a little. 'Let's make a run for it.'

Peter grabs Pooh and shuffles after me.

'We must have left the back door unlocked.'

John is looking around, a worried frown on his face.

'Didn't you put the key in the wellie like you always do?' I ask, pushing him aside so Peter can get out of the rain.

'I thought I did, but it was wide open.' He slips something in his pocket.

The idea of being robbed is such an alien concept in these tiny villages that we search for an alternative explanation.

'What was that?' Peter points to John's pocket.

He pulls out the note. 'The chimney sweep. I must have got the date wrong. Both chimneys are done.'

I can tell when John is lying. 'He should have locked up afterwards. I'll mention it when I see him.' John says nothing. 'Are you OK? You are very white,' I ask.

He looks up as if he has only just noticed me. 'Yes, maybe I'm getting Peter's cold. I'll put the kettle on.'

Peter has gone through to his bedroom. He comes back with a parcel. 'Mummy was here! She left me a birthday present!'

I shoot John a look. 'Are you sure, Peter? Surely, she would have said.'

He waves an envelope. 'Of course, I'm sure. There's a card as well.'

My darling Peter, I am so sorry I missed you. I came down with your birthday present to surprise you. You must have gone on holiday. I have to go, but I'll be back at Christmas. How are you getting on at school? Can you speak French now? I am missing you, but Daddy will look after you. All my love, Mummy xxx

Peter is fighting back the tears. 'She should have said she was coming. I would have stayed to see her.'

I hold on to the breakfast bar to stop it from swaying. 'It was a surprise,' I say, struggling to get the words out.

The room turns cold.

'Richard brought her, didn't he?'

I look at John and know the chimney sweep story is a lie.

'Yes, he did,' he says.

I hope he is doing the right thing. Lying to protect Peter now might make things worse later.

The breakfast bar has stopped swaying, so I let go. 'They've gone now. When Mummy comes for Christmas, she will be on her own.'

Peter looks again at his mother's letter. 'I'm sorry I missed her, but I'm glad I didn't see Richard. Can I open my present?'

He disappears back into his room.

I take John's hand. 'The note was from Richard, wasn't it?'

He nods.

'We need to know how recently they were here,' I say. 'I'll go out to ask around. Can you phone Eimear?'

It doesn't take long to find out. Our nosey neighbour saw everything and was quivering to tell me. When I get back, John is with Peter.

Pooh snuggles into him, pretending he doesn't mind the smell of sick. 'They came to get me, didn't they?'

'It looks that way.'

Peter pulls Pooh closer. The experience has taken years off him and he is a small boy again. 'I'm scared. Will Richard try again?'

John reaches for his hand. 'I don't know, but if he does, we will stop him. Remember what Eimear said, you are in control. That means if you don't want to, you don't have to.'

Peter doesn't look reassured. 'That's just talk. We can't stop Richard if he wants to do something.'

I interrupt while John is still thinking about how to answer.

'Richard and Cathy left about half an hour ago.'

A frown deepens John's already worried expression. 'That was close. Do you think they will come back?'

'I don't think so. Bruno was delivering the neighbour's shopping. He speaks a bit of English. They said something about needing to catch the ferry.'

John gives a wry smile. 'Typical Richard. I bet he got one of those booze-cruise tickets. Eimear is on her way. She'll know what to do.'

Eimear smiles, but her green eyes pierce each of us.

'John, you said Richard left a note. Do you have it?'

He takes it out and hands it to her. After reading it, she excuses herself to make a phone call. When she comes back, she is more relaxed, makes small talk about the holiday, and then leaves, promising to come back for supper tomorrow.

'Can I see the note?' I ask.

He hands it to me. *You can run, but you can't hide. I'll be back.*

Cathy, heading for Calais

Richard is scaring me. I have never seen him so angry. 'Is it because I brought the games console with me?' I ask.

He grabs the gear stick. Cogs grind, and the engine screams. 'I couldn't give a fuck about that.'

He is trying to drive and type on his phone, and almost hits a lorry. If we make it back to England alive, I'm leaving him. My mind races, trying to make sense of it. It's me that wants Peter back, but Richard that comes up with some hair-brained plan to kidnap him.

'It's not a kidnap. You are his mother. You have parental responsibility.'

That was on the way down, when some things he was saying made sense. Now, with so many near collisions on the motorway, my life flashes before my eyes. When we were at uni, he was getting off on making John the cuckold. I always knew he was unstable, but I called it unpredictable, exciting — the things John was not. Everything was going to plan until Peter's letter. When John told me that Peter was staying in France, and he was not leaving Francine, the power balance shifted. Richard was no longer in control. Getting Peter back would give him the reins again. I do not know what the texting is about. Right now, I don't want to know.

We finally make it to Calais. Richard hands over the passports. Border Control studies the screen in front of him before returning the tickets and picking up the phone. A British officer pulls us over. He takes our documents and summons a WPC. They take us to separate rooms.

'Let's start with your full name.'

'Catherine Demelza Cartwright. My mother was a Poldark fan.'

I've said it so often it has become the second part of my name, like "Duchess of Cornwall".

The officer writes it down without comment. 'Where have you come from?'

'Saint Etienne.'

The questions keep coming. Where am I going? When did I come to France? Why? What is my relationship with Richard? The officer leaned in closer when I mentioned I had come to France to visit my son. She presses me on why the visit was short.

'He was not there. I suppose my husband took him on holiday.'

Another officer enters the room and hands the WPC Peter's letter.

She changes tack. 'How would you describe your relationship with your husband?'

When they finally release me, I ask about Richard. 'He's still helping us with our enquiries.'

The WPC's tone softens. 'It could take some time. You are not obliged to return to the UK. You may prefer to go back and talk to your husband. Are you insured to drive this car?'

'It's my car.'

'In that case, you are free to go. We will take Mr Patterson home.'

Back in the car, there's a massive signpost in front of me. France left or ferry right?

26

Peter

Daddy always tucks me into bed. Tonight I don't want him to go. I snuggle up to Pooh and try to sleep. The nightmare returns.

A humming in my head becomes a car engine, and I am in the back seat. The couple in the front start as Daddy and Francine, then change to Mummy and Richard. They are wearing fancy dress costumes and laughing. She turns, showing me her pig mask.

'I'm Piglet,' she squeaks really high.

'And I'm Pooh,' adds Richard in a gruff voice.

The voices sound like cartoon baddies.

'No, you're not!' I scream. 'Take me home!'

'I am taking you home,' growls not-Pooh. Not-Piglet laughs.

'I want Daddy!'

'I'm your daddy, and I want you!'

The car swerves as not-Pooh turns, pushing a horrible mask into my face. The warmth spreads in the bottom of my bed.

Not-Piglet squeaks. 'We're getting near Calais. Where are the passports?'

'In the bag on the back seat,' growls not-Pooh.

I pull out the newest-looking one just before not-Piglet pulls the bag onto her lap.

'There are only two, yours and mine.'

I post mine through a gap in the window where the wind catches it, and it's gone.

'You stupid bitch, I told you to put them all together.'

'No, you said you didn't trust me and that you would do it yourself.'

Richard jerks the car into a lay-by. 'Give me that!'

He rummages in the bag before throwing it back at Mummy, then drags me out. The warm dampness freezes in the chill wind. Richard pulls out the bedding, dropping it in the puddles at the side of the road. He gives up and pushes me back into the car, throwing the wet bedding in after me.

'We'll knock him out, cover him in blankets and hope they don't search the car.'

I run into Daddy's bedroom screaming and tell him about the nightmare.

Eimear comes over the next day and explains what's happening.

'The nightmare is Peter's brain telling a story that could have happened. It is trying to work out what it would do if it was real.'

Daddy puts me down so I can fetch Pooh. 'What can we do to help?' he says.

'First, we have to remove the danger. That I have already done. I phoned Thames Valley Police. They have charged Richard with attempting to abduct a minor and released him on bail.'

'Can they do that? I mean, Cathy is his mother.'

Eimear nods. 'Indeed, but it is all about choice. Peter's letter made it quite clear he wanted to stay in France.'

Francine interrupts. 'I didn't think children could choose.'

'You are thinking of consent. The Courts and Social Services have a legal obligation to consider the wishes of the child.'

'You seem to know a lot about it.'

'I've worked in child protection all my life. Thames Valley knows me. That is why they stood to attention when I contacted them.'

Francine says what we are all thinking. 'Will he try again?'

'Not without a passport. That is what you must help me make Peter understand. The deciding factor was the menacing note Richard left.'

Dad asks if that will cure the nightmares.

'Yes, but it will take time.'

She turns to me. 'Peter, we can have a proper talk tonight.'

'I've got another question, Eimear, but you may not know the answer,' says Francine.

She smiles at her. 'Try me.'

'Why is he not having nightmares about Oradour?'

'That's an excellent question. Peter, do you have nightmares about that?'

I shake my head. She nods.

'First, they wouldn't do any good. It has happened. The subconscious does not need to work out what to do *if* it happened, because it already has. Second, past-life nightmares only happen when the soul is seeking to return to that time because there is an unresolved issue. Peter was not seeking that. An ill-advised school trip forced him back.'

Francine jumps on the idea. 'Tell them, Eimear. Tell them they shouldn't be taking children there.'

'What can I say? Some children in your school are reincarnations of those the Germans massacred? It is true, but they would still laugh at me.'

In my room, Eimear comes straight to the point. 'Mummy and Richard came to take you back to England.'

I hang on to Pooh. 'I won't let them. They can't make me.'

Eimear helps Piglet climb in beside us. 'That is why we are talking — we are here to keep you safe, to keep you in control.'

Pooh whispers something, so I nod. 'Richard does things nobody expects. It is like he is two people. Winnie said it's because people like you never looked after him when he was little.'

'Pooh is right. He wants to help everyone. Just now, we are concentrating on helping you. Fixing Richard is someone else's job.'

I hold Piglet's ears to stop them twitching. 'Richard does what he wants. He doesn't deserve to be fixed.'

'Everyone deserves to be fixed. Not everyone can be.'

I laugh. 'Now you sound like Pooh.'

Eimear laughs too. 'Do I? That's the nicest thing anyone has said to me!'

She is serious again. 'The police want to speak to you. There's nothing to be afraid of. It is just to be sure that it is you choosing to live here, not Daddy or Francine.'

If you want to scare someone, say there's nothing to be afraid of. 'I'm not going back even if the police want me to.'

'You don't have to. The police will come here.'

I have to wait for ages, but just before Christmas, two police officers arrive. Eimear must have known they were coming because she was there when they arrive.

'Graham, I thought you had retired!'

The older police officer laughs. 'I thought you had too, Eimear!'

He turns to Dad and Francine. 'DI Jones, but you can call me Graham.'

The younger one holds out her hand. 'Sophie.'

Her boss shoots her a look.

'DC Chandler,' she adds, blushing.

Graham is old-fashioned, which is what Francine calls sexist, like men thinking it's a woman's job to brew tea.

Daddy makes tea, so I go to help him. 'Why do they want to talk to me?'

'Mummy has said she wants you to live in England. Because Francine and I said no, they want to ask you what you want.'

'But you told them.'

'They want to hear you say it.'

'Will you be there?'

'In the next room.'

He gives me the tea tray to take through.

Graham takes his cup. 'Has Mr Patterson been to this house before?'

He means Smarmypants. Daddy says he came at half term when we were away.

I put my hand up. 'He also came to help with the move.'

Graham gets all narky. 'Can you explain, Mr Cartwright, why Mr Patterson helped you bring your son to France, then two months later, he comes to take him back?'

197

It's all going wrong because he makes it sound like Daddy and Richard were kidnapping me. I look at Eimear for help, then she takes Graham outside to tell him off. He comes back quite different.

Eimear is smiling. 'Peter, Graham has agreed that I can be in the interview with you. Are you OK with that?'

What a relief!

'We are going to play a game a bit like solicitors.'

That's the one where you can't answer when someone asks you a question. The person on your right is your solicitor. They have to say for you. If you say anything, you are out.

We go into my bedroom where Eimear kicks off her shoes and stretches out on my bed. 'I am Paul.'

'Who is Paul?' I ask.

'Peter, it's a game. I am your pretend twin brother. The police want to know why you don't like Richard. I know, because you told me. Now you are my solicitor.'

Graham asks "Paul" questions, and I have to answer.

Never play solicitors with Eimear — she would win every time! We played for two hours, and she didn't speak once. When the game is over, Graham calls her Eimear again.

He opens the door for her. 'Eimear, that is the best interviewing method I have ever seen.'

She smiles. 'It is to help people remember things they have forgotten.'

27

Cathy

I don't know what to do. I never handed in my notice. After the fiasco in Calais, I thought I should have, but it doesn't matter now — they sacked me. I try to phone Richard, not to see him, but to get answers. I want to tell him I'm dumping him. That's why I'm round his house, to say it to his face. Police have stretched tape across the top of the drive. I try to duck under it, but a police officer puts out an arm to stop me.

'This is a crime scene. You can't go through.'

'I'm looking for Richard.'

The police officer pulls out his notebook. 'If you mean Mr Patterson, then we all are. What is your name?'

He takes my details and asks me to call them if Richard contacts me. Fat chance of that. What does he mean this is a crime scene? What crime? When Richard came back from the Far East, he said it was like the Wild West. I didn't know what he was talking about, but it sounded dodgy. He was bragging, trying to convince me he was a big deal in the banking world. Now I'm wondering, has he got caught up in some international banking scam? It would explain why he wasn't at home, but they never asked me in Calais if I knew anything about his finances. They seemed more interested in Peter.

I'm home, pushing the ready meal around my plate, refilling my glass. The doorbell rings, making me jump up and knock over the wine. Two police officers find me dabbing Pinot Noir off my blouse.

'It's about Richard, isn't it? Have you found him?'

DI Jones offers me his business card. 'No, we were rather hoping you could help us.'

He takes Peter's letter from his briefcase. 'Can you explain how this came to be in Mr Patterson's possession?'

The uneaten food eyes me with a hint of suspicion. 'I was upset when my husband came to tell me my son didn't want to see me. He gave me a letter.'

Jones takes out his notebook. 'Please answer the question.'

Why is he being mean to me? 'I am trying to. Richard and I are friends. I showed him the letter — he must have kept it.'

The WPC wades in. 'Please explain what you mean by "friends".'

I blush. The police must have worked out we were lovers. I mumble something stupid, which she puts in her notebook. 'Did you expect your husband to say no when you asked him to return your son?'

She writes another meaningless response. 'Who had the idea of going to France?'

I waffle on about John's inheritance, buying a holiday home, making a fresh start. None of it seems to interest them.

Jones cuts across his subordinate. 'Do you have any idea where Mr Patterson may have gone?'

While they talk, I replay my sorry life in my head, then I remember the holiday cottage.

'He sometimes borrows a cottage in Devon. Would you like me to find the address?'

I go to look. The police must guess why I have it. If he jumped bail and is hiding there, he will not want me to give them his address.

I go back downstairs. 'I'm sorry, I can't find it. It's about somewhere. I'll pop it into the station when it turns up.'

They don't look happy, but without a search warrant, what are they going to do? It's not like it's me that is being investigated. None of it makes any sense. They can't be investigating me not kidnapping my son.

They've gone. The meal is cold, but I can't be arsed to reheat it. Instead, I pour more wine. Not the best idea for problem solving, but it blurs the edges, so I only see the basics.

Killer facts.

Written in large on the top of a piece of paper. The wine stain gives it a Gothic vibe.

One: <u>PETER LOVES ME.</u> (big letters, underlined)

Two: John does not want to leave Francine. (Can I do something about that?)

Three: I am invited to France for Christmas, but without Richard. (Not a problem — he's gone missing.)

Four: Police arrest Richard, and he jumped bail. (Why?)

Five: Richard did nothing wrong by going to France. (They can't arrest him for <u>not</u> kidnapping Peter.)

Six: Richard jumped bail. (Crossed out, I've already put that.)

Six: Richard was boasting when he got back from Hong Kong. (Insider trading?)

Seven: My guess is Richard has gone to Dartmouth. (Not a killer fact, but a killer hunch.)

I turn over the paper.

Killer Solutions.

One: Invite myself to France for Christmas.

Two: Go to Dartmouth.

I finish the wine and pick up the phone. I hear a voice so familiar, a voice that hesitates when he hears mine.

'Hi, Cat... Yes, he is... Well, he's just gone to bed, but I'm sure he's still awake.'

Footsteps and whispering, then Peter's voice. I don't hear the words, just the sound, letting it waft over me, pouring into the dried creeks of my soul. I cannot even find meaningless questions to ask, just to keep him talking. He dries up in the face of my silence.

'Would you like to speak to Dad?'

He, too, has run out of words.

It's my fault. 'Yes, please. Love you.'

I don't think he heard the second part — I listen to him padding through and whispering, 'She wants to speak to you.'

John has had time to compose himself. Now he sounds normal.

'Hi, Cathy. I'm putting you on speaker so Francine can hear.'

Why the warning? Does he think I will hit on him?

'Peter wants me to come for Christmas. Are you still OK with that?'

They both say yes.

'Are you sure? Won't it be too awkward?'

This time it's Francine who answers. 'Not at all. It will be wonderful for Peter to have both parents with him for Christmas.'

Putting the phone down, I pick up a fresh bottle of wine, change my mind, and put it down again. Not that I've started on my journey back, but I have stopped running away. The second killer solution will be harder.

Dartmouth

I should have taken the motorway. The rain thrashed against the relentless beat of the wipers. What took us four hours back in the summer took me seven. I only stopped to pee and get something inedible at a roadside cafe.

Now I am slithering over the decking where six months ago I was sipping champagne and watching the sun set over the Dart. I remember Richard saying the patio door needed fixing. If I slip in that way, I can put off the front-door conversation.

The room, dark except for a single desk lamp, smells of overheated paper. Richard is bent over a shredder with boxes everywhere. Calmly, he picks up a wad of paper, peels off a few sheets, and feeds them into the machine. I stand watching him until he finishes the box and turns to fetch another.

'Cathy! What the fuck are you doing?'

Instead of a sassy "I could ask you the same question", all I manage is to whisper his name. For the first time, I see fear in his eyes.

'Who did you bring?'

'Nobody.' The word comes out as a croak.

He throws the box aside and strides up to me. 'I don't fucking believe you!'

'It's true.'

He stares at my tears. 'You know you are just stupid enough to be telling the truth. Where's your phone?'

'In the car. Do you need it?'

He laughs. 'Like a dose of clap.'

I'm lost.

'They followed you,' he explains

'Who?'

'Fucking hell, Cathy.'

'The police?'

He does a slow, ironic hand clap.

'I'm sorry.'

Am I apologising for leading the police here or because I am dumping him?

'Grab these.' He throws a box of papers towards me, points to another, picks up three more, and pushes past me.

'Where are we going?'

'The boat.'

'It's raining.'

'Well spotted.'

'It's dark.'

'Fucking hell, Cathy, if you can't say something I don't already know, shut the fuck up.'

'I'm leaving you.'

For the first time, I catch him off guard.

'Nice timing.'

'I'm sorry.'

'Can you help me take these to the boat before you go?'

I follow him. He dumps the boxes he is carrying, takes mine and jumps aboard. 'Undo the stern.' He is already busy with the forward mooring.

'Where are your waterproofs?'

He puts his hand to his mouth in mock shock. 'I forgot them. I hope I don't catch a cold.' He grabs the push pole. 'Help me push off, then do me a favour and push off yourself before the police track you down.'

'I didn't know you could sail.'

'There's lots you don't know about me, sugar tits. You should have spent more time with your knickers on. I could have given you lessons.'

He turns, ducks under the boom, and raises the sail.

Back at the house, I find a light. He's covered every surface of the room with piles of paper, some untouched, some reduced to confetti. It looks as if he only stopped when the shredder was full, tipped it out and carried on. Of course, I can't make out any of it. He has been far too systematic. The only thing left was a smell of paper and empty file folders with Chinese writing on them.

I need to pee. On the way to the bathroom, I see the blue lights.

Jones and Chandler push past me with a perfunctory wave of ID. It doesn't take them long to establish that I am alone.

'Where is he?' The older police officer can smell the kill and has no intention of diluting it with politeness.

'Out on the boat.'

The room still smells like Office Land on Black Friday, and it's making me feel nauseous.

'In the dark, in winter, with a storm brewing?'

Nodding, I look for somewhere to sit before I faint.

He pulls out his phone. 'DI Jones. I want coastguard round at East Point PDQ. Fugitive in small craft. Get the chopper up with lights. This is a manhunt.'

The WPC pulls out her notebook. 'Did you tell him the police were on their way?'

'I didn't know you were coming,' I whisper, looking for something I can blow my nose on.

'Don't touch that!' Jones has snapped off his phone and bats my hand away from the pile of shredded paper.

He turns to his subordinate. 'I want all this bagged.'

Pulling out another phone, he waves it in my face. 'Didn't know this address? Didn't know we were following you? You had geolocation activated.'

'Where did you find my phone?'

'On the passenger seat. You didn't lock your car.'

'We weren't expecting visitors.'

'Really? I wonder. He wasn't, but you?' He runs the corner of my phone down my arm. 'I can't make my mind up about you. Whose side are you on?'

Something snaps.

'Get off me!' I turn to Chandler. 'See that? I want to make a complaint. That's a microaggression.'

The predatory expression on DI Jones' face has gone. He turns to his subordinate. 'For the record, DC Chandler, I was returning Mrs Cartwright's phone, which she foolishly left in an unlocked car.'

She writes it down.

'Sandie, would you be kind enough to find a chair for Mrs Cartwright? She does not look well. Perhaps a glass of water while you are there.'

As soon as the younger officer leaves the room, he changes again. 'Either you are an excellent spy, or a terrible one. My money's on the former. In Reading, when you said you couldn't find this address, your phone was on the coffee table. You were telling Mr Patterson that we were asking for his location, that you hadn't given it to us, but it...' he looks at his notes, 'it will turn up.'

The WPC returns with a chair and a glass of water. 'Sophie, I'd kill for a cup of tea. Can you see what's in the kitchen?'

I take a sip of the water. 'Richard deactivated his phone. Why else would I have driven all day in the driving rain to speak to him?'

'You know perfectly well that a phone is never off. An agent only deactivates compromised phones. You knew if you drove here with geolocation active, we would follow you.'

I have still not forgiven him for touching me with the phone. In the kitchen, there's the sound of a kettle being filled.

'I don't know any of those things, but DI Jones, if you think either Richard or I are spies, you seriously need to watch fewer Bond movies.'

He pulls the shredder close to my chair and sits on it with care.

'Call me Graham. May I call you Cathy?' I shrug. 'What are you, Cathy?'

'A married woman with an eleven-year-old son who thinks she is still a girl who can two-time the boys in the playground.'

He smiles. 'Nice try. Maybe you are right. The thing is, you let him go, and you let yourself get caught. We cannot arrest Patterson until we catch him, but I can arrest you now.'

I flush. 'What for?'

'Assisting a fugitive in his escape.'

Sophie returns with two mugs of tea. She offers me one, but I shake my head and pick up the glass of water.

She hands the other to Graham. 'Two sugars.'

'Thanks pet.'

She ignores him, fetches another chair and sips the rejected tea.

'Mrs Cartwright is now going to tell us the full and unexpurgated story of her and Mr Patterson. I hope you have a spare notebook.'

I tell him everything I know. He does not seem that interested in the sex, but pulls me up when I get to the Cheung Kong contract.

'How much do you know about it?'

'Quite a lot. My boss was the developer. I checked the legal contracts.'

'What was Mr Patterson's role?'

'I don't think he had one. He just worked for one of the hedge funds managing the spread.'

'I'm not a financial wizard. Can you explain?'

'The fund managers buy forward in Hong Kong Dollars. They release funds at different stages of completion. Nobody knows what the exchange rate will be, so the hedge funds take a view and offer to buy Hong Kong dollars at a certain price, regardless of the rate.'

'Sorry, pet, you've lost me.'

'The developer controls his costs irrespective of currency fluctuations. The fund managers make money betting on the future rate.'

'Is that the work you did for your boss?'

'No, it was more contractual stuff. What operated under UK legislation, and what under Hong Kong law. We put as much under the second as we could get away with because it was more tax efficient.'

'You are losing me again.'

'Sorry, you wanted everything I know.'

'Of course. Figures bother me. I'm more of a people man. What do you know about Mr Cheung?'

'Very little. He was a Hong Kong entrepreneur. The story was that he was pro-Beijing. He got planning concessions and an offer of a place on the post-handover executive.'

'In exchange for what?'

I shrug. 'Money, I suppose.'

'Doesn't sound very communist.'

Sophie coughs and looks at her watch.

Graham nods and turns back to me. 'Maybe you can write all this technical stuff down for us at the station. Mr Cheung has become a person of interest to us. There were several takeovers that made him extremely rich, facilitated no doubt by his new political power.'

'I'd heard he was extremely wealthy and well connected politically, but for Sir Evelyn, the Hong Kong market dried up after the handover. We switched our attention to Dubai. What has all this got to do with Richard?'

Graham looked at Sophie. 'I am not at liberty to say. Our government became interested in him because of his association with Mr Cheung. Ministers believed it would assist our understanding of the Hong Kong executive.'

'You mean MI6 recruited him?'

'You might very well think that. I couldn't possibly comment.'

'Stop trying to sound like that bloke from *House of Cards*.' Sophie suppresses a smile. 'If Richard was working for MI6, why is he on the run?' I ask.

Graham leans forward as if he is going to put his arm across my shoulder.

'Cathy, can I be frank? You benefit from the stability of a happy family life with John. That did not stop you looking for, shall we say, additional benefits elsewhere.' He holds up his hand to stop my objection. 'Let me finish. Mr Patterson had an equally stable and mutually beneficial relationship with Her Majesty's Government. Regretfully, that did not prevent him from seeking additional relationships.'

'He became a double agent.'

'Your words, not mine.'

'I did not know he was a spy. I thought he had got caught up in some money laundering or insider dealing business, and had fallen foul of the law.'

Graham stands. 'I believe you. The problem is that the law does not operate on belief, it requires proof. I need to take you back to Reading police station for further questioning. I want fraud in on all this contract stuff.'

My shoulders drop. 'Graham, I am done in. I couldn't possibly drive back to Reading tonight.'

He smiles. 'We wouldn't let you. You might do a runner like Richard. You are coming back with us.'

'What about my car?'

'Devon Police will pick it up, run it past forensics, give it a full valet, then return it to you good as new.'

'Better in places,' I add automatically.

'Sorry?'

I shrug. 'Oh nothing. It is something Peter says. It is from a story his dad reads him.'

'*The House at Pooh Corner,*' Graham explains. 'I used to read that to my kids.'

In an instant, this scary police detective hunting down international spies becomes a dad. One who has read his children so many bedtime stories, he knows them by heart. I allow him to put his hand across my shoulder as he leads me to the car.

Before we get to the main road, I am asleep, dreaming of spies and double agents.

Jenny, 1943

I arrive back at the safe house. Only a few months ago, I would have fallen into Jean's arms, told him Ricardo was still about, and that he had just raped me. Today, Jean doesn't even notice there's anything wrong.

He kisses me without emotion. 'There is a message from London.'

I smell Esther on his skin.

'They're sending a Lysander,' he says. 'A new radio transmitter, money, arms, and explosives. Now the Germans have taken over the

Free Zone, we have to prioritise intelligence gathering and sabotage.'

With little difference between the two zones, the young man who made his reputation as a passeur is now irrelevant.

'I'm sorry,' I whisper.

He looks at me. 'Don't be. I've moved on. I've volunteered for sabotage. More my metier than combat.'

Is he thinking about me killing the guard, or his inability to kill Ricardo? I wonder if the Italian is dead yet.

'We've never had a Lysander before. Where will it land?'

'Between us and St Sulpice. The clearing beyond the wood.'

'Can they land a plane there? It's tiny.'

'It slopes south west. They will land up the hill. We turn it round and it takes off immediately. You will be on board.'

'WHAT?'

'That was the main part of the message. SIS has replaced SOE.'

So, I too am being replaced. I volunteered as a courier for SOE and became a spy. Now SIS has taken over Special Operations, it wants to vet the operatives it has gained.

'When is the flight?'

'Next full moon, if the skies are clear.'

A nail paring of a moon watches us through the window. Less than two weeks. I turn to leave.

'Was there something you wanted to say to me?' he asks.

'No. I have to go to work.'

After my shift, I return to the woods. Someone has locked the hut door, so I go to the back to look through the window.

'Looking for someone? I rent it by the hour for working girls.'

'Fuck me, Ricardo. You scared me!'

'Surprised to see me? Strange, since I live here.' He unlocks the door and stands aside. 'Come in. I've opened a fresh bottle of wine. There was something wrong with the last one. It gave me the runs.'

The silent emptiness of the woods surrounds me. The silent emptiness of my soul fills me. Inside the hut are pain, conflict, argument. Outside is death; inside is life. I kiss Ricardo on the cheek as I pass the door. He has not washed for days, has no change of clothes, and the cyanide proved to be a powerful emetic. The contrast with the smell of Esther on Jean's skin could not be greater. They both smell of my Yardley's lavender soap. I imagine them bathing together.

Ricardo offers me wine. This time I take a long pull on the bottle.

'I have to leave.'

The emptiness in my soul left by Jean's new love draws Ricardo into its orbit. Louis had reason to embargo any plans to turn Ricardo into an Allied asset, but I have nothing else.

He takes a large swallow of wine in his turn. 'Leave? Have you been called up for STO? I thought that was only for men.'

Pétain has just introduced *Service du Travail Obligatoire*.

'No. It also includes young single women, but I'm not going to Germany. I am going to England.'

I rarely catch him off guard, so I press my advantage. 'Ricardo, the tide is turning. Germany cannot win this war. In North Africa, Rommel is being squeezed between the French and the Brits. Russians are advancing on the Eastern Front. US troops are already in southern England waiting to liberate France.'

'How do you know all this?'

'I am a spy.' The four words dance like butterflies around the dank cabin. They settle on the walls, opening and closing their wings in time to the blinking of Ricardo's eyes.

'Not a brilliant one. You forget I am an informer. Schneider will pay me well for turning you in.'

'The Germans will not believe you. Remember the radio codes?'

The bottle stops halfway to his lips. 'How did you know about those?'

Alliance had warned Jean only two weeks ago to change his frequency and call sign. I made sure Ricardo gave away the old ones.

I shrug, taking the bottle. 'Like I said, I'm a spy. Your problem is that the Germans now believe you deliberately supplied false information. As far as they are concerned, you are already batting for the other side, so you may as well let me recruit you. That way you will get Allied protection.'

There's a long silence. 'Tell me more.'

'The RAF is sending a Lysander. We unload the cargo and any passengers, you and I jump aboard, and they take off. They will only be on the ground about five minutes.'

Another long silence. 'Why should I trust someone who tried to poison me?'

'Why should I elope with a man who raped me?'

Neither of us answers the other's question.

'What are the alternatives?'

'You stay here until either the resistance or the Germans find you, or you starve to death.'

'I could kill you.'

'That might make your wait longer.'

'I could frustrate the landing.'

'That's very easy to do. If any part of the routine is not right, the Lysander is under strict instructions to abort the mission and return to England without landing.'

'Let me think about it.' He moves in to claim his reward.

I turn my head. 'When you have washed,' I tell him. 'I'll bring you food and a change of clothes.'

28

Cathy, 2005

They found the boat first. As soon as they told me it had capsized, I knew.

'We recovered some papers.'

Graham is trying to keep me updated.

'Are they any help to you?' I ask out of politeness.

'Until the case is closed, we keep everything. For now, the focus is on finding Richard.'

He now uses first names. 'Do you know where to look?'

'That's where the papers are useful.'

'Was there an address?'

He laughs. 'They are useful because we can plot the tides and currents the night he went missing.'

'So, you are looking for his body?'

'That is the focus of our enquiry, yes.'

Caversham crematorium is almost completely empty. The pallbearers and ushers stay inside to boost the numbers. Graham and Sophie are here, along with a third person standing alone at the back.

A stranger approaches me. 'Did you know...' she glances at her notes, 'Richard?' I nod. 'It's just that nobody else seems to, and usually a friend or family member gives a eulogy.'

'A eulogy?'

She looks apologetic. 'Well, just a few words. How they knew him, something they liked about him.' I stare. 'If they can think of anything,' she finishes lamely.

Knew more positions than any other man I've bedded, I think to myself.

'Just as long as it is appropriate,' she adds.

After a few meaningless sentences about the river of life, she invites me to step forward.

'Richard and I go back a long way. We were at university together. His favourite film was *Who Killed Roger Rabbit?* He used to call me Jessica.'

The silence presses down on me, each sentence sticking in the mud of emotions I cannot feel, forcing me to continue.

'He wasn't really bad. He was just drawn that way.'

Enough is enough. I pretend to be overcome with emotion and shuffle back to my seat. The stranger standing at the back slips out.

France

John offered to pick me up at the airport, but I needed an escape route, so I rented a car. My desperate desire to hold Peter in my arms overrides any misgivings about the holiday. I cannot escape that I am now the ex, and the love nest John was building is now Francine's domain. We are all adults and are doing this for Peter. I promise I will be nice.

'Mummy!'

Before I can get out of the car, Peter flings himself on me. 'It's going to be just like Christmas in Reading with you, me and Daddy.'

'Not quite.'

'No, because Francine is here. I said you could sleep with me so you won't be lonely, but Daddy said I am too old, so they have put a bed up in the loft. If it is too cold, you can sleep on the settee in front of the fire. That's the best place in winter. I'm not allowed to sleep there because I have my bedroom, and Daddy and Francine stay there until it is time for them to go to bed.'

I tip the boy and his words onto the pavement so I can get out of the car. John and Francine are waiting by the door. Their smiles are warm, if a little forced. It's Francine who steps forward to hug me. I'd forgotten how small she is. And young. They sweep away the unfair thought on a wave of welcomes that carry me into the kitchen.

Francine bustles about making drinks whilst Peter crawls all over me, and John tries to catch my eye to make sure I am OK.

'Eimear is coming for supper,' Francine says, placing a mug of tea in front of me. 'I left the bag in. John said you like it strong. Would you like milk?'

The kitchen door opens, and an enormous bunch of mistletoe enters, followed by Eimear.

'I'm a bit early because I thought someone might want to put this up before supper.'

Whilst the others are busy with the mistletoe, she whispers to me.

'I understand you went to the funeral.'

'How did you know? I've not told anyone yet.'

Her smile avoids my question. 'Why don't I tell them?'

I try not to look too relieved. 'Would you mind? How much do you know?'

'More than you.' She winks.

Eimear dabs the corner of her mouth with her napkin. 'John, you have excelled yourself once again, but an old lady does not have the appetite of youth. While you all enjoy seconds, let me tell you the story of Richard. I will start with the war, as that might help you see how the two stories interweave.'

I help myself to more roast potatoes and pass the bowl to Francine.

'Like all of you, Ricardo did not survive the war.' There's the faintest flicker of her eyes towards me. 'Just as in this life, he was chiefly interested in looking after himself. When the Germans had the upper hand, that meant supplying information to them. Towards the end, Jenny tried to recruit him as a double agent.'

This time, the glance in my direction is longer.

'Why did she do that?'

'Peter, don't talk with your mouth full,' I admonish him.

Eimear continues. 'It was Louis' idea, but he changed his mind when he saw the risks. Meanwhile, SOE had recalled Jenny to London.'

Now it's my turn to ask why. Graham had talked to me in the car on the way back from Dartmouth. I was falling asleep, and it all got muddled up with the book Peter had given me.

'Politics,' Eimear explains. 'The Dordogne was of major importance to the Allies. They wanted all intelligence to go back to SIS, not SOE. Since Jenny was an SOE agent, they wanted to replace her with someone from SIS.'

John looks puzzled. 'Surely the intelligence service and operations executive were on the same side?'

'You would think so, wouldn't you? It was not just London that had issues. Jenny and Jean were no longer getting along. That I think contributed to Jenny's proposal to Ricardo that he went back with her and worked for the British.'

'But you said he didn't survive the war.'

'He didn't. If he had, he would have gone to Greystones.'

'What's that?'

'Lord and Lady Leybourne gave over part of their estate in Kent for foreign agents. They came for debriefing, training, or simply respite from the onslaught of Gestapo counter intelligence. After he died, Ricardo's spirit went there and developed an affection for the place. When the war ended, they converted Greystones into an orphanage. To begin with, it was for children of the intelligence community whose parents had perished. Later, it took war babies, mostly from unmarried mothers. It survived as a children's home until the abuse scandals, when it closed.'

'What has that to do with Richard?'

'Ricardo was reborn as Richard and placed there in 1966. He learnt to live on his wits,' Eimear explains.

'But he sounded so posh,' John objected. 'Didn't he go to public school?'

'He did. Wilson introduced a system of scholarships to put disadvantaged pupils into public schools.'

'That doesn't sound very socialist,' I complain.

'Maybe he thought a few clever working class kids would bring the posh ones down a peg or two,' John suggests.

'The experiment didn't work, at least not for Richard,' Eimear continues. 'Nature blessed, or perhaps cursed, him with exceptional intelligence. He passed his eleven-plus when few orphans managed. He won a scholarship to a public school where he learnt to appear affable whilst being extremely manipulative.'

John looks at me. 'I know.'

I nod to show that, too late, I know too.

Eimear carries on. 'All of this I know from my work with the community. Until DC Jones contacted me, I did not know what had happened to him after university.'

'What do you mean, your work with the community?'

'In the seventies I worked in Child Protection. My doctorate was a study of the practices at Greystones. Later, I worked for Berkshire County Council Children's Services. That is how I met DC Jones. West Berks noticed Richard after he returned from Hong Kong.'

'Why would they notice him?' Peter asked.

'That is where it gets interesting. Cathy, you will have heard of Mr Cheung, the property developer?' I nod. 'Setting aside the cultural differences, he was very similar to Richard. He grew up on the streets of Kowloon. Any parenting he had was at the hands of the triads, who put him to work picking pockets. As soon as he was tall enough to reach the pedals, he started driving maxicabs.'

'What are they?' Peter asks.

'Twelve-seater minibuses that run unregulated bus services on the peninsular. The Chinese mafia control their unofficial routes. Cheung grew up to control one of the most profitable bus franchises, then branched into property development. That was when he met Richard. He had developed more of a reputation for ducking and diving than finance. That is why he started working in the planning department for the outgoing British administration. He was supposed to be safeguarding British interests post-handover, but it gradually became apparent he was batting for the other side.'

Francine looks confused.

'Working for the Chinese government,' John explains.

'After Hong Kong, he did the circuit, posing as a British business executive, but all the time he was conducting industrial espionage for the Chinese.'

'How did the police find out?' Peter asks.

'That is something they will not tell me. Graham just said that he couldn't say because it would prejudice the other investigations. All he would tell me is that Richard was under surveillance, and him leaving the UK triggered an event that re-awoke their interest. That happened when he came out in August, and again at half term. I'm a bit of a techno-numpty, but apparently when he is at home he can communicate securely from his computer. MI6 sent fake messages, which he picked up on his phone. On the first trip, he waited to get home before replying, but the second time, he replied from France. Border police used Peter's attempted abduction to hold him whilst they carried out the trace. Back in Reading, they only had the attempted abduction, which was not enough to hold him in custody. As you know, they released him, and he jumped bail. Cathy guessed where he was hiding, went to confront him, and found him shredding evidence. Realising she had led the police to his hideout, he tried to escape by boat. A storm blew up, the boat capsized, and apparently, he drowned.'

Apparently? I was at his funeral. I remember her reply to my question. "How much do you know?" "More than you," she said. Eimear picks up her glass, takes a sip of wine, and waits.

Peter is the first to speak. 'I thought it would make me happy that I will never have to see him again, but I don't know if I'm allowed to think that now he has died. I'm pleased that I can visit Mummy now. That's OK, isn't it?'

Christmas Eve

I'm up early the next day. If I wanted to make an impression to win John back, I would not do it like this. The loft is freezing. I spent most of the night gazing at the skylight, waiting for a signal that morning was not far off, and I could make myself a hot drink.

Concentrating on basics — like not dying of hyperthermia — takes my mind off the future. Why did I come to France? That is easy. To spend Christmas with Peter. What then? Go back to England? What for? Everywhere I look, I find gaping voids. The largest and irreversible one is Richard. Just like that, he has gone, and yet he is still here, controlling me. I am tied as surely as I used to be during our bondage sessions.

217

He is not controlling you.

I don't even bother looking round. If that is Jenny talking to me, she can bloody well show herself like Esther does to Peter. I sit up, put on a jumper, and climb back into bed. I am free, but fuck, it's cold!

Like the frost that is forming on the inside of the skylight, realisation creeps in. The same thing happened with my father. Suddenly, he was gone, and Mother still blames me. I suppose she loved him. She bore him two children, and she was still with him right up to that fateful morning in Cooplands.

'I'll never forgive you.'

She knew what she was saying. Never forgive her daughter for taking her husband away from her or for forcing the break-up of the family.

I had freed myself from my father's unwanted attentions, but in doing so, I had lost the parts of his love I still needed. When a child loses the love of one parent, she turns to the other. That morning in Cooplands I lost that too.

Boys would have to wait. I was at an all-girls' academy. This suited my little sister, whose crushes on teachers, then prefects, settled into a cocoon of sisterhood. This, whilst not exempting her from the transience of teenage relationships, steered her through school.

All I had was studies. To be the best, to get to university, to get a degree. For what? To stick it to my father who I drove away, or my mother who turned her back on me?

Cathy, stop. You are making yourself a victim.

I turn to the voice. This time it has a body. She is sitting on the end of the bed smoking a Gitane and wearing a red beret and a trench coat.

'Take it off. You look ridiculous.'

No, it's too cold. When is Jean going to light the fire?

'When he gets out of Francine's bed. Anyway, I thought ghosts didn't feel the cold.'

Cathy, he will never get out of her bed unless you do something about it. Accept it and move on.

There's a noise from downstairs. 'I don't know. Right now, I'm going to make a brew.'

29

John is coming in with a basket of logs. 'Hi, Cath. I'm lighting the kitchen stove; we'll soon have it cosy.'

I think of the central heating in England. 'Fancy a brew?' I ask.

'No thanks, I had one in bed. Warmest place.'

I say nothing, cupping my hand round the mug and watching him light the fire. I want to ask him how things are going with Francine. To look for signs of buyer's remorse. He feels my eyes burning into his back.

'You can set the table. Bread in the bin, butter and cheese in the fridge, jam in the cupboard. Francine is going out for croissants.'

On cue, Francine comes in one door whilst Peter appears at the other.

'Hi, Cathy. Sleep well?'

'Not really. I'm not used to the cold.'

'Me neither. We haven't got the hang of heating the entire house yet. You could sleep in the living room if you don't mind the sofa. To be honest, it is the warmest room in the house when the weather is like this.'

'I might do that if I won't be in your way.'

She comes up and pecks me on the cheek. 'You are not in our way.'

I see John's smile out of the corner of my eye, and Francine's flicker, looking for approval. She is trying, and I should do the same.

'Croissants all round? John, give that bread to the birds. I'll get fresh.'

'Chocolatine!' Peter has latched himself onto me, but his eyes follow Francine.

'Of course. I've ordered a *bûche* for tonight. Do you want to come and help me carry it, darling?'

The last word stings. John shoots her a warning look, which she registers and covers by saying something else.

'We don't do Christmas cake in France. A *bûche* is a cake in the shape of a log.'

'I want to stay with Mummy.'

'Of course. I won't be long.'

She has gone, but her presence lingers. I look at my husband and son, remembering the scene last Christmas.

'Daddy, what are we doing tonight?'

'We've invited Eimear and Paula for supper, but they won't stay long. Paula is not very well.'

'Who's Paula?' I ask.

Peter answers. 'Paula is Eimear's girlfriend. Like Aunty Jan and Alice, but really old. Will there be games?'

John shuts the stove door. 'I thought we could tell stories round the fire. We can do games on Christmas Day, after you have opened your presents.'

'I'm doing a story. I'm going to make up my own Winnie the Pooh Christmas story.'

'That's sounds lovely, but breakfast first!'

After Christmas dinner, we go to the living room. Eimear is wearing a long green dress embroidered with silver thread that catches the firelight. She has sat her partner Paula near the fire, but the old lady still pulls her pale blue cardigan about her as if she expects someone to steal it.

I'm wearing the skirt and blouse I used to wear for Richard. This time it's for Francine's benefit, and maybe John. You never know, and there's nothing wrong with looking your best at Christmas. Peter pulls me onto the settee so he can snuggle up. To show they are an item, Francine waits for John to sit in the armchair, then settles on the floor in front of him.

Peter is itching to tell his Winnie the Pooh story. He tells about how the animals go to visit Christopher Robin on Christmas Day. It's amazing, but seems to last forever. We keep clapping before he's finished. He comes back to sit on my lap after, and I try not to cry. Peter looks at Francine as if he wants a cuddle from her too, but doesn't dare when I am here.

Francine stands. 'Who's next?' Nobody answers, so she goes to fetch the wine. 'Anyone for a top-up?'

I hold up my glass.

I have a story.

A young girl steps out of the fire.

'Esther, you said you were not coming!'

Peter rushes straight through her and finishes up in Francine's lap. I feel Jenny also watching the party and wonder if she, too, will make an appearance.

My family comes from Alsace where they tell many stories. The symbol of my region is the stork. You often see them nesting on chimney tops. Today, we celebrate Holda, the goddess of Birth and Death. She welcomes the dead to her kingdom before sending them back to the land of the living to be reincarnated as babies. The souls come down to earth as raindrops, where they gather in lakes and springs to play while they wait to be reincarnated. Holda's messengers are elves who she sends out in silver boats to catch the souls with a golden thread. When they catch one, they take it to a new mother.

Tonight, if you look out of the window, you will see Holda dressed in red and white, and wearing a goose-feather cape. She is giving out gifts and happiness from her magic chariot. Soon the days will get longer and the storks will return, bringing human babies to be born in the spring.

Peter claps. 'That was a lovely story, Esther. Don't go away, I want to tell it again for the grown-ups who can't hear you.'

Eimear stands. 'There is no need, Peter. We all heard. It's Christmas Eve. Magic happens tonight.'

'It's true,' I whisper to Peter as he rushes back to me.

Full of compassion, Eimear is stroking Paula's arm to wake her. 'I need to take my wife home. Thank you so much for inviting us.'

I give Peter a squeeze. 'That means it is your bedtime, young man.' For once, he doesn't make a fuss.

'Esther, can you give me my bedtime story?'

Of course.

Peter comes back in his pyjamas for his goodnight kiss. I ask if the ghost had told him another story.

'Yes, about a girl who fell into a well. There's another world down there. Like *Alice in Wonderland.* The girl is very kind and helps people, especially an old lady living alone. Eventually, the girl gets homesick, so the old lady gives her a gift and shows her how to return to her mother. Back home, every time the girl speaks, a gold coin falls out of her mouth. That's the gift. But her mother is greedy, so she sends her other daughter down the well. The sister is lazy and doesn't help the old lady at all. The witch beats her and sends her home with a curse. Every time the sister speaks, a frog comes out of her mouth.'

It sounds very Germanic. Hard work rewarded, and laziness punished. If the ghost is part of that Alsace family, it would explain her love of German folk tales. I miss Peter so much. That's why I give him an extra tight hug. It's also because I want Francine to know I'm his mother. Peter gives me a half smile as he looks at Francine out of the corner of his eye, then snuggles into me. Eventually I release him and he scuttles off with Pooh and Piglet.

Looking around, I try to make as much sense of everything as the alcohol will allow. The whole thing is beyond weird. John has been restoring this place for two years. Last Christmas we snogged on this sofa and talked about moving down for good. OK, I wasn't straight with him about leaving Richard, but I was going to. It's just that Richard is not a person you can say no to. My plan was to kid Richard that I was staying, then sneak away without giving him my French phone number. Now it seems ridiculous. Eloping with your husband to escape your lover rather depends on your husband not having one of his own.

I am not the only one to be affected by alcohol and the spirit of Christmas. Since I arrived, John and Francine have been careful in hiding overt displays of affection from me. This does not extend to Francine marking her territory by sitting at John's feet, or discreet rhythmic noises when they think I am asleep. Now Francine is sitting on his lap. What hurts is not the intimacy, but that she is so tiny she can get away with it. The last time John and I sat like that, it lasted five minutes and gave him a dead leg.

It looks like John has fallen asleep. To make conversation and pretend things are normal, I talk to Francine. 'That was weird — Esther joining the party. Delightful story, though. Very Christmassy.'

She shifts position, so she is facing me. 'Yes, she usually just talks to Peter. Eimear says it is something to do with him being a child, closer to the other side.'

The nod is to pretend I understand. 'Do you think it will stop when he reaches puberty, like *Peter Pan*?'

'I don't see why it should. I still see her.'

With those words, I am sober. 'That's the bit I don't understand. If you take the view that ghosts are souls unable to rest in peace until something rights the wrong, how can there be two of you? I mean, if she was reborn as you, wouldn't the old you just disappear?'

Francine laughs. 'I had almost exactly the same conversation with Eimear. You need to ask her, or ask me again when I have had less wine.'

There's an openness and honesty in the way she looks at me, not hiding the fact that she has replaced me in John's heart, but not showing any triumphalism either. She smiles with a genuine desire to be my friend.

'Can you try to explain? It's important. I've started seeing the English spy.'

Francine raises an eyebrow. 'Interesting. I'll try. First, there is only one me. My soul is a part of my living body and will be until I die. When that happens, my spirit floats until it finds another vehicle to inhabit. It takes on the appearance of its old physical presence and can persist even after the new body has been born.'

'But does Esther have a soul?'

'No. Well, yes, but it is in me. I am her living self, which is the receptacle of our soul. It is like she is a photograph of me, but one that was taken seventy years ago.'

I stare into the flames.

'Sorry, I didn't explain it very well, did I?' Francine says.

'Yes, you did. It's just weird.'

'Tell me about Jenny.'

'Well, it used to be just voices, but yesterday I saw her.'

'Wow! Where?'

'Upstairs.'

John is now awake and listening.

'What did she look like?'

I laugh. 'Like the resistance girl in *'Allo 'Allo.*'

John joins the conversation. 'Maybe that is what you expected her to look like.'

'Maybe. Without the cigarette. I could have done without that.'

'That was what the smell was!' John exclaims. 'I thought you had started again, but didn't like to say.'

'I think she wanted to tell me something, or maybe tell Esther.'

'Couldn't she just tell her herself?' Francine asks.

'I don't know. Perhaps it has to pass through us now they have been reborn.'

She yawns. 'Maybe, but I am far too tired to work it out. I'll help you with the bedding. You've certainly got the warmest room tonight.'

'Don't worry, I can do it. You two go up.' I insert the word "two" like a drop of vinegar on an open wound. It hurts, but I am training myself to bear it.

Putting a last log on the fire, I slip under the covers on the sofa. Francine is right — this is the warmest room in the house.

When I wake, Jenny is staring back at me.

I couldn't let him go. Will you?

'I don't know.'

Do you still love him?

She is making me cry.

Do you still love him?

'You know the answer.'

So, you know what you have to do.

To give me space to think, and to clear my head, I dress and step out into the frosty night air with no idea of the time. The darkest hour is just before dawn. Jenny drifts in front of me. We leave the village, but before long, a house takes shape in the darkness in front of me.

A warm, twinkling light illuminates the windows, and the sound of music fills the air. A room with a gramophone player, girls in black dresses and white pinafores, men in German uniforms. I find myself inside listening to the languid tones of Marlene Dietrich.

Vor der Kaserne. Vor dem grossen Tor. Stand eine Laterne. Und steht sie noch davor.

Jenny, now in a waitress uniform, is carrying a tray of drinks. She serves them and comes to me.

Ask not for whom the lantern shines, it shines for me. I operated undercover as Mademoiselle Maille. To those soldiers, I was Lili Marlene.

She motions for me to sit at a table with her.

Do you still love John?

The question makes me angry. 'Who are you, Jacob Marley?'

You know who I am, but if you must give me yet another name, make it Jiminy Cricket. I ask again, do you still love John?

I hate her, but I nod.

Do you want him back?

I nod again.

Does he love you?

A frown deepens across my forehead. 'I don't think he hates me.'

I suppose that's a start. Not much, but a start.

'What shall I do?'

The right thing.

With that, she is gone.

30

Esther, Boxing Day 2005

It's early and Peter is in his room playing the computer games he got for Christmas. Pooh and Piglet are watching.

The world is changing, Piglet. I do not understand it anymore.

Piglet edges closer to his friend. *Only bits of it, Pooh.*

Peter is changing, but only bits of him. That was a lovely story he wrote.

We will always be in that story. Piglet tells Pooh.

Pooh rubs his nose in the way he always does when considering one of life's mysteries. *Peter wasn't in the story; why was that Piglet?*

Because he wrote it. You can't be in your own story.

The nose scratching has brought Pooh no nearer to enlightenment. *Why is that?*

Because that would make it real life, Pooh.

Pooh stops scratching. *Real life scares me. I think I'll be in a story, then I will be the story waiting on the shelf until someone is ready to listen.*

Leaving them talking I drift through to John and Francine's room. The sofa where Cathy sleeps is empty. I wait. The house, too, is waiting to tell us stories, stories we are in.

When John's phone rings, the house freezes, ears erect, nose twitching, whiskers quivering. He reaches for the phone as the house scuttles into its own stonework.

'John?'

He sits up. 'Cathy? Where are you?'

'I don't know. I couldn't sleep, so I went for an early morning walk and got lost.'

The house is so silent I can hear the tremble in her voice.

John rubs his eyes. 'Which way did you go?'

By now, Francine is awake. She snatches the phone from John. Until now, Cathy and Francine have been circling each other like prizefighters, where John was the trophy. Francine won. Now she is behaving like they are sisters.

'I turned right at the crossroads.'

'What can you see?'

'Pigs. There's a lane to the left, but it doesn't go anywhere.'

John is out of bed, getting dressed and shouting towards the phone. 'I know where you are. Stay put, I'll come and get you.'

'Thank you, darling.'

Francine hears that, shuts off the mobile and tosses it towards John. 'I'm going with you.'

He fumbles to retrieve the phone. 'There's no need. Cathy's at Soupiece, so I'll only be five minutes. Put the coffee on.'

Francine is already out of bed. 'I'm going with you.' *John has a lot to learn if he thinks that by leaving Cathy, he has got his trousers back.* Francine says to herself as she hops on one leg, trying to pull on her jeans.

A week later, the New Year's Eve party is taking place. They have invited Eimear and Paula to play cards.

Paula wins. She can't remember what happened on Christmas day, but she knows every rule in the game they are playing. Francine puts the cards away while Eimear gets Paula ready to go home. John sends Peter to clean his teeth.

'We haven't made New Year's resolutions yet.'

Peter is stalling, and it works. Francine is the first to answer.

'I want to find out as much as possible about the house.' She turns to John. 'What about you, my love?'

Cathy looks daggers at her, but John hasn't noticed. 'I am going to return to my hobby of brewing. If I can, I would like to start a brewery. Your turn, Peter.'

'I am going to get a girlfriend. Esther doesn't count because she is a ghost.'

'But you are too young! At least wait until you are a teenager!' his mother protests.

'I'm not talking about sex. People can be friends without sex. I want someone my age to talk to. Girls are better listeners than boys.'

Eimear joins in. 'It's good to have friends your own age you can talk to. Make lots of friends. Don't make one into a girlfriend. If you have friends who are girls, one day, one of them will become a special friend.'

Peter pouts. 'You always say things like that. What's your resolution, Eimear?'

'I think I'll come out of retirement. There's a lot I can do and still look after Paula.'

She looks at Cathy, inviting a response.

The spy takes the bait. 'Do you only work with children?'

'Not at all. We can talk in private if you stay longer.'

'Actually, I am going to. In fact, that was my New Year Resolution: to move to France.'

In the stunned silence, Peter rushes up to hug her.

I am betrayed. Now I know why the English spy has been appearing to her living self. They are hatching a plot to frustrate my plans to bring John and Francine together. In my rage, I fly into Peter's bedroom and start pulling things off shelves. Peter comes in to see what is making the noise.

She can't!

'I don't understand. Who can't what?'

That English spy, she can't stay!

'She's not a spy; she's my mum.'

What about my living self? Francine loves you as much as she loves your father. The two of you have become her whole life, my whole death.

I don't know what to say. She is my mummy and I want her to stay. I also want to live with Daddy and Francine. I'm only a kid, but I can see it is one or the other. What must Francine be feeling right now? I have to go back.

I follow him back into the kitchen. John is shaking, waiting for Cathy to give him the "can we give it another go?" speech. Richard's death has broken the spell, and Cathy has become the naïve Wren parachuted behind enemy lines. The brave passeur will claim her heart, like he claimed mine. She knows him in ways my living self has yet to learn. She loves him, as she must have done many years ago. Cathy thinks John loves her. Why else did he do all he did to remove her from Richard? Cathy will appeal to John's sense of duty. He will do the right thing for his wife and son. Cathy is dismissing Francine, telling her to get over him. It will be as he had planned when he first came to France.

I give up. Letting out a mournful wail, I spiral up through shredded clouds towards the gibbous moon.

A treachery of ravens mobs me. *Go back! Go back!* Black fur-lined beaks tear at the spaces where once flesh hung. I cannot abandon my living self. Francine is shaking. Beside her, Peter is inviting her to cuddle him. The man we love is behind her. In front, the woman she tried to befriend. This is how she repays us. She will reclaim the two men in our life. My living self will return to her flat, to the library, and become that lovely little old lady that everyone says is helpful.

The house bleeds. Ruby rivers create images in the ancient stones.

A bearded warrior weeps.

A naked girl with a stillborn child lies motionless.

A hooded priest burns.

A musician with his cello is interred alive.

A nun prays.

An airman bleeds to death.

A million other images escape the walls to form streams that gather into rivers flowing red into the sea.

Cathy looks at Francine. 'Now that Richard is gone, I am free to love again. John, you tried to warn me. I should have listened. Well, here I am. I am listening now.'

'Too late.' John's face is like thunder.

Cathy ignores him.

'I know. Stay my friend. I hope I have redeemed myself enough to deserve that. I need something to cling onto.'

Cathy turns to Francine. 'This is "truth or dare". Now it is your turn.'

My living self gives a watery smile. 'I do not know the game, but if you are asking for my thoughts, I will give them to you. I am asking myself why this is so hard. You have given me the person I wanted most in the world. I was happy to borrow John to provide him with happiness and find some for myself. John could not do that. He tried to make sure you were OK first.'

'You don't need to tell me.'

'I'll never understand how you could give John up. It's something I could never do. Either you do not love him, or you love him more than I realise.'

'It is more than you realise.'

'That scares me. You could still change your mind. I will be on my guard and will fight for John if necessary. I can no longer play the mistress, so instead I will pay the price for exclusive rights: dedication, loyalty, fidelity.'

Finally, John looks at both of them. 'You are talking about me as if I was not here. You cannot decide between you who I will love.'

'We weren't doing that.' They speak in unison.

'You were.'

Francine looks drained. She has also had too much to drink and needs to sleep. If she goes to bed and leaves John and Cathy alone, will Cathy take him back as quickly as she gave him away? She takes the risk.

'I am sorry, I cannot keep the sleep away any longer. Goodnight, Cathy. See you soon John.'

Cathy also gets up. 'We all need to sleep.' She kisses them both and disappears.

The holidays are almost over. Peter will soon go back to school. I wonder how he will explain having two mums. They are in the kitchen talking, the English spy staring at my living self.

'I'm staying in France to be near Peter. It is not to get John back.'

Francine is crying. 'I'm sorry that I don't trust you and even sorrier that I don't trust John. It is so unlike me.'

I don't trust her. She will try to get John back.

Peter hears me. 'No, she won't; she just said so.'

And you believe her?

'Of course, she is my mummy.'

I have no answer to that, so we listen to the conversation in the kitchen.

The spy takes Francine's hand. 'It's obvious why John fell in love with you.'

'I was certain you would take John and Peter away from me,' Francine says. 'When I was little, I found a stray puppy. One day, the owner knocked on the door. My mother answered, went into my bedroom, took the puppy and handed it back. All mother said was, "It is not your puppy; it never was." That was how I felt on New Year's Eve.'

Cathy squeezes her hand. 'I almost bottled it. I retreated to take a run at the chasm I had to leap. Back from the cliff edge, I lost my nerve. I was back in the land of John and Cathy. Someone whispered in my ear, "Stay, you can make John stay too. You can make him do whatever you want." If I believed the voice, it would crush you, but I didn't care.'

'You were going to, weren't you?'

She nods. I knew it.

'Why didn't you?'

'It would have crushed John, too. It was the thought of living with a corpse which propelled me over the abyss.'

Francine whispers, 'Thank you.'

For once, the spy looks guilty. 'I am sorry I kissed him like I did. It was wrong.'

'You were saying goodbye.'

'Yes, I was.'

'Thank you again. May I kiss you?'

Cathy leans forward, and my living self places a soft kiss on her lips.

I lose my temper, sending the contents of Peter's desk flying.

What is she doing?

He grabs the pen mug before it hits the floor.

'Your living self is making friends with my mummy. You should try it sometime.'

I am shimmering with anger. *She's got John. She should say thank you very much, have a good journey back to England.*

Peter turns to me, hands on hips. 'Maybe Francine was thinking of me.'

You?

I stop pacing through his homework and look at him.

He stares back. 'Yes, me. Cathy is my mummy. She may not be perfect, but she loves me. You may not want to hear this, but Francine is not my mummy.'

I stop flying around and settle on the bed. *I know.*

He presses his advantage. 'Francine loves me; she wants what is best for me. That means me seeing my mummy.'

John walks into the kitchen. 'Breakfast is served!'

The spy and my living self are still kissing.

He stops. 'I hope I am not interrupting.'

It breaks the spell. They pull apart, and Francine laughs. 'Not at all, but that is my line.'

John puts the croissants on the table. 'What is?'

'Breakfast is served!'

'Ah, yes. Just don't say I should take these...'

Francine shoots him a look to stop him from finishing the sentence. 'John, that's enough!'

Cathy does not know what they are talking about. I do. It's what my living self said when she retrieved her knickers after their first time.

I give up. Peter joins them for breakfast. They are sorting out practical arrangements. Francine offers Cathy her old flat in Touriac.

The spy hesitates. 'You'll be burning your bridges.'

Francine puts down her mug. 'I did that a long time ago. John, take Peter and Cathy to see it. I want to go to Perigueux to start my research.'

31

Cathy, January 2006

The street door is down a narrow alley. My first impression is of going back to the flat John and I had as students. You can't compare a mediaeval French market town with Bristol, even the posh end. I punch in the access code and push the door against the flotsam of junk mail. Behind is a spiral stone staircase that makes our house in St Etienne seem modern in comparison.

'John and Francine's house.'

I say it aloud, trying to adjust. John has taken Peter round the corner to get an ice cream from Ariane, so I mount the uneven steps alone. He must be finding this as awkward as me. When I am with him, he tries not to show his love for Francine, but I can tell. One day, Peter will look at a girl the way John looks at his librarian. I imagine I will find that much easier than this. Why? I love John and Peter. I want them both to be happy. Wrapped in all this altruism is a part of the old me, the part that thinks that perhaps my sacrifice has earned a little personal happiness.

Turning the key, I step inside to Francine's world. Her smell is everywhere. Neat shelves filled with books ordered and catalogued. A writing desk, papers left out as if the owner was called away at short notice. Resisting the urge to read them, I open the bedroom door. The bed is as large as Francine is small. I wonder whether they made love here. It does not matter — this bed predates John. Not a virgin then. Why should she be? Much as I would like to be friends with her, I don't suppose we will ever discuss her previous lovers any more than we will compare notes about John.

Closing the door, I turn my back on her love life. Even if it's a cheap swap for John, the flat is OK. Francine is kind to give it to me. God, I miss him, but I can't let the thought settle. I'm done with all those clichés about making my bed and lying in it. Locking up, I go to find Peter tucking into an enormous ice cream sundae.

Back at St Etienne, I go up to the loft to fetch my stuff. Before mounting the scaffold, I need to do one more thing. Esther is waiting for me.

'Hello,' I say.

She is sitting on the bed and her profile is quite clear. And pretty.

Can you see me?

I nod. We sit in silence. 'I know who killed you,' I say.

Esther nods too.

So do I.

Silence envelops us as fog might close around a departing ship. I cry.

'Why did you not tell anyone?'

I was dead.

'You could have told Peter.'

What could he say if I did? "You know the man my mum is having an affair with? Well, in his previous life he killed my dad and stepmum. I know because a ghost told me."

Esther's outburst silences me. This is surreal.

What I don't understand is how Ricardo knew about the Lysander.

'I do.'

The ghost does not move.

Tell me.

'I was jealous. Sex with Ricardo was just about getting information, but I loved Jean.' I clench my fists until the nails pierce my palms. 'He loved me.'

TELL ME!

Her head turns. A gaping wound, blood dripping from the skull that had once held her brain, replaces the beautiful profile.

'I was jealous.'

It comes out more of a scream than a confession. The remaining eye fixes on me, forcing full disclosure.

'He loved me, but he loved you more. I couldn't stand that. Nobody had ever loved me like he did and you took it away. He said he didn't want me in his bed anymore and I should live with that Italian informer.'

I am breathless from so many confessions.

Do you know who Ricardo is today?

Of course I do. Pierre, Peter, Jean, John, Ricardo, Richard. Like a riddle, it's obvious when you see it.

So the English spy was a double agent feeding information back to the enemy.

'It wasn't like that. He wasn't supposed to kill John.'

No, only me. You want to save the brave resistance fighter, but the little Jew-girl dies.

'I told you, it wasn't like that.'

Esther turns, so she is beautiful again.

We all came back. That means we were all killed. Tell me what happened after I died.

1943, Woods near St Etienne

Jenny is waiting for the Lysander. Somewhere in the woods, Esther and Jean are at their stations. The L formation of flashlights and the moon are the only guidance the plane has to land behind enemy lines. Her plan is to wait for her replacement to get out, then Ricardo will break cover and kill Esther. Between them, they will overpower Ricardo, and Jenny will persuade the pilot to take him back instead of her. She only has one minute. Usually they just swing the tail of the plane around and it takes off straight away.

The gibbous moon disappears into a bank of clouds, taking Jenny's plans with it. No moon, no landing. Two shots ring out in quick succession. Her first instinct is to run towards the reports, then she changes direction. Of all the places she might find Ricardo, the crime scene is not one. She makes for the shed and bursts in.

'What the fuck have you done, Ricardo?'

The Italian looks up and smiles. 'Ciao, Bella. You wanted someone dead, so did I. Two rats on one skewer.'

'That was not the deal.'

He shrugs. 'I changed my mind. Germany will not lose this war.'

The packing crate is between them. On it sits the gun he is cleaning. In a few rapid movements, she re-assembles it, then points it at him. He smiles and claps with slow, ironic movements.

'Bravissimo! I had forgotten you are a trained member of His Majesty's armed forces.'

He spreads his hands on the crate, showing he is unarmed.

'But you will not shoot me. Jean did not have the balls, and neither do you. You have never killed a man.'

She rests the muzzle on his temple. 'Oh, but I have.'

The report is so loud in that tiny shed that her eardrums rupture. She places the barrel in her mouth, tastes his blood, and pulls the trigger again.

Printed in Great Britain
by Amazon

33308061R00134